Also by Judith Ingram:

A Devotional Walk with Forgiveness

Remember, the past
isn't always behind you ~
Please enjoy this book!
Judith Ingram

Judith Ingram

Bridge to the Past
Book One in the MOONSEED Trilogy

Judith Ingram

Vinspire Publishing
Ladson, South Carolina
www.vinspirepublishing.com

Bridge to the Past

ISBN: 978-0-9851232-7-7

PUBLISHED BY VINSPIRE PUBLISHING, LLC

This book is for my mother
Elizabeth

Judith Ingram

Prologue

I sometimes wonder whether Katherine's coin would have gone to someone else had our school chosen a different day for a field trip to Fort Ross.

I remember that January day being cold and drizzly. White cotton mist clung to the red cliffs overlooking the Pacific Ocean, where seagulls dipped and soared and disappeared into the blurred horizon. Wind howled up the cove and lashed across the bluff where we huddled over our lunches. It swept sand into our eyes and stung our lips with salt and eventually drove us into the shelter of a modest souvenir shop. A little bell jangled as we piled through the doorway into welcome warmth, announcing ourselves with adolescent giggles and the shrill self-important chatter of sixth-grade girls.

I hesitated just inside the door while my classmates streamed around me and funneled into the narrow aisles. I watched them, backpacks bobbing and heads conspiratorially close as they moved away from me. I doubt they paid any attention to the recorded music meant to create a soothing ambiance: a native flute cascading through silvery notes, a hand drum pulsing softly. Aromatherapy-scented clouds drifted and mingled with the ocean fog we brought in on our jackets.

I struck off for the furthest corner of the shop — a loner as always. I liked being alone, or at least that was my act. I knew my grandmother's wealth and notoriety set me apart from the other Academy girls, and that was fine with me. I didn't care about their silly parties or their sleepovers. I didn't need a best friend to sit with at lunch. I ignored the fact that there was something about me, something that the other girls sensed and instinctively shunned, but like I said, that was my act. I prided myself on my independence.

I reached a colorful display of Native American basketry and began an exaggerated study—aware of the whispers and guffaws behind me. I blinked hard and stuck out my chin, trying to remember how excited I was to visit Fort Ross. I loved history, and the fort—now an historic park—was the site of the first Russian settlement on the California coast, about ninety miles north of San Francisco. I forced myself to focus on the display baskets. They were intricately woven and quite beautiful, the larger ones frilled with feathers and seashells. I reached out a fingertip, and the silky feathers bowed to my touch and sprang back, tripping my imagination.

I saw black-haired women sitting in the deep shade of redwood trees, choosing feathers to decorate their baskets while they laughed and gossiped together. Young girls were wedged between their mothers and grandmothers and aunts, watching the women's hands and learning their craft, listening to their stories—

Hairs pricked up on the nape of my neck as I suddenly felt I was being watched. I jerked my head around. My classmates were intent upon a postcard kiosk and paying no attention to me. Shivering, I pulled my jacket closer and moved along the aisle, trailing a hand over glossy covers of coffee table books about Russian and California histories. I opened a few to old drawings of Fort Ross and the coastline cliffs just after the Russians had settled the area. One picture in particular caught my attention: a child playing with her doll on a rough covered porch. I imagined her mother just inside the open door, arms dusty with flour up to her elbows as she punched down bread dough and called to the girl to stay on the porch and to keep her dress clean, for heaven's sake—

This time my entire body jerked around. My gaze flew to a colorful display of Native American blankets draping the back wall of the shop. A life-size wooden statue filled the corner behind an old-style brass cash register and glass display case. The statue's body was draped in blanket material like the wall behind it, its face chiseled into rough features that looked uncannily human.

Intrigued, I took a step closer and froze. Eyes like twin black currants gleamed at me. The statue came to life as the colorful drape moved and an arm lifted. A finger like a gnarled tree root pointed at me and crooked.

The native flute seemed suddenly loud as my classmates broke off their chatter to stare. With a grunt, the statue heaved herself off her stool and lumbered to the far end of the glass case. Like a sleepwalker compelled to obey, I approached her.

She slid open the case and selected a copper coin the size of a half-dollar. She laid it on the glass in front of me.

"You buy." Her voice was dry and cracked, like the weathered crevices pinching her face. "One day, it changes your future." She inched the coin forward with her tree-root finger and watched me.

The coin wasn't currency but a commemorative piece of some kind. A flag was etched into the gleaming copper and writing too strange to decipher at a glance.

I swallowed and looked up. The woman's eyes seemed

to have no pupils—only inky depths that I feared could suck the thoughts right out of my brain if I kept staring. I swallowed again.

"How much?" I whispered.

She shrugged and regarded me without expression. I fumbled through my backpack for crumpled bills and piled all my money on the counter: forty-three dollars and eleven cents. I pushed the money toward her, reddening as the other girls snickered and whispered behind their hands.

The old woman nodded, and her eyes disappeared briefly into the folds of her face. She sighed and laid the coin on my open palm.

"Today, tomorrow, yesterday," she said. "They are all the same."

I stared at her, but she didn't look at me. Instead, she scooped up my money and sidled over to the cash register.

* * *

During the long bus ride back to San Francisco, my hand stole repeatedly into my pocket to rub the coin as if it were Aladdin's lamp. I refused to let the other girls hold it. By the time I got home, I had decided to keep the coin and its promise of magic a secret from my mother and my grandmother. I climbed into bed that night still clutching it and fell asleep with my thumb circling its rim, feeling automatically for a curious nick cut deep and worn smooth over time.

It was the cold, silent hour before dawn when something woke me. A descending moon poured a dazzling stream of silver through my window, making me squint as I opened my eyes. The silver pooled beside my bed, and in the center of the pool, not three feet away from me, stood a girl watching me.

She was small and slight, close to my own age, with a curtain of dark hair spilling down her back. Her eyes were intent on me, gleaming black in the moonlight. I stared back at her in mute astonishment, more fascinated than afraid.

I tried to sit up but found my arms and legs manacled by the paralysis that comes with sleep. As I struggled to free myself, the girl's image quivered and began to separate, like ripples in a reflecting pool. In another instant, she had dissolved. I was staring at my bedroom wall through an empty shower of moonbeams.

Part One

WINTER

Victoria

Chapter One

My grandmother kept a silver dollar in her jewelry chest. Sometimes she'd let me hold it while she told me the story of how the coin had changed her destiny. A rich lady had come into her parents' bakery one day to order a wedding cake for her daughter. My grandmother had waited on well-to-do patrons before, but she'd never seen anyone as fine as this woman. She could recall with detail the woman's unspoiled white gloves, the dainty scallop of lace trim on her hat, and the blue and gold threads embroidered on her tiny black velvet purse. While my grandmother stood, struck dumb with awe, the woman opened her purse and pulled out the silver dollar.

"For your dowry, my dear." She pressed the coin into my grandmother's hand and winked as if they shared a secret. "I hope someday you'll make your mother as happy as my daughter has made me."

It was the first money my grandmother had been allowed to keep for herself. She told me the sheer weight of the silver on her palm had made her hungry for more. That single coin, she claimed, coupled with the vision of that fine woman, had started her on a path of destiny and the ultimate building up of the Prescott retail empire.

Brought up as I was on the story of my grandmother's silver dollar, having held it in my hand and witnessed her success, I couldn't be blamed for believing that the strange souvenir coin from Fort Ross could alter my future as well. From the day the old woman sold me the coin, for ten long years, I carried it with me everywhere. In my purse or in my pocket, the coin found its way into my hand as easily as a key slipping into its lock. I came to depend on the smooth feel of its copper under my thumb, on the calming effect of its embossed flag and letters. The perfect circle of its rim, save for the odd nick, reassured me of an enchanted future I spent long hours imagining.

Perhaps it was the sheer intensity of my longing for a different life that imbued the coin with its special power. In any case, when that day finally arrived for the old shop woman's prediction to come true, I would fail to recognize it. I would rub the piece out of idle habit and make my wish carelessly, angrily, never dreaming that the coin was ready at last to work its magic.

* * *

That day in early March dawned gray and cold. I awoke in a sheen of sweat, struggling up from the depths of a recurring nightmare I'd had since childhood. The child's voice still whispered in my head as I opened my eyes and realized I was alone in the bed. The bathroom door stood open; the rooms were silent. Ryan was either having his coffee or had already left for work.

I turned my gaze to the window where a gloomy San Francisco fog pressed against the glass, sheeting it with a fine crystalline veil. I shivered and burrowed deeper into the warm sheets, but the grim daylight followed me. Eventually, resentfully, I threw back the covers.

I encountered Ryan perched on a kitchen barstool, reading the newspaper and downing a mug of coffee. His alert, groomed appearance and his pleasant "Good morning, Vicki" earned an unintelligible grunt from me. I fixed myself a cup of tea and sat hunched on the stool beside him, scowling into the fragrant steam rising in curls from my cup. He cast me a long look and put his paper aside.

Pushing off the barstool, he crossed the kitchen and tipped the coffee pot into his mug. He kept his eyes on his task and spoke with tired patience that annoyed me further: "If you hate your job so much, Vicki, why don't you just quit?"

I looked up at this replay of an old conversation. Ryan leaned against the counter—his long legs crossed at the ankle, his head tilted thoughtfully to one side. His well-shaped mouth dipped slightly in a frown.

"Eleanor doesn't own you," he continued. "You have the right to leave Prescott's any time you want." He raised his mug but kept his eyes on me as he took a sip.

Excuses rose to my lips like soda bubbles. "I can't quit, Ryan. Eleanor would be so hurt." He raised an eyebrow, and I stuck out my chin. "Okay, I owe her. She gave Mother and me a home when we had nowhere else to go. She gave us a place in her company—"

"Made slaves of you!" Ryan spat the words. "When she isn't ignoring your mother, she's belittling her. And don't tell me she was doing *you* a favor by turning you into a fashion model. At twelve years old! For her precious department store. Eleanor's bottom line is always whatever is best for Prescott's."

"I know, but—"

"She uses you like she uses everybody. And she's so vain, she won't even let you call her Grandmother!" Ryan wagged a finger at me. "Don't mistake her interest in you

15

for any kind of love, Vicki. Eleanor Prescott isn't capable of the feeling."

His brutal honesty stung. Without thinking, I snapped back, "So now you're an expert on love? Trust me, Ryan, you wouldn't know love if it snuck up and bit you on that well-shaped behind your lady clients admire so much!"

The harsh words shocked even me. The surprise in Ryan's eyes darkened quickly into anger.

"That's not fair." His voice was cold. He stared hard at me, and I looked away, down at my cup. "Just what am I supposed to do, Vicki? You hardly let me touch you anymore." Then, agitated, "Why did you marry me if I'm so repulsive to you? Can you answer me that?"

There was hurt beneath his anger. I couldn't look at him. Ashamed, confused by my own anger, I thrust myself off the stool and shoved open the sliding glass door to our balcony. Fog slipped around me, hiding me like a magician's cloak as I stumbled across to the railing and clung to it, grateful for the shock of cold, damp iron against my hot palms.

A few minutes later the front door slammed, rattling the sliding glass pane behind me. I stared into the eerie blindness of the mist and wondered, not for the first time, why I didn't love my husband.

Ryan Ashton was probably the most attractive man I had ever met, with wavy hair the color of summer honey and hazel eyes warm and intelligent. His long limbs and slender build might appear too lean if not for the sculpted muscles achieved as much through the fortune of heredity as through disciplined physical effort. His body in motion called to mind the prowling restlessness of a jungle cat—graceful and sensual, primed for quick action.

He had a tiny white scar in his left eyebrow, which he was in the habit of raising when curious or skeptical, and a smile that could stop my heart. That perfect mouth leaned toward stubbornness, but could speak with charm enough to soften the flintiest of souls—even Eleanor's. His social ease at thirty-two contrasted with my painful shyness at twenty-two and undeniably attracted me to him. Within the confident circle that Ryan created for us, I felt, if not exactly loved, at least safe.

Despite his social competence, however, Ryan remained an intensely private man. Ten months of marriage had convinced me that I might never know him completely. Moreover, I knew I remained as much a mystery to him as he was to me. In that tragic sense, our marriage was a perfect match.

I rubbed away useless tears and looked down. Fog hid the street below and the surrounding buildings that normally anchored our apartment in place. I felt eerily adrift, alone on my tiny island of gray cement and black iron railing. Muffled city noises floated around me like the phantom murmurings of a ghost ship. An errant breeze ruffled my hair and brushed my cheek like a gull's wing.

I shivered and pulled up the collar of my robe. Thrusting my hands deep into my pockets, I encountered the familiar shape of the old souvenir coin. Instinctively, possessively, my fingers curled around it.

Obeying ten years of habit, my thumb began to circle the coin's rim while emotions gathered like a storm in my chest. Dark words whispered in my head of secrets and longings and a bitter ache I couldn't name. My fist tightened around the coin until my nails dug painful half-moons into my palm. The fog pressed against my face, blind and weeping, and suddenly I cried out, "I wish I were *anybody* but Victoria Reeves-Ashton! Please, God, just let me wake up some morning *a completely different person!*"

The impersonal mist swallowed my cry. On a defeated little sob, I swung around and slumped against the railing. The glass door caught my reflection and threw back the familiar image of a young woman, tall and slender, with a luxuriant mane of blond hair she'd inherited from the Rhineholdt side of the family. Her eyes were a stunning emerald green—Eleanor's eyes. The woman in the glass was an icon for Eleanor Prescott's department store chain. People knew her as Victoria the Beautiful. Victoria the Successful. Victoria the Fortunate.

I knew her as Victoria the Caged. Victoria the Timid. Victoria the Incomplete.

The woman in the glass watched me with sorrowful eyes. I looked away from her pain and released the coin, letting it drop to the bottom of my pocket. I rubbed my palm where my nails had scored the skin.

Still avoiding the woman's eyes, I walked past her into the empty silence of our apartment and slid the door shut.

* * *

Our weekend excursion to Rosswood was decided with astonishing speed.

Ryan came home that evening full of energy and waving a colorful brochure. "Rosswood Estate," he said. "A family-owned vineyard two hours north of here, in Sonoma County. We're considering a resort project on a site nearby. Larry wants me to check it out." He opened the brochure to show me a pretty Victorian house. "He offered us the weekend escape package at this Summerwood Cottage bed-and-breakfast. Interested?"

It may have been the word "escape" that sold me on the idea. Or perhaps the coin was already working its magic. For whatever reason, I agreed to the impromptu trip with a ready enthusiasm that surprised us both.

The following evening I carried my suitcase into the corridor and watched Ryan lock the front door of our apartment. We took the elevator down to the parking garage, stowed our luggage and coats in the Jaguar's trunk, and within minutes were nosing into the writhing snakes of Friday night traffic headed across the Golden Gate Bridge into the gathering darkness of the North Bay hills.

* * *

We stopped for dinner in Petaluma, at a restaurant just off Highway 101. Branigan's Steak House was cozy and rustic, with lacquered wood tables and red-leather menus boasting the best steaks in Sonoma County. A waitress with fringed white boots and a cowboy hat perched above improbable platinum curls took our order for two steak platters. She gave me a smile and Ryan a longer one, letting her eyes travel down to his waist before she turned away.

Unaffected, Ryan pulled the Rosswood brochure from his pocket and flipped it to the back panel. He tapped his finger on a little map.

"Rossport," he said. "That's the nearest town, looks like two miles from the estate. Built in the mid-1850s on a tributary of the Russian River. I'll want to get a look at that. Plus, I'm anxious to walk the site." He tore off a wedge of warm bread and applied butter in a single, careful stroke. "I want to get a feel for the terrain, you know? Give the design a chance to come alive on its own." He popped the bread into his mouth and chewed thoughtfully.

I dropped my napkin onto my lap and smoothed it

19

with my hands. "It's your trademark approach, Ryan, that makes your designs so good and you the best architect Larry has." Ryan's scarred eyebrow lifted faintly at the compliment. I reached for the bread. " 'Let the land speak, and it will present you with the key to itself.' "

At hearing his own words, Ryan stopped chewing and stared at me.

"Here you go, folks."

The waitress shoved sizzling platters beneath our noses. She positioned Ryan's with such care, I suspected that another couple would be getting their platters somewhat later than they should.

"Anything else I can get for you two?" I looked up, but her eyes were all for Ryan.

He treated her to a heart-stopping smile. "No, thanks, Marsha. I think we're good."

I glanced at him in surprise. Then I noticed her name printed on a plastic bar pinned to her blouse. She planted her hands on her hips and beamed a long-toothed grin at Ryan.

"I'll just bet you are, sugar," she purred. My eyes widened, and she winked at me. "Enjoy yourselves." She turned with a toss of her platinum curls and sauntered back to the kitchen.

Ryan reached for the pepper and tapped it briskly over his steak. "You know, Vicki," he said conversationally, "you're welcome to come to the site with me, although I think you'd be bored. It could take hours."

I twisted my water glass on the shiny tabletop. "That's okay. I brought along my sketchpad. You know, just in case..." I trailed off with an embarrassed shrug.

Ryan set down the pepper and waited. I sipped my

water.

"You're good, Vicki. You could be better if you'd ignore your grandmother and start trusting your own instincts." Ryan picked up his fork, frowning. "Eleanor isn't God Almighty. And she sure doesn't know anything about art. Besides, I think she's just piqued because you won't learn the retail business from her." His tone gentled. "Don't let her discourage you. It's your own voice you should be listening to."

Ryan made it sound so simple, as if Eleanor were the problem. As far back as I could remember, though, I'd had trouble bringing my paintings to life. Although technically correct, my artwork showed little imagination. Whenever I lifted my brush to the canvas, I found myself back in the seventh grade with Sister Annette chirping over my shoulder, "Good, Victoria, but too tentative. Too weak. You must *believe* in your subject if you expect others to see what you see!"

Sister Annette might disagree, but I preferred control to creativity. Obeying the rules kept you a lot safer than wandering off on your own path. One careless brush stroke and you could discover a secret, something dark and horrible and dangerous, and express it on canvas before you could stop the impulse. You might suddenly find yourself drawing hands with no arms...or faces with no eyes...or big blue flowers with no stems crowding in over your head, shutting out the world...

Control. I gripped my hands in my lap under the table until they stopped trembling. Then I reached for my knife and fork. With careful precision I sliced off a wedge of steak I did not want and laid it squarely on my tongue.

* * *

Ryan and I finished our meal and drove north on Highway 101 for nearly an hour before we exited onto two-lane Springstown Highway. Within minutes of leaving 101, the darkness of the country hills enveloped us in a blanket of silence. According to the map, the highway would take us all the way to Rossport, but we would need to turn off before reaching the town. With the tributary on our right, Rosswood Road should appear on our left and take us directly to the estate.

I stared out the window, knowing we must be passing vineyards but seeing only my own face staring back at me in the glass. The darkness beyond was absolute. Thick clouds conspired like jealous guardians to keep even the faintest starlight from slipping through and touching the earth.

I sighed and burrowed into my seat, resting my head against the soft leather. I closed my eyes. Ryan's favorite playlist filled the car with the rich velvet of Nat King Cole's voice and lulled me as I pondered the paradox that was my husband.

He was a skilled businessman, clever with people and bold enough to carve a successful niche for himself in the world of architecture. But his confident charm concealed an extremely private man who enjoyed vintage love songs and created beautiful, sensitive designs for buildings and homes. Although he kept it hidden, I might glimpse this secret self in a dreamy look or in a spontaneous moment when he spoke with passion about his work. At such times he seemed closer to my own age and somehow more vulnerable. To be honest, I probably discouraged those moments because the idea of Ryan's vulnerability always made me uneasy.

My thoughts slipped unexpectedly to my father. Ryan didn't know about my father. No one did. My mother told everyone that Jack Reeves had died in a car accident when I was a toddler. But Eleanor told me the truth one day when I was ten years old.

She'd caught me playing with my mother's cosmetics — powder in my hair, lip-gloss smeared across my mouth, my eyes a raccoon's mask of glitter-green eye shadow. She hauled me off the vanity bench and slapped me.

"What are you doing?" she shrieked. "Practicing to be a harlot like your mother? Her own husband couldn't stand her!" Her fingernails bit into my arm. "You think that man was your father? He wasn't, and he didn't die in a car accident. He ran out on your mother because she's a slut, and you're turning out just like her!"

I fought my way out of her grasp and ran into the hall, fingers in my ears and screaming. When I got to my room, I slammed the door and locked it. Then I took down my father's picture from the dresser. I looked into the face I loved, and I told him I hated him. I told him it was all his fault that my mother and I were so miserable living in my grandmother's house.

Instead of hate, however, a secret hope was born. I began to sleep with his picture hidden under my pillow, and I dreamed of the day when he would arrive at Eleanor's front door and demand to see me. He would hold me in his arms and tell me I was his child in all the ways that mattered. Then he would take me to live with him somewhere in the country. I would quit school so I could keep house while he worked to support us. In the afternoons I would set out tea and wait for him in our beautiful rose garden, anticipating the moment when he would appear, and I would see that special look of love in his eyes.

Years of fruitless longing chipped away at my fantasy until all that remained was the single image of waiting for my father in the rose garden. In my mind or in oils I painted on canvas, the picture was always the same—a gleaming teapot on a small round table, matching cups and saucers, folded napkins, and always the rosebuds, curled tight and expectant in their green sheaths, waiting for love to make them bloom.

The Jaguar slowed down. I opened my eyes and glimpsed the turnoff from Springstown Highway onto Rosswood Road. A moment later the car's headlights picked out "Rosswood" arching in black iron letters over our heads. Soon the pavement narrowed and began to twist. Redwoods crowded close on either side, framing the road ahead into a tunnel that channeled the Jaguar's beams. I spotted a deer standing on the edge of the trees, ears pricked forward, staring at us with glassy eyes.

Then we were on a narrow bridge. I knew from the map that we were crossing Two Trees Creek and were only minutes from Summerwood Cottage.

Chapter Two

Snug in a hollow of forested hills, the bed-and-breakfast inn glowed from within like an enchanted Victorian dollhouse. Our tires left pavement and crunched on gravel as we approached the house and stopped before a white arbor gate. The door of the house opened. Warm light silhouetted a woman's figure briefly before she came down the stairs and raised her hand in greeting.

"You must be Mr. and Mrs. Ashton. I'm Alice Andrews. Welcome to Summerwood Cottage!"

Her voice was hearty, and she walked with the long strides of a country hiker. "Walks like a farmer," my grandmother would have sniffed.

I stepped from the car and found my hand swallowed in a firm handclasp.

"Everybody's out just now, getting dinner in town. Here," she offered, moving to the rear of the car where Ryan was unloading our suitcases. "Let me help you with those."

Toting coats and baggage, Ryan and I followed our hostess through the gate and up a brick path that neatly cleaved through lawn. Light from the open door spilled across the porch and momentarily dazzled me as we crossed the threshold into the house.

With a proud flourish Alice waved the garment bag she carried. "Welcome to Summerwood," she repeated.

We stood in a small foyer bathed in light that drifted down from a high ceiling. Thick carpet patterned with rose blossoms cushioned our feet. A pert bunch of wildflowers resting on a table at my elbow touched the air with a sweet, grassy scent.

A parlor opened on our left, overstuffed with armchairs and loveseats. Mismatched tables overflowed with magazines and leafy plants, and busy chintz curtains draped the windows in generous folds. Ryan nodded with interest at a bookcase crammed with volumes, many of which, Alice claimed, told the history of Sonoma County.

"Through there is the dining room," she said, pointing at the far end of the foyer. "Coffee and juice are set out at seven, along with the morning papers. We serve breakfast at eight."

She started toward a narrow staircase, which ascended along the right-hand wall to an open passageway on the second floor. As we mounted the steps behind her, I noticed the banister, intricately carved with a motif of climbing rose vines. "Oh!" I stopped to finger the delicate grooves. "How beautiful!"

At the top of the stairs, Alice turned to look. "Yes, indeed. Those carvings are original." Pride warmed her voice. "This house is 150 years old. The original owner's son carved those banisters when he was a boy. Later he was sent to Russia for a formal education and became an artist, well-known in his time—Leon Rostnova."

We joined her at the top of the stairs, and she pointed to an archway leading off to the right.

"That's the new wing we added on seven years ago, when we opened Summerwood as a bed-and-breakfast. Now this," she waved to the open passageway on our left, "was all part of the original house. Your room is the third door."

We padded along a rose-patterned carpet identical to that in the foyer. The beautiful banister continued on our left, overlooking the foyer, and three doors stood in a row on our right. The first door was shut and bore an enamel plate painted with the name *Strawberry Patch* in elaborate script.

"Each room has its own name and decor," Alice explained. "Just for fun." She stopped before the second door, which stood open. "This is the bathroom you'll share with the guests in Strawberry Patch.

"Nice." Ryan spoke up behind me and pointed to the vanity top. "Where did you get those tiles?"

"Shanklin and Sons, in Santa Rosa." Alice's look was curious. "You know tile, Mr. Ashton?"

"I'm an architect, so I work with vendors and designers. I'm always looking for new sources."

"Maybe you could give us some ideas about this old attic we're thinking of converting. It's such a waste of space as it is." Alice moved to the third door, which also stood open. "This is your room. We call it the Tree House."

I entered first, taking in the quiet earth tones and simple wood furnishings. The heels of my shoes sank into a thick carpet patterned with ivy leaves. Ryan followed me in and set our suitcases at the foot of a four-poster bed, its mattress high and spread with a neat quilt of calico squares. Potpourri teased the air with a faint woodland scent.

Alice came in behind us and laid the garment bag on the bed. "You can't see it now, but an enormous oak fills this window during the day and makes you feel as if you're living in a tree." She pointed to a basket of nuts sitting on a writing table near the window. "You may want to tempt the squirrels with those. If you're patient, they'll come right up to the sill for you." She rubbed her hands in a gesture of finality. "Well, I guess that's it." She smiled brightly and crossed to the door. "Oh, and I've saved some hors d'oeuvres for you. Come on down to the parlor whenever you're ready."

* * *

In my dream, I am a child hiding behind the sofa in Eleanor's library. It is the middle of the night, and the bear is searching through the upstairs rooms, looking for me. If I am to escape, I have to do it right now, before he comes downstairs.

I rise and tiptoe across the room, past the Queen Anne coffee table and Eleanor's favorite armchair. I am at the door, soundlessly turning the knob. Pausing to listen. Nothing.

I creep into the hallway. Light gleams faintly through the heavy glass imbedded in the front door. I take a cautious step toward it, and then another, balancing with arms extended like a tightrope walker. Beneath my bare toes a floorboard creaks.

The bear bellows angrily, and the front door slides away from me, shrinking down a dark corridor. A closet appears in the wall on my right. I dive into it, pull the door shut behind me, and claw my way through an army of coats, choking on the heavy smell of winter wool. Against the back wall I slide to the floor and pull up my knees, arms trembling, heart lunging against my ribs like a caged animal.

I hear the bear lumber down the staircase, but then it's quiet. I fix my eyes on a thin bar of light showing beneath the closet door. A shadow crosses the bar, accompanied by a wet, snuffling noise. Shaggy hair pushes under the door. A moment later, claws scratch at the wood.

The wall behind me has turned to stone. The coats are gone. I am in a cave where something foul has been buried. I smell it on the air, thick and ripe. Trying not to breathe it in, I crawl toward the deeper darkness, my hands and knees sinking into cold, soft dirt.

Something touches my shoulder. I can't scream; my chest burns with the effort. Bile rises into my throat, hot and stinging, choking me —

"Vicki! Wake up!" The touch on my shoulder hardened into a grip that shook me. "*Vicki!*"

Light burst like hot red needles through my eyelids. I cried out and threw up my hands, trying to block the pain.

"It was a dream, Vicki. You're all right." Ryan's hand touched my hair, pushing it back from my face. "Was it that same nightmare, the one you've had before?"

I nodded, not trusting myself to speak. I opened my eyes and squinted up at him.

He was propped on his elbow, his chest bare above the bed sheet, his tawny hair tousled from sleep. Looking beyond him, I recognized our newly familiar bedroom at Summerwood.

"Want to tell me about it?" His steady voice drove my nightmare off into shadows. I had no desire to bring it back.

"No." My voice quivered with the warning that tears were close. I rubbed fists into my eyes and tried to smile, but my chin trembled.

Ryan frowned and studied me. "Okay if I turn off the light?" he asked finally.

I nodded, and he switched off the lamp. I felt the bed jiggle as he settled himself beside me and laid his hand over mine. We lay quietly while the darkness slowly thinned. Soon I could trace the hairline perimeter of the window shade, see the faint shadow patterns of the oak branches waving outside.

Ryan began to stroke my fingers, one at a time, rounding the tips and dipping into the deep vales between. In answer, I moved against him and rested my head on his shoulder. He smelled warm and sleepy, and when his arms came around me, I welcomed them. He stroked my hair and my back, and I shut my eyes and breathed him in, trying to still the quaking vestiges of my nightmare with his calm. Ryan put his mouth against my hair, and when his arms tightened, I didn't pull away—so great was my need for the solid comfort of his body. When his lips moved down the curve of my cheek, I kept my eyes closed and tried to relax. I promised myself that this time would be different.

I couldn't say exactly when the cornflowers appeared. One moment Ryan was kissing me, and the next they were simply there, making room for me as they always did. In an instant they absorbed all my senses, and Ryan and our bedroom disappeared. I was drifting on a gentle blue silence, free of my body, resting in the familiar companionship of the cornflowers.

At some point I slipped from their embrace into a dreamless sleep that carried me through to the morning.

Chapter Three

I opened my eyes to sunlight poking around the edges of the window shade. Ryan was nowhere to be seen. A glance at the bedside clock shocked me with the knowledge that I had thirty-three minutes to get myself showered, dressed, and downstairs in time for Alice's breakfast.

Late as I was, I dawdled shamefully before the mirror, debating about the right clothes to wear. I had learned at an early age to mask my social unease with an expensive, carefully assembled exterior. I finally settled on a yellow turtleneck sweater, dark green corduroy trousers with a wide leather belt, and a doeskin jacket. I twisted my long blond mane into a French braid, hooked simple gold hoops into my ears, and stepped back from the mirror to observe the effect.

Eleanor's emerald eyes glinted back at me. I lowered my lashes and raised my chin, tilting my head to the side as I had been taught. The effect was immediate, a transformation into the sensual, self-assured woman who modeled lingerie for Prescott's department stores. Porcelain skin and fine-boned features, another legacy from the Rhineholdts, added to my façade of casual confidence.

With a tutored poise, I opened the door and stepped into the passageway.

Bacon-scented air humming with conversation, laughter, and an undercurrent of Celtic harp music drifted up from downstairs. No one seemed to notice my descent. I spotted Ryan in the parlor, his back to me, talking with a short balding man. I approached them and touched my husband on the sleeve.

He turned, coffee cup in hand, and his hazel eyes scanned my face in a quick, frank appraisal. I shrank a little, not certain what to expect. In the first months of our marriage, Ryan had been patient with my sexual shortcomings, making an effort to be kind and attentive during the day, taking things slower at night. Lately, however, his patience had widened into distance. He spent more time at the office, and I'd heard rumors about Jessica, one of his architect colleagues. I once made the mistake of asking him about her. His denial had been cold, sharp, and final. The subject of Jessica never came up again.

This morning Ryan was being kind, perhaps for the benefit of the balding man. He smiled and drew me to him with an arm around my shoulders.

"Tom Fisher, I'd like you to meet my wife, Vicki."

The man swept me up and down with an appreciative gaze and extended his hand. "Vicki. A real pleasure." He pumped my hand and smiled. "Ryan has been telling me what a talented lady you are."

"Thank you. But what you see is really the photographer's talent, not mine." I extracted my hand. "I just stand wherever they tell me and smile."

"Oh. No, I meant your painting. I teach community college art, so I'm interested in raw talent. Ryan says you have a style that's subtle but strong on detail. He says you're very good."

I opened my mouth without a clear idea of how I should reply. Fortunately, the tinkle of a bell announced breakfast and saved me the effort.

We funneled into the dining room, and Ryan found

seats for us on the window side of Alice's table. I glanced around, recalling someone's comment that this room had once been the master bedroom. I tried to imagine it without the long table and chattering guests, with a chest-of-drawers against the wall instead of a sideboard filled with ceramic dishes. A fire would be crackling, just as it was now, in the corner behind Alice's chair at the far end of the table, and the walls would be papered with a dainty floral print. No, candy stripe, with flowers in a bowl on the dresser and another beside the bed…

Ryan touched my arm, snapping me back to the present. A young woman sitting opposite Alice at our end of the table introduced herself as Stacey Andrews. She had curly red hair, and her lively brown eyes made it easy to guess she was Alice's daughter.

I glanced around the table, recognizing people who had come in the previous evening while Ryan and I had sampled hors d'oeuvres in the parlor. Seated on my left were Margaret Dougan and her husband, Angus, an elderly Scottish couple whose daughter had gone to college with Alice. Across from them were young honeymooners, Chris and Lisa Knight. Like us, they were from San Francisco. Chris was an architectural student at UC Berkeley, and last night he and Ryan had polished off the remaining hors d'oeuvres while they discussed design theories and professors they both knew.

Lisa recognized me from my photos and confessed that, while she couldn't afford the dresses on the third floor of Prescott's, she couldn't resist visiting them any more than she could resist the ground-floor confection counter for that small but exquisite box of Belgian chocolates.

Tom Fisher found seats for his wife and daughter

directly across the table from us. Amanda Fisher was an angular girl just budding into adolescence, with straight blond hair pulled into a ponytail. When her father introduced me as Victoria Reeves-Ashton, her blue eyes rounded with recognition and wonder.

"Is this your first visit to Sonoma County, Vicki?" Stacey was buttering her toast, and she gave me an encouraging smile.

"As an adult, yes," I replied. "But in the sixth grade our class went on a field trip to Fort Ross, over on the coast." Amanda watched me with such rapt attention I directed my comments to her. "The sight of that Russian fort overlooking the ocean made a lasting impression on me. I even bought an old copper coin from there, an authentic souvenir from the 1887 Sonoma County Fair. I carry it with me everywhere, for good luck."

As proof, I produced the coin from my trouser pocket and held it out.

"It's funny you should mention Fort Ross." Stacey examined the coin and passed it into Amanda's eager hands. "This house we're sitting in was built by a Russian agriculturist who came over with the Russians when they built the fort. His name was Petrov Rostnova, my great-great-*great*-grandfather. He married a Native American named Morning Star, and when the fort folded, he stayed on to farm." She picked up her juice glass and waved it through the air. "*Voilá*. Rosswood Estate."

Stacey sipped her juice and nodded at Amanda.

"Amanda has been coming up with her folks since she was six and knows practically as much about the Rostnova family as I do. Right, Amanda?"

Amanda flushed and gave Stacey a grateful look.

"Well, about the house, anyway."

"Right. She's an expert on Rosswood House." Stacey glanced our way. "Have you seen it yet? It's a *must* before you leave."

Ryan slid a knife through his ham. "We're touring the winery today," he said. "The mansion is on our agenda for tomorrow." He gave Amanda his best smile. "Perhaps Amanda would consent to act as our tour guide?"

Amanda dropped her gaze to her plate, but a dimple peeked out at the corner of her mouth.

"If you do, Amanda, be sure to show them Alexander's portrait." Stacey pointed her fork at Ryan. "He was Petrov's elder son. Alexander hated having mixed blood. He looked like his father and could easily pass for Russian. He fashioned Rosswood House after the grand family home his father had left behind in Vladivostok. I think he built the house to convince everyone that he was more Russian than Native American. As if anybody cared."

She shrugged, and in the silence that followed we all turned our attention to breakfast. Soon Margaret Dougan's soft Scottish brogue piped up beside me: "Stacey, dear, tell the Ashtons about Elise. She still lives there, you know." Margaret sighed. "Gentle creature, her mind isn't what it used to be." She shook her head. "Poor wee thing."

I looked at Stacey.

"Elise Delacroix," she said. "My great-aunt and quite a good artist in her day. You'll likely meet her tomorrow if you visit the art gallery at Rosswood House. She's often there, entertaining visitors with her stories of old Sonoma County."

Margaret laid a spotted hand on my arm. "Elise is the only grandchild left of Alexander and his wife Isabel." She leaned confidingly close. "Now *she* wasn't Russian at all. Isabel was Spanish. Her rich father disowned her when she married Alexander and went to live in that big Russian house of his. Alexander's first wife died, you know. Some say he drove her to her death because she couldn't give him a son, but don't you believe it. Alexander had a bad reputation, that's all. He couldn't have been as wicked as they say."

She sighed. "Of course, there was talk about his daughter, too. They say Katherine was terribly headstrong, just like her father before her. Katherine, that's Elise's mother, you understand." She squeezed my arm. "There was talk of her doing in her own husband. But no one can be sure. There was never any proof of such a thing. And now Katherine herself is dead and buried in the little yard behind Isabel's chapel. May God rest her soul."

Margaret crossed herself and sighed. Abruptly, she reached for the teapot and gave me a bright smile.

"More tea, dear?" she asked.

* * *

I opened the front door of Summerwood Cottage to midmorning sun so unexpectedly dazzling that I fumbled immediately for my sunglasses. As I stepped out, however, the air nipped my cheeks with the cool bite of winter not yet surrendered to spring. Along the porch I caught sight of Chris and Lisa Knight cuddled on a sturdy-looking swing, their feet pushing lazily against the balustrade. I turned quickly away to give them privacy but also to preserve my own solitude. I had left Ryan in the parlor happily foraging through old maps and books on Sonoma County, his notebook already filling with his strong, precise script. I wanted this time alone to explore.

I stepped off the porch into full sunshine and turned for my first real look at Summerwood Cottage. It seemed a house built to endure, designed with ranch style practicality without sacrificing the elegant charm of its Victorian heritage. Despite the delicate fish-scale shingles peeking out from under the eaves of a pitched roof, its horizontal planks and window trims were plain and functional. Buttercup-yellow paint contrasted gently with the thick white turn posts and sturdy balustrade of the spacious porch where the honeymooners kissed. Carefully groomed shrubs concealed the foundation, and green lawn fanned out from the house like a neatly hemmed apron.

In the center of the lawn stood the only tree visible inside the white picket fence. Although it wasn't a great height, I knew instinctively that the tree was old. The tips of its naked, horizontal branches offered cuplike flower buds beginning to burst open, identifying the tree as a dogwood.

A gravel path edged the lawn and led me through neat rows of heavily pruned rose bushes. Like the dogwood, the roses were already breaking the season of dormancy, hiding their naked thorns inside flushes of new bronze leaves. Each raised bed featured a brass nameplate, and some of the names I recognized: Katherine, Isabel, Morning Star.

The gravel path ended at the edge of the rose beds, but I continued along a rough dirt path to the back of the house. Rounding the corner, I stopped suddenly still at the magnificent sight of an ancient oak tree. Of course, this was the tree that filled our window upstairs and turned our bedroom into a tree house. Its huge trunk, gnarled and rutted with age, reminded me of the enchanted trees in fairy stories my mother read to me as a child. A bark-covered root high enough to sit on emerged from the ground and dipped back amid masses of azaleas and rhododendrons on fire with neon pinks and crimson reds.

Struck by the wild beauty of the place, I drew closer to the oak and realized, with a pang, that this might be a private garden off-limits to guests. As I stood hesitating, an acorn thumped me on the head, and I jerked my gaze upward. A large gray squirrel sat perfectly still on a branch not far above me, peering down at me with a dark, glistening eye.

I grinned at him. "Is this your polite way of asking me to leave?"

To my astonishment, he scrambled down the trunk and darted directly into my path, where he sat up on his haunches and regarded me with a solemn gaze.

Intrigued, I said softly, "Well, hello, little fellow."

He didn't move, only stared at me, even as I took a cautious step toward him.

I looked him straight in the eye. "Come up to my window later, and I'll have a treat for you. All right?"

Perhaps he really understood me. In any case, he dropped to all four paws and chattered loudly at me, twitching his tail in stiff jerks. Then, without warning, he leaped behind the trunk of the old oak and disappeared, leaving me to stare stupidly after him.

Chapter Four

Rosswood Winery lay nestled in a valley of its own. Buildings of rough stone telling their age clustered on the valley floor, hemmed in on all sides by gently rising slopes endlessly striped with dormant grape vines.

The name "Rosswood" arched over the entrance to the compound in wrought iron letters as we drove through. A low stone wall displayed the now familiar blue-and-gold crest of Rosswood Estate. We drove a short distance down a paved road bordered with oleanders to arrive at a parking expanse surfaced in gravel.

A low roll of dark clouds had swallowed the brilliant morning sky, and I thought I felt a raindrop as I climbed from the Jaguar. Ryan took my arm, and we hurried toward the closest building, a stout structure of gray stone partially veiled with ivy. Inside, the room was large and surprisingly homey. A cheerful fire blazed in a massive fireplace at the far end beside a curved counter with barstools. Wine bottles and gift items crowded the wall on our right, and the left side of the room offered little round tables where tasters could sit and enjoy a panoramic view of the hills.

We spotted Chris and Lisa Knight at the counter, where two men poured out wine and explained a little of their origins. We joined the honeymooners, and Ryan accepted a sample offer of wine. Far from being a wine enthusiast, I declined.

Chris raised his glass to us. "Guess we're bound to run

into some familiar faces," he said. Lisa commented on the unusual crispness of the chardonnay, and I nibbled on a cracker, wondering how soon we could leave. If the tour didn't take too long and the weather held, I still hoped to get a few hours alone for wandering and sketching, while Ryan took off on his own to visit the building site.

One of the men behind the counter hung up his apron and pulled on his jacket. Apparently our tour guide, he stepped around the counter, and eight of us followed him out the door. We trooped across the parking lot to a block of dead-looking grape vines clinging tenaciously to long spans of thick wire.

Our guide—Randy, according to the name stitched over his jacket pocket—explained how the unique characteristics of the Napa-Sonoma region made it ideal for growing grapes. I noticed his light brown hair just matched the color of his eyes, which sparkled when he talked. It struck me that he looked somehow familiar.

Someone in the group asked about the rose bush planted at the head of every row.

"Roses grow a lot like grape vines, with the same basic requirements for optimum growth," Randy explained. "But roses are less hardy and show stress sooner than the vines. So we monitor the roses and can remedy soil or pest problems before they affect the grape crop. They save us time"—he flashed me a grin and a wink—"and they're very pretty to look at."

Lisa glanced sideways at me. Ryan slipped an arm around my shoulders and kept it there as we followed our guide to the center of the compound.

For the next ten minutes Randy explained how the grapes were stripped of their stems and cleaned, and then stripped of their skins and fermented in huge insulated tanks. He led us to a long building with corrugated metal siding.

"This is where we age the wine," he said, and rolled back a heavy door. Unexpected cold rushed out. We followed him inside, through a maze of dark aisles deep into the building where the smell of wine and old wood hung thick in the air. I trailed on the edge of the group, glancing over my shoulder and trying to guess how far we were from the outside door.

Randy stopped us in an aisle endless with barrels stacked high above our heads. Someone asked about the letters scratched in chalk on the barrelheads, and I wished they would stop asking questions so we could leave. It was getting difficult to breathe. I imagined the aging wine sucking oxygen from the air, leaving barely enough for us.

The questions droned on, and Randy's answers grew faint. I concentrated on breathing regularly and fought the heavy wine smell for my share of oxygen. My heart fluttered like a trapped butterfly. I pressed one hand against my chest and the other against a barrel. To my horror, the wood under my hand hardened into stone; the stacked barrels darkened into the walls of a cave. I knew this place. I shut my eyes on a thin shriek of terror as my knees buckled. Expecting to hit the cold dirt of the cave floor, I fell instead into someone's arms, and I blacked out.

* * *

In my dream, I am in a forest so dark I can scarcely see the trees. Ahead I see dim light, and I move toward it. I have an appointment to keep, and I'm afraid I will be late.

I emerge from the trees to a beautiful night sky soft as velvet and pinpricked with stars. A full moon rises above the redwoods, showing me a path that runs alongside a creek. I follow the path without question, fascinated as it uncoils itself just ahead of me like a shimmering silver ribbon. The path begins to climb, and soon I am high above the creek, my bare feet magically impervious to pain as I clamber over rocks and forest debris. The moon goes ever before me, leading me upstream, guiding me to the appointed place.

I reach the top of a rise, and there below me is an old wooden bridge. Moonlight paints its worn rails and sagging planks with an ethereal glow, lifting it out of the darkness. The magic ribbon continues to uncoil itself until it reaches the very edge of the bridge. I realize with a tremor of excitement that this is the appointed place. On some level I understand that this bridge has been waiting here for years, waiting patiently for me —

A loud screech split my dream wide open. Images fled into shadows. Momentarily suspended between worlds, I had to fight to locate my body and then force my eyes open. Afternoon daylight showed me our bedroom at Summerwood. I was lying on the bed alone and cocooned in the luxurious warmth of a quilt.

Another screech jerked my attention to the window and forced a weak laugh. My squirrel—I was certain it was my acquaintance of the morning—perched outside the window and peered in at me, his body quivering with comic intensity.

Clutching the quilt around me, I slid off the bed and padded to the window. The squirrel bolted but stopped three branches away. With tail fluffed and jerking, he turned sideways and chattered as I unlatched the window and pushed it upward.

"Hello. Come for the treat I promised you?" I picked out a walnut from the basket and held it out on my palm.

He stayed put, cocking his head a little for a better look but making no attempt to come closer. I laid the walnut on the sill, just inside the window, and retreated to the bed to wait.

A full minute passed, then another, while my visitor and I watched each other. A soft breeze rustled the oak leaves between us and lifted the curtains. I kept my breath shallow, the rise and fall of my chest carefully hidden beneath the quilt.

At last he moved. In fits and starts, he worked his way back to the sill. With a long last look at me, he snatched up the walnut and scampered back to the safety of the third branch. There he paused to roll his prize between his teeth and his paws, making certain it was sound, and in an instant vanished down the trunk of the tree. I jumped up, but in the time it took me to get to the window, he was gone.

The breeze returned, cool and fresh against my face. I sank to the window seat with a sigh and stared up at gray-bellied clouds, while my mind cast back over the events that led up to my odd dream.

I remembered being trapped in the bowels of the winery and fighting for breath. The next thing I knew, I was stretched out on a hard bench. Ryan was rubbing my hands and calling my name.

I opened my eyes to the glare of an overcast sky. A face I recognized popped into view—Charlotte Rainey, one of the guests from Summerwood.

"That's it. She's coming around." Charlotte's practical voice ushered me further into consciousness. "Keep her lying down until the color's back in her cheeks."

Without asking, Charlotte stepped forward and felt for

my pulse. My head rested on Ryan's lap, and he smoothed the hair back from my forehead.

"Vicki?" Charlotte spoke loudly into my face. "Feeling better? Ryan caught you before you hit the floor. You'll be okay." She touched my shoulder. "That place was stuffy. I felt a little faint myself." She took my arm and nodded at Ryan. "Okay to sit up now? Gently."

They raised me to sit between them. My head buzzed for a moment, and when my vision cleared, I saw that others were standing a few feet off, glancing at me and murmuring quietly. Mortified, I hid my face in Ryan's shoulder. His arm tightened around me.

I felt the bench give as Charlotte rose and addressed the others. "She's okay now. Let's move on." I couldn't bring myself to look, but footsteps moved away, and voices took on normal speaking volumes, receding into the distance.

I kept my face pressed into Ryan's shoulder, and he held me quietly. At length, I sat up straight, rubbing my sleeve over my eyes, and pulled away from Ryan. He let me go.

I steeled myself for a glance at his face. Expecting his usual composure, I was not prepared for the frank bewilderment in his eyes or the vulnerable quivering of his mouth. The sight of his distress triggered a wave of anxiety I tried to quell with a quick rush of words.

"I feel so silly, fainting like that. I can't imagine what happened."

He shook his head and looked away. I wrung my hands together in my lap.

"It was so stuffy in there, Ryan, even Charlotte felt faint. You heard her say so—"

"But it wasn't the stuffiness, was it?" Ryan's tone was

harsh. I looked at him. "I saw you, Vicki, before you fainted. I saw your eyes! Something about that place scared the living daylights out of you."

His intensity gripped me, and in that moment I almost told him everything—about the bear that had pursued me through nightmares since childhood, about the cornflowers that took me away from him whenever we made love, about my own mother's wary distance from me. About the fantasy rose garden where I still waited for my father.

About the dark chamber in my dreams where a terrible secret lay buried.

The words I wanted to speak rose in my throat and stuck. Instead, others tumbled out, delivered in a high, tight voice: "Don't be silly! I wasn't frightened. I felt dizzy because the air was too thin." Then, helpfully, "Maybe I didn't eat enough lunch."

My gaze faltered and slithered away from the utter disbelief in his.

We sat in silence. I dug a hole in the dirt with the toe of my shoe, and then smoothed it over.

Ryan spoke. "I don't know how to help you, Vicki." His voice had regained that cool composure I recognized. "If you won't talk to me, then I wish you would talk to somebody else. And soon." He paused and waited for me to look at him. "I'm concerned about what might happen to you if you don't get to the bottom of whatever this thing is." His voice roughened. "We both need to know what's got you so scared that I can't even touch—"

He stopped and blew out a breath.

"I'm not saying it's your fault," he continued gently. "I know I get busy and leave you alone a lot. I know I'm older than you. I've tried to give you time to get more comfortable with me. But it's not enough, is it?" He frowned and looked off to the distant rows of naked vines. He added softly, "Things haven't turned out exactly the way we planned, have they, Vicki?"

His tone of baffled disappointment cut deeper than angry words ever could. Tears sprang to my eyes. I blinked them back and dug another hole with my shoe, deeper this time, concentrating as if it were all that mattered in the world.

Chapter Five

We left the winery and returned to Summerwood. Ryan had tucked me under the quilt before he drove off to visit the proposed construction site as planned. My nap refreshed me, and with a few daylight hours still remaining, I pulled on my jacket and let myself out the front door.

The late afternoon sky hung low with clouds, and I pulled up my collar against the cold whip of a rising wind. My shoes crunched on the gravel drive and silenced abruptly when I reached the paved road and turned right, heading for Two Trees Creek. In a canvas satchel slung over my shoulder, I carried my drawing pad, pencils, and charcoal, along with a handful of nuts on the possibility that I'd see my squirrel again.

Less than ten minutes of walking took me to the edge of the creek. On my right was the bridge Ryan and I had crossed over, driving to and from Summerwood. I struck out to the left, following a dirt path close to the water. A blanket of silence weighted the air, as if the forest held its breath. Not even birdsong broke the stillness. Instinct from some primitive corner of my brain warned me that rain was coming.

The path rose. I began to feel warm under my jacket as I scrambled over low rocks and skirted scrubby plants hostile with stickers. I could no longer see the creek, but I heard its gurgle and smelled the fetid dampness of decaying plants. Over time the water must have carved its narrow swath through dense forest, for redwoods crowded down on my left and jumped the chasm to crowd the opposite bank as well. Beyond the tallest trees, a hawk soared high and silent against the clouds.

Now uncomfortably hot, I welcomed the sight of a wide flat-topped boulder jutting out over the creek. Dropping my satchel, I tiptoed as close as I dared to the edge and looked down about forty feet to the glimmer of moving water. Steep banks buried under lush tangles of green and red growth muffled the edges of the creek, which was running high with the captured runoff of a rainy winter.

I backed up carefully and sat with crossed legs, enjoying a wide view of the sky and woods. I reached for my satchel and pulled out my pad and a pencil. On impulse, I also extracted five hazelnuts and set them in a row on the flat surface behind me. Then, pencil poised above a clean white page, I closed my eyes and inhaled deeply, deliberately flexing and relaxing my muscles in sequence—arms and shoulders, thighs and calves, and finally my toes.

I opened my eyes slowly and let my gaze drift. A coarse breeze made them water, and the landscape blurred. Gray sky and green treetops blended together in watercolor patterns. Strangely, the gray began to dominate. It swallowed the green and brightened to a solid glare. The pulse at the back of my eyes beat quickly and sharply against the brightness.

The glare softened, and images emerged from the pulsing, shifting like a slide show in front of me. Black-haired girls chased each other up hillside paths. Dark figures danced around a campfire. A line of people walked single file across a peculiar bridge, the men carrying spears and poles, the women balancing babies and baskets of food on their hips, with small children clutching at their skirts.

The bridge itself was a curiosity, rough and mounded, as if two gigantic trees had been laid side by side between the opposing banks.

I stared for so long my eyes began to burn. I blinked and teared up, and the images vanished. I found myself gazing at a bank too thick with brush to allow for footpaths or campfires, and too high to be the same bank I had just seen. All my senses seemed electrified and painfully intense — my skin hummed, my eyes smarted from the glare, and even my hair roots stung at the wind's gentle tugging. My brain pulsed with too much blood, and I wondered if I could be having a stroke, out here alone by the creek where no one would ever think to look for me.

Crack! Noise like a gunshot exploded right behind me. I screamed and jerked around in time to see a squirrel leap to the top of a nearby rock. Four hazelnuts in a row and bits from the fifth explained the noise, which sounded as loud as a cannon as I surfaced from my dreamlike state into solid reality. I stared, slack-jawed, as the squirrel calmly finished his meal from the safety of his rock and eyed me with wary interest. Then I began to laugh. I held my sides and giggled helplessly, leaking tears that were half mirth and half hysterical relief.

The squirrel's imperturbable presence settled me. My nerves calmed to a normal pitch, and my heart slowed its runaway gallop. I wiped my eyes with my sleeve and gave my small guest a shaky smile.

"Sorry if I scared you." My voice seemed a clumsy intruder in the quiet forest. The squirrel raised himself a little and regarded me solemnly. I swept a hand at the row of hazelnuts. "You're welcome, you know. I brought them just for you."

Of course I believed it was my squirrel. It didn't matter that probably thousands of squirrels lived in the woods and all looked alike. In my current frame of mind, it was easy to believe that this squirrel not only remembered me but had deliberately followed me here.

He sat perfectly still, and I decided not to engage in another waiting game with him. I shoved my unused pad and pencil back into my satchel, looped the strap over my shoulder, and rose carefully, easing the blood back into my cramped legs. The squirrel leaped out of sight behind his rock.

I looked at my watch. Ryan would probably be back by now and wondering what had happened to me. On legs still unsteady, I stepped off the flat boulder and started back along the path to Summerwood.

An ear-piercing screech spun me around. Not two yards away stood my little friend—feet spread and tail bristling. To my amazement, he scampered off a few feet, turned, and screeched again.

His message was clear.

Shifting my satchel, ignoring a voice in my head that told me I was bordering on lunacy, I began to follow the squirrel along the overgrown remnants of a path. He darted in and out of sight just ahead of me while I shuffled along through dead leaves and tripped over exposed roots and refused to think about anything at all, until, suddenly, we topped a rise, and I knew we had reached our destination.

I saw the bridge just as I had dreamed it during my

nap at Summerwood. Without the moon's softening effect, the structure looked dilapidated and dangerous. Its split-wood rails gaped in places; its middle sagged where supports were rotting away. Someone had nailed a board across its entrance and posted a warning. I could see the yellow caution triangle from where I stood.

I gazed down at the bridge with a curious lack of surprise. Rather, I felt profound satisfaction to see that it existed in real time and space. In a way I did not yet understand, I knew it was my link to something — or to someone — terribly important.

* * *

"Ryan says you went for a walk today, Vicki." Stacey's smile was friendly as she passed me a basket of bread. I was seated at one end of a long table in Loggers End, an historical hotel-turned-restaurant in the town of Rossport. Stacey, our hostess from breakfast, sat on my right. Ryan sat across from me beside Chris and Lisa Knight. Stacey's two older brothers, one of them our winery tour guide, sat with their girlfriends at the far end of the table. To my relief, no one mentioned my embarrassing fainting spell at the winery.

"Where did you walk?" Stacey scooped a wedge of butter onto her plate and handed the butter dish across the table to Lisa.

"I followed the creek upstream." I thought I sounded convincingly casual. "Two Trees Creek, right?"

"Right. It's really full this time of year." She slathered butter on a wedge of bread, popped it into her mouth, and added, with difficulty, "How far did you go?"

"I ended up at a bridge. It looked really old and falling apart." My throat closed over the words, and I reached for my water glass.

"Whoa! That bridge is over a mile upstream from the road, and there's not much of a path left. I'm surprised you found it."

Mercifully our salads arrived at that moment, making it easy not to respond. I could just imagine telling Stacey that a squirrel had shown me the way.

"That bridge has an interesting history," Stacey continued. "It's supposed to be haunted." I choked on my salad greens, and she chuckled. "It's just an old Native American legend. Living around here, you're bound to run into old stories about bridges and rocks and trees and such. See, they believe all nature is spiritual, that even inanimate objects have spirits. They also believe that certain spots are sacred—like that bridge and especially the hill where Rosswood House sits."

I forgot my food and stared at her. Recognizing an attentive audience for what was obviously a favorite topic, Stacey lowered her voice confidingly.

"Every spring the native people used to gather on their sacred hill to celebrate the end of winter and ask their gods to grant another year of good hunting. When Alexander defied their traditions and built his house on the top of their hill, well, they believed their spiritual world was thrown out of balance. Something would have to happen to the house or to Alexander to restore natural harmony." She stabbed the air with her fork for emphasis. "When Alexander was killed, they made a big deal out of it. They claimed he was being punished for his disrespect."

She shoved lettuce into her mouth and continued talking around it. "Their sacred hill is an important part of the Two Trees Creek legend. Have you heard that one yet?"

I shook my head, and she nodded, poking through her salad with her fork.

"Well, every year, like I said, they made a pilgrimage to this sacred hill. One year the creek was really full from the rainy season, and the people couldn't get across. The water was almost flooding the banks. Of course, this was a long time ago, and the banks weren't as high as they are now. But the water was just too dangerous to cross, running too fast and too deep.

"Anyway, they camped beside the creek and chanted and danced all night. See, it was really important for them to get across the creek and up to their hill before the first new moon of spring. That's when the *supernaturals* were supposed to come down and mingle with them.

"Along toward morning, so the legend goes, a thunderstorm rolled in. Lightning struck down two giant redwoods, one on either side of the creek. Each tree fell toward the other bank, and the two rolled together to form a bridge across the water. The people took it as a good omen. So they painted themselves up and crossed the bridge for their sacred celebration on the hill."

The waitress removed our salads. I watched her bring platters of chicken, and I asked Stacey, "Do you believe the legend is true?"

She gave me a curious look. "No one's ever asked me that before." After a moment she shrugged. "Who knows? A lot of this old native stuff is based on something that really happened, but it gets added to over the years. The native locals keep the stories alive. They say a bridge was built by the white settlers over the very spot where the old redwood trees used to be. That's the bridge you saw today, and you can see how old *that* one is. The two trees, if there

53

ever were any, are long gone."

She grinned at me and pulled a wing off her roasted chicken. "Anyway, that's how the creek got its name, and why they say that whole place is haunted."

* * *

That night I lay awake long after Ryan fell asleep. I watched the shadows of the oak tree quiver and bow against the window shade, and I fingered my old copper coin against my palm. Stacey's words played in my mind along with images I had seen that afternoon. I turned them over and over, trying to make rational sense of them.

As the hour deepened, my eyelids grew heavy, and I wandered into that netherworld where reason loses its form and the impossible takes on a queer kind of logic. The coin grew quiet in my hand. I nestled into my pillow, sighed, and drifted into sleep.

In my dream, I am sitting on the flat granite rock that juts out over Two Trees Creek. I had been sketching, but when I look down, the paper is untouched. I press harder, drawing with heavy strokes, but I cannot get my pencil to leave a mark. The page remains stubbornly blank.

The pencil slips from my fingers and rolls to the edge of the granite. It drops into the water and begins to bob along upstream, against the current. I jump to my feet and race along the left bank, trying to keep the pencil in sight.

I am suddenly on the rise overlooking the old bridge. Night has fallen, and a bright moon hovers just above the trees, showering silver over the bridge's broken rails and sagging planks. The moonlight thickens into white mist that curls around the bridge until the bridge is hidden. Minutes pass. The mist thins, and with a shock I see a young woman standing at the rail.

She is small and wearing a white gown. Dark hair falls like a curtain down her back. I try to move toward her, to call out, but I am mute and rooted where I stand. All I can do is lift my arms helplessly.

The mist thickens once again, and in the last moment before she disappears, the woman looks up. Our eyes meet, and then she is gone.

Chapter Six

If one thought of Summerwood Cottage as a sparrow, small and plain, then Rosswood House was a peacock.

Built on the crest of a hill, the mansion stared out over my head from white-curtained windows, imposing its gilt Victorian grandeur and Russian aristocracy upon the mild countryside. A two-story tower built on the second floor, directly over the front entrance, gave the house an imposing, three-story appearance. Vying with the tower for structural dominance, a Russian Orthodox onion dome rose on the left side of the house. Beneath the dome, arched windows curved around what I imagined must be a stunning room. Tall bay windows lined the ground-level floor, the royal blue and gold colors of their trim repeated on every window and roofing detail I could see. A porch freshly painted with a glossy coat of cerulean blue matched the entrance steps sweeping down to the drive where I stood, transfixed by the magnificence of Alexander Rostnova's house.

Ryan surprised me from behind by taking my elbow and pointing.

"Look at those windows!" he exclaimed. "Different styles on each floor. See, Gothic at the top of the tower, right under that French mansard roof. Brilliant."

I turned to face him. He was shading his eyes as his gaze ran expertly over the lines and angles of the house, assessing and memorizing. I smiled.

"It's a beautiful house, Ryan," I said. "I wish I could

appreciate it the way you do, see it the way you see it."

He looked at me, lowering his hand from his eyes. "Do you, Vicki?" His voice was charged with the same excitement that sparkled in his eyes. "I could teach you. In fact, I'd love to teach you."

His intensity startled me. I took a step back just as he was reaching for my hand.

"Some digs, hey, Ashton?"

Chris Knight strolled up, hand-in-hand with Lisa. Ryan held my gaze a fraction of a second longer before turning.

"Chris." Ryan put out his hand. "Lisa. So you let this character drag you out on a Sunday morning to poke around an old house?" He flashed her a smile even I couldn't detect as anything but spontaneous and warm. "Must be love."

Lisa's broad grin at Ryan's words included me.

"I've been dying to get a look inside this place," Chris said. He released his wife's hand and touched the small of her back, but I could see his attention had shifted. "The blueprints for the house are copied in one of those old books at Summerwood. Mrs. Andrews showed me. Did you see them?"

As if on cue, the two men turned together and started up the steps. Lisa gave me a wry look.

"I think we've lost them," she said. Her grin was indulgent. "By the way, your husband is terrific, Vicki. He's taken such interest in Chris this weekend, even though he's only a student. You're a lucky woman."

"Yes," I said shortly. "Well. I guess we should join them."

We followed the men up the steps and through the

doors into a magnificent circular foyer. The first thing I noticed was a wide staircase curving down from a great height to spill a royal blue and gold Aubusson runner onto the foyer's gleaming hardwood floor. Polished mahogany climbed the walls in a generous wainscoting and textured the ceiling with a checkerboard pattern. Tapestries depicting scenes from the Russian countryside alternated with tall, elegant mirrors to line the walls above the wainscoting and gave me the feeling of almost being outdoors.

I caught a sweet scent and tracked it to a bowl of freesias perched on a pedestal table in the center of the foyer, where guests could sign a register. As Lisa and I joined our husbands at the table, I spotted Tom Fisher and his wife, with Amanda standing off to the side looking bored. She straightened when she saw us. After whispering to her mother, she approached us shyly, one arm twisted behind her back and hooked to the elbow of the other arm flopping at her side.

"Hi," she said. She dimpled a little in her uncertainty.

Ryan turned. "Miss Fisher! You remembered our date." His smile turned her cheeks a pretty pink. "I can't wait to see this magnificent house of yours."

"It's not *my* house!" Amanda laughed, releasing her poor arm and clasping her hands in front of her. "There is a tour guide. Over there." She pointed to a woman who stood rather primly behind a red velvet rope suspended between brass poles. "But I could show you some stuff that's not on the regular tour. My mom said it's okay."

Ryan gave her a wink. "Delighted," he murmured. Amanda hid a smile behind her hand and edged over to where I was standing.

"Did you sign the book?" She perused the list of names scrawled in loose columns on the stiff cream pages.

"I think my husband did." I tapped the page. "Here. Mr. and Mrs. Ryan T. Ashton."

She looked up and made a moue at me with her small mouth. "You should sign your own name. People won't know it's *you* if you're just Mrs. Ashton."

I took the pen she offered and smiled. "Okay, you're right. Where do I sign?"

Beaming, she pointed to the next line and nearly blocked my vision as she watched me sign my name: Victoria Reeves-Ashton, San Francisco, California.

"I've been to San Francisco lots of times," she said. "We live in the East Bay. My dad teaches at Diablo Community College—"

"Look, they're lining up," Lisa interrupted. Ryan and Chris were standing with the Fishers, and we hurried to join them. Amanda kept up a steady stream of chatter.

"You've never been here before, right? Well, I have, lots of times." The docent removed the velvet rope, and Amanda dropped her voice to an energetic whisper. "Wait till you see Isabel's bedroom upstairs. It's *seriously* awesome! Violets were Isabel's favorite flowers, so they restored her bedroom in violet and blue colors. Alexander was handsome, but I think he looks mean—"

Amanda bit off her words when Mrs. Fisher frowned over her shoulder, just as the docent began her presentation.

"Welcome to Rosswood House. Today you'll get a taste of the Russian, Spanish, and Native American heritage that belongs not only to this house and estate but to Sonoma County and much of California as well. We'll begin with the library."

She led us through double doors into a room smelling of beeswax polish and old books. Green velvet drapes were drawn back to admit natural light through a pair of tall, stately windows behind a massive desk. Built-in shelves lined with an impressive number of volumes, a small number of them locked behind glass doors, rose from floor to ceiling on two walls. A pair of high-backed armchairs pulled close to a marble fireplace attracted the recluse in me — I imagined the snug read they would promise on a cold, rainy night.

The docent called our attention to framed pictures grouped on the wall beside the fireplace. "Petrov Rostnova began the Rostnova dynasty in California. That's our earliest picture of him, there in the center."

I crowded close with the others to study the portrait of a young man in his early twenties, fair-haired and wearing a uniform I did not recognize. Fashionable sideburns sprouted along the sides of a face made handsome with regular features and a well-formed chin. The mouth was full-lipped, and I fancied a sensitive nature there. Light-colored eyes, narrow-set and thoughtful, were fringed with lashes so pale they almost disappeared.

The docent continued. "Petrov was an agriculturist from a wealthy Russian family. Educated in Moscow, he was sent to Fort Ross in 1832 to help make the fort profitable. Efforts to farm the coastal area had been largely unsuccessful, and the Russian-American Company was struggling to save its considerable investment in California and Alaska by growing food crops. Despite their efforts, the fort failed and was sold to John Sutter in 1841.

"Petrov remained in California after the fort closed. He

married a Pomo Indian girl and settled in this valley to farm. They had two sons, Alexander and Leon, and a baby girl who died in infancy. His wife died soon after the daughter was born. Women from her tribe cared for his sons while Petrov worked the farm."

She indicated the photo of an old house I barely recognized as Summerwood, smaller and quite drab.

"Petrov lived with his sons in the house he'd built for his wife, Morning Star. Some of you may recognize the house as Summerwood Cottage. With the help of native labor, he planted wheat and corn, but profits were disappointing. Unfortunately, Petrov was more idealist than pragmatist. He had no business sense. When gold was discovered in 1849, he left the farm and his sons in the care of his wife's relatives to pan for his fortune. He was successful enough to return eighteen months later and book passage for his sons back to Russia to receive a formal education."

She pointed to another portrait. "This was painted just before the boys left for Russia. The tall blond boy is Alexander, who was eleven when he left California. His brother Leon was eight. You can see that Leon was dark, like their mother."

We took turns moving closer to study the two solemn-faced boys standing on either side of their father. Petrov sat with his hands posed awkwardly over his knees. He looked shockingly old for a man who was probably only in his late thirties.

"In later years Petrov became a friend and mentor of Luther Burbank, who settled in Santa Rosa. They both experimented with new varieties of roses and grapes. That's a picture of them standing on the front steps of

Summerwood." She indicated a photograph of two men, one of them white-haired, squinting against the sun. "The boy in the background is Petrov's grandson, Nicholas, Alexander's eldest son. He died in a tragic riding accident when he was twelve. And here is a picture of Petrov with Herbert Greenspan and other members of the Monte Verde Viticultural Society, taken at the State Fair in 1872."

The docent gave us a moment to study the pictures. Then she led us from the library into the dining room. After the dark paneling and solemn rows of books, the dining room seemed bright and airy, with walls papered in soft blue and beautiful moldings painted a glossy cream. The polished table gleamed with eight place settings of gold-rimmed china, crystal, and silver flatware arranged in careful symmetry on linen placemats edged with lace. A magnificent crystal chandelier caught its reflection in the table's surface and sparkled against the beveled glass doors of an ancient china cabinet and a tapered curio beside me.

"Some of you may recognize the Lomonosov porcelain." The docent nodded at the blue-and-gold dishes and figurines displayed in the curio. "Most of those pieces were purchased in Russia and brought to California by Leon's Russian-born wife, Ana. The table china, however, is Spanish. Isabel, Alexander's second wife, brought this set with her when she became his bride. The crystal goblets and flatware were added to the family collection sometime later."

Lisa nudged my elbow. "Better not make any sudden moves in this room," she breathed. "This china looks incredibly fragile. But so beautiful."

I murmured agreement as she bent over the table, and I glanced around for Ryan. He and Chris were looking up, inspecting the elaborate ceiling moldings. Ryan's face had recaptured its excitement, echoed in Chris's face as he nodded and listened attentively to Ryan. Amanda materialized beside me, and we moved together with Lisa through a small serving room and from there into a spacious kitchen.

The docent's seamless presentation pointed out the fireplace with a massive stone hearth, a black stove made of heavy cast iron, and a rough wooden table flanked with low benches. We filed into a dark hallway so narrow we could scarcely walk two abreast. Four small bedrooms opened off to the right, identified by our docent as servants' rooms. In contrast with the rest of the house, these rooms seemed as bare and impersonal as monk cells, each with a narrow bed, a simple headboard, and a wooden crucifix nailed to the wall above.

Passing a locked door to the wine cellar on our left, the docent led us into a gunroom at the end of the hall. When Amanda tapped me on the arm, I willingly left the glass cases displaying firearms and the paraphernalia that went with them, and followed her across the room. Here other cases displayed bows and arrowheads nestled in rivers of white satin. Above the cases hung framed photographs and drawings of the Native Americans who had lived in the area. Amanda pointed out the photo of a large Native American woman flanked by two small white children.

The woman stood on the steps of a wooden porch, her white dress stretched across a heavy bosom and ample hips. Small black eyes peered out from a deeply creviced face; her black hair hung in two thick plaits. In contrast to her great size, the children seemed small and insubstantial. They looked about five years old.

"That's Katherine and Nicholas," Amanda said. "Nicholas was the boy in the other picture, the kid hanging on the railing behind Luther Burbank. He and Katherine were twins. He died when they were twelve. Then there was only Katherine and her baby brother."

The blond-haired boy was dressed in a white shirt and short pants that looked as though they'd fall off his skinny frame if they weren't held up by suspenders. He was clasping the woman's hand with both of his, his pale eyes solemn as he peeked out from behind her generous skirt. The girl was as dark as he was light, her black hair held back by a ribbon tied into a bow. Her ankle-length dress had a high collar and long, tight sleeves. She held both arms stiff at her sides and looked as though she wouldn't have stayed for the photo if the woman's hand had not been clamped on her shoulder. No one in the picture was smiling.

Ryan came up behind us as Amanda pointed to the woman.

"That was their nurse, Dora. They say she was a witch, and she taught Katherine all she knew about medicines and magic spells and stuff like that."

Margaret Dougan's soft brogue drifted back to me: *They say Katherine was terribly headstrong, just like her father. There was talk of her doing in her own husband...*

Ryan asked Amanda a question, but my attention was on the little girl in the picture. Her fists were clenched and her mouth pinched in a flat, stubborn line. Even through the grainy myopia of the old photo, a defiant spirit flashed in her dark eyes.

I studied those eyes and wondered if what people said about Katherine was true.

Chapter Seven

In her excitement, Amanda all but pushed me into Isabel's bedroom. It was the circular room I had admired from the drive and was situated in a corner of the upstairs hallway, directly beneath the onion dome. Our group breathed a collective gasp of wonder as we stepped across the threshold into sheer Victorian elegance.

My gaze caught immediately on the high ceiling, which echoed the curve of the onion dome and was carved like a cathedral's, accented with pale blue and gold. The graceful half-circle of windows filtered light through snowy lace panels. A thick comforter striped in royal blue and purple covered the bed's high mattress and complemented the canopy and bed curtains. A bold crucifix hung above the bed, incongruous against the dainty flowers of blue and violet that danced across the wallpaper.

The bedroom unquestionably belonged to a lady. Across the room from us Isabel's dressing table displayed silver-backed brushes, crystal perfume bottles, and small porcelain boxes. A tall silver vase offered a spray of hatpins. I longed for a closer look, but another velvet rope guarded Isabel's treasures against visitors with curious hands and clumsy feet.

The docent pointed to a small table beside the bed. On the wall above the table hung a painting of Mary holding the infant Christ.

"Isabel was Spanish and a devout Catholic," the docent

said. "Here she prayed and lit candles daily for her family. She also had a small chapel built on the property, which you are welcome to visit after you leave here today."

Lisa was examining a framed embroidery sampler when Amanda touched my sleeve. I turned, and she pointed through a low archway to a small sitting room behind us.

"Look in there." Her whisper was pitched high with excitement. "That's her. That's Isabel."

Above the carved ivory mantel of a small fireplace rested the portrait of a stunningly beautiful woman. Her dark, wavy hair was piled loosely on top of her head, softly framing a perfect oval face and luminous eyes of a color somewhere between dark blue and violet. She wore a black silk dress with a froth of lace at her throat, caught by a round decorative brooch of some kind. In her lap she held a nosegay of violets. I remembered Amanda saying that violets were Isabel's favorite flowers.

"Isn't she gorgeous?" Amanda breathed. "She was Alexander's second wife, the mother of the twins we saw downstairs. Remember?"

I nodded and wished the familiar velvet rope weren't forbidding us access to the sitting room. Amanda pointed to another portrait hanging on a closer wall.

"That's their wedding picture. Alexander's handsome but he looks a little mean, don't you think?"

The wedding couple were posed with the solemn expressions of old-style portraits. Alexander sat in a straight-backed chair, and Isabel stood behind him, her hand on his shoulder. He looked remarkably like his father — tall and lean, with blond hair and classic features. But I saw what Amanda meant. The pale eyes seemed flat and cold, the mouth grim. There was no trace of the vulnerability I had seen in young Petrov's picture, that soft, romantic look that made you believe he could fall in love with an Indian maiden and care for roses.

"This is a wedding photo of Alexander and Isabel, taken in 1876." The docent stepped up to the portrait, and the rest of the group gathered behind us. "Isabel Cuerello was seventeen and betrothed to the son of a rich hacienda owner when she met the handsome Alexander and fell hopelessly in love with him. Defying her father's wishes, she secretly married Alexander, who was quite a bit older than she and already widowed. Her father, don Miguel Cuerello, was furious. He promptly disinherited Isabel and at the same time forbade his family from ever speaking to her again. Alexander was reputed to be a cold, distant man, so it's possible that Isabel led a lonely life after her marriage into the Rostnova family."

The docent led the group into the hall, but I stayed behind for a moment longer. I gazed up into Isabel's fresh young face and imagined her dreams of an idyllic future doomed to disappointment. Had she, too, fallen in love with only a handsome smile?

At the door, Amanda fluttered her hands. We hurried to catch up with the group just as they entered a room midway down the open corridor. Large circus animals decorated the walls of the room. "This was the nursery and playroom for all the Rostnova children," the docent explained. "Those spiral stairs in the corner lead up to the tower room, which served as a schoolroom before the schoolhouse in town was built."

Of course, this was the two-story tower over the front entrance to the house. Ryan and Chris were the first ones up the spiral staircase, even before the docent finished her paragraph. I contented myself with wandering around the room, studying the circus animals up close and noticing curious irregularities, as if they had been painted by a child. Pieces of a wooden puzzle were arranged on a low table to look as though a child had only just left the room and would soon return to finish it. Shelves built low on the wall displayed an assortment of toys, mostly wooden and painted in colors once bright but now faded and chipped. Dolls of various sizes sat in a row like children on a school bench, their dresses limp with age, their heads balding in patches, their glassy eyes wide and staring.

Our next stop after the nursery was Alexander's large bedroom at the end of the hall. I crossed the threshold to the sight of tall windows facing east, but the light they gathered seemed lost in the darkness of the paneled walls and massive furniture. A bed covered in burgundy satin sent up four posters like arrow-tipped spears. A tall wardrobe spanned one corner, its contents secreted behind heavy doors secured with brass locks. In the opposite corner a stone fireplace sprawled floor to ceiling, its blackened maw swallowing light beams that ventured too near.

The docent paused before the portrait of a woman in her late twenties with rather bulging brown eyes under a brown velvet hat. This was Alexander's first wife of ten years, Anastasia Styvolsky, whom he had married in Russia and brought back to California. The docent launched into a history of the distinguished Styvolsky family, and I suddenly didn't want to hear the story. To listen seemed somehow disloyal to the sweet young Isabel.

I slipped unnoticed into the hallway and leaned over

the banister, trying to see down into the round entry hall. Apart from an occasional laugh from Alexander's room, the great house seemed deserted and deeply silent, except for a soft, rhythmic ticking.

I turned and confronted a tall grandfather clock. Its elaborate face of etched brass displayed not only the time of day but also the phases of the moon through a small window above the fulcrum of its hands. Behind a beveled-glass door, a polished pendulum swung in precise, unhurried strokes.

Herded along with the group, I had passed by this quiet sentry without noticing it earlier. Now, as we faced each other, I felt curiously humbled, as if I were standing in the presence of an old and wise being. The monotonous metering of its pendulum brought to mind a song I had learned in grade school: "My grandfather's clock was too large for the shelf, so it stood ninety years on the floor…"

The docent's voice preceded her into the hallway. She glanced at me in surprise as she gathered the group before the clock.

"This clock was a wedding gift from Anastasia's family. It stood originally in the parlor at Summerwood Cottage, where the couple lived during their first years of marriage. When Alexander built this house, it stood in the downstairs foyer for many years before being moved upstairs to this present location. To my knowledge, the clock has never failed to keep time in over one hundred years."

As the group murmured appreciatively, Ryan touched my elbow. "You disappeared," he said.

I shrugged and let his comment pass. "You and Chris seem to be getting along rather well."

Chris had rejoined Lisa, who was walking just behind the docent. I saw Amanda craning her neck, looking for me.

"I like Chris," Ryan responded. "He's bright and full of ideas, some of them not very practical but at least original. I've been thinking we may be able to use him at the firm when he graduates."

We finished touring the upstairs floor and started down the great staircase. Halfway down, the docent stopped us and pointed to the wall above the entrance doors, where the Rosswood crest hung—a royal blue shield sprinkled with tiny gold stars and a gold crown at its center, overlaid with an *R* in elaborate gold script.

"That's the Rostnova family crest," she said. "When Alexander returned from his education in Moscow, he dreamed of building a house exactly like his ancestral home in Russia, right down to the family crest. This house was called 'The Russian House' by locals for years, and the surrounding forest 'The Russian Woods.' Over time, the names changed to Rosswood, 'Ross' being another word for 'Russian.' Fortunately for the family, when the Rostnova name passed out of existence in California, they could keep the family crest with its *R* for Rosswood instead of Rostnova.

"The great earthquake of 1906 caused such a shift in the earth's crust that many local hot springs dried up, including those at Cougar Canyon and Golden Springs Valley. As the tourist business declined, Springstown became a logging town and shipped its lumber downriver to help rebuild old San Francisco. The town's name was officially changed in 1922 to Rossport because most of the lumber came from Rosswood lands, and the family was the biggest employer of local labor."

Amanda caught up with us as the docent proceeded down the stairs to the foyer. "She forgot to mention the crown," she whispered. "One of the family's ancestors was a cousin or an uncle or something to the czarina of Russia. I guess the family thought that made them royalty, 'cause they put that crown in their crest."

I nodded, thinking how it must have pleased Alexander to lay claim to a Russian crown, however obscurely.

At the hospitality table the docent turned to face us.

"Ladies and gentlemen, this concludes our formal tour of Rosswood House. Before you leave, please be sure to visit our art gallery and gift shop located through that door." She pointed to her left. "Today you can meet Elise Delacroix, one of our local artists and Alexander's last surviving grandchild. She always has some interesting stories to tell about growing up in Sonoma County." She waved her other arm to the right. "Also, please feel free to visit at your leisure the chapel and formal garden located on the east side of the house. Thank you all for visiting Rosswood House."

Amid polite applause, several of the group clustered around the docent to ask a few last questions. I was about to ask Ryan if he wanted to visit the chapel and garden when Amanda clutched my arm.

"You can't leave yet! You haven't seen the art gallery or met Elise Delacroix. She's the best part of the whole tour because she's *real!*"

Ryan smiled at me over Amanda's head and lifted an eyebrow. I smiled back. Together we meekly followed her into the gift shop.

Chapter Eight

Amanda prodded us through the narrow aisles with barely enough time to glance at the souvenir sweatshirts and boxed sets of Rosswood Estate wine. The gift shop opened abruptly into the art gallery, a long high-ceilinged room naturally bright with an uninterrupted wall of windows. Paintings studded the wall on our right and caught my interest, but Amanda was already pointing to a cluster of people at the far end of the room, their attention riveted on a tiny white-haired woman seated in their midst.

We quietly joined the group and picked up the thread of Elise Delacroix's story.

"The Indians didn't like it, of course." The old woman's voice was surprisingly deep. "Alexander had built his great house on their sacred hill, the place set apart for meeting with their gods. And so, the Indians watched and waited for the mighty ones to take their revenge."

Elise dropped her voice to a stage whisper. "It happened on the night of his daughter Katherine's wedding. Alexander had been celebrating at The Green Bottle, the old tavern in town. It was nearly midnight when he left, drunk as a skunk by all accounts, but he'd gotten himself home in that condition plenty of times before. His horse, Ebony Fire, could be trusted to find the way. The sky was dark—the night of a new moon—and no one ever knew what really happened."

She paused dramatically and glanced around her silent audience. "Farmer Ferris drove his wagon down the road next morning and recognized Ebony Fire standing off to the side. Everyone knew the Russian's horse—he'd raised it from a colt to be the most beautiful, most intelligent stallion in the county. Ferris climbed down from his wagon and tried to catch the horse's reins, but it was spooked and wouldn't let him get near. Then he spotted Alexander lying in the gully, his neck twisted at a peculiar angle and his eyes staring up with such a look of wild evil that Ferris thought for sure he was demon-possessed. Then he saw that the man was dead. Ferris couldn't make himself go down there alone. He jumped on his wagon and high-tailed it back to town to get help."

Elise settled back in her chair, and her voice regained a normal pitch. "The Indians said one of their mighty ones appeared on the road and cast a spell on Ebony Fire to make him throw his master. It's a fact that the horse went so loco they had to shoot him. Christian folk said it was the devil come to claim Alexander's soul for his evil deeds and for marrying his daughter to the wicked Anton Kamarov, who also came to a mysterious death two years later. Who knows?"

She spread her hands and shrugged. "But it wasn't coincidence that brought the terrible drought to an end that year. The rains began almost from the hour Alexander was found dead. Two Trees Creek began to rise, and cougars were seen once again on the ridge—a good omen. Folks never could agree if it was a demon or an angel that appeared on the road that night. But they couldn't argue that their troubles ended at the same time the arrogant Russian lost his life." Elise nodded. "The Indians say the gods look after their own. They always have and still do. Tomorrow night—the first new moon of spring—they will come again to their sacred hill, looking for believers."

Elise raised her hands, signaling the end of her story. We all clapped, and she nodded and smiled graciously. Someone helped her rise from her chair, and I turned to Ryan, who quirked his eyebrow and gave me a skeptical smile. I was about to respond when a hand clamped onto my arm.

Startled, I turned and looked fully into the face of the little storyteller. Elise was staring hard at me, her grip on my arm almost painful.

"My dear," she said urgently, "do I know you? You seem so familiar, but I can't quite place you." She searched my face anxiously. "Tell me. Were we at school together?"

She released my arm and leaned heavily on her cane but continued to study me. This close to her, I thought I detected a hint of the Asian about her features, in the slant of her dark eyes and the roundness of her face, perhaps from her eastern Russian heritage. Her gaze grew more intense, the recognition in her eyes so convincing that I could do nothing but stare back at her in mute astonishment.

I noticed her hand on the cane began to tremble. Soon her small figure shook all over, yet she continued to stare at me with that unnerving intensity. I was afraid she would fall. Indeed, a docent rushed past me and caught her shoulders just as the tiny storyteller began to pitch forward.

"That's all right, dear. Time for you to rest." The docent glanced around briefly and said, "This happens sometimes." Murmuring encouraging words about a spot of tea and some nice banana bread, she led away the trembling old woman and disappeared with her behind a door marked "Private."

My legs wobbled, and I dropped gratefully onto the velvet chair Elise had vacated. People milled around, throwing me surreptitious glances and murmuring to each other.

I grabbed Ryan's hand with both of mine and looked up at him. "What does it mean?" I whispered. "She *recognized* me!"

Ryan squatted beside my chair. "It means nothing. She's old and confused. You probably look like someone she used to know."

Amanda had backed away from us. She stood close to her mother and stared at me with round eyes.

Lisa approached, frowning. "Vicki, what happened?" She glanced at Ryan as he rose and stood behind me. "Something about that old lady knowing you?"

"She doesn't. It's a mistake." Ryan's voice was firm, like his grip on my shoulder.

"Are you okay?" Lisa peered into my face. "Can I get you a glass of water?"

I shook my head and laughed weakly. "It was too weird. For a moment I felt certain I must have known her in a previous life or something. I can't explain it."

I realized I was speaking very loudly.

Lisa nodded and brought a chair close to mine. She sat down. "My grandmother got pretty scary sometimes. Out of the blue, she'd start calling me Martha and my sister Sarah, like we were her sisters. I'd swear at those times she could look right through me, like I wasn't even there. It was the creepiest feeling."

She grimaced, and I shuddered. We laughed quietly. I glanced around and saw Ryan standing by the wall of paintings, talking with a docent. He nodded and shook hands with the man.

I rose from my chair as he approached.

"Feeling better?" He scanned my face and nodded. "Good. There's something I want you to see."

He took my elbow and guided me toward the painting he had apparently been discussing with the docent. Lisa came with us, but I was hardly aware of her as I stopped short before the painting, paralyzed with shock.

There in the painting stood the old bridge. There was the moon, the curling mist, and the young woman poised at the rail. Her dark hair fell behind her shoulders and down her back, just as I had seen her in my dream. But even more shocking was the second figure in the painting, a woman with long blond hair, standing on the rise above the bridge. She gazed down at the dark-haired woman with her arms outstretched. Her face was in profile, and I couldn't be absolutely certain of her features...

"That's amazing," Lisa said. "Vicki, she looks just like you!"

* * *

"You don't believe a word I've said."

I drew the quilt tighter around my body and huddled further into the corner of the window seat in our bedroom at Summerwood. Alice, bless her, had fixed us some hot tea, but its soothing effects were already fading, and the terrible shivering had returned. Ryan's cup sat cold and untouched on the floor beside him. He'd pulled up a chair from the writing desk and was sitting forward — hands clasped, elbows resting on his knees — as he listened to my story.

My speech was halting at first, labored, as if each word were being pulled up from a place deep inside my body. I told Ryan everything — how I had lost my mother's love at the same time the bear began chasing me through my nightmares. I told him about the blue cornflowers that took me away from him whenever we made love, and about the fantasy rose garden where I waited for the father who wasn't mine.

Then I told him about my vision at Two Trees Creek, which Stacey later confirmed as a legendary event in what she called a haunted place. I described my dream of the bridge and how I knew, with inexplicable certainty, that the dark-haired woman emerging from the moon-mist was Katherine Rostnova. It was she who had visited me on that enchanted night when I was twelve years old, who would be waiting for me when I slept again tonight.

I cried through most of my narrative, wiping my runny nose on my sleeve and not caring, desperate to get my story told. But part of me held back from the grip of emotion and slipped quietly outside the quilt to clinically scrutinize the scene of a woman telling her story and a man observing her. The man was tense and silent, and I could see he didn't believe her, didn't believe in Katherine or the bridge. He was going to ply the woman with logic and tell her she was crazy.

"Vicki, it's all so...fantastic." Ryan spread his hands and leaned back in his chair. "I'm glad you told me. I can see all this has been tearing you up. And no wonder."

It was undeniable, that edge of skepticism in his voice, the slight arch of his brows over cool, reasonable eyes. I was surprised at how much it hurt me.

"You don't believe a word I've said."

"Now, wait just a minute." He held up his hand like a policeman. "I didn't say that. Let's start with the last part, about the bridge and this woman." He chose his words carefully. "You say you dreamed about her before you saw the painting this afternoon."

I nodded. "And Elise knew me," I added.

"Well, that's the point, isn't it? The docent told me Elise painted that picture years ago. She thought she recognized you because you look remarkably like the woman she painted. Doesn't that make sense?"

"No. She painted me because she knew me somehow. And she recognized me today. I'm sure of it."

"But how? How is that possible?"

"I don't know. I just know it's true." His eyes narrowed at my stubbornness, and I looked away. I traced a finger over a seam in the quilt and wondered idly if the patches had been sewn together by hand or machine. I had always wanted to learn how to quilt.

"Vicki, that doesn't make any sense." Ryan's tone was irritatingly patient. "You must have seen a copy of that painting in one of those Sonoma County books lying around here. The parlor downstairs is full of them. You might not even remember seeing it, but you dreamed about it and put yourself in as the second figure because you already look so much like her. Doesn't that make more sense?"

He was so intense that I had to look up at him. His brows were dipped in a fierce V, and his gaze bored through mine with such force I could almost feel it at the back of my skull.

I realized that even if I held out for what I believed to be true, I could never explain myself to his satisfaction. My conviction would lodge itself between us as one more barrier.

I tugged at a loose thread escaping from a seam in the quilt. "I suppose you're right," I said, despising myself for my cowardice. "The way you explain it sounds very logical."

"Yes" was all he said. But I heard the relief in his voice.

I pulled at the thread, and to my dismay several stitches came loose. I fixed my gaze on Ryan's face.

"Do you think I'm crazy?"

He had the grace to meet my eyes.

"No, I don't think you're crazy." He spoke kindly. "I do think you went through some pretty bad times, though, when you were a child—everything you said about the nightmares and the bear chasing you through Eleanor's house. And there's that business of the cornflowers, how you can disappear inside yourself when I touch you. I wonder—" He cocked his head and stared at me with sudden speculation I found unnerving. "I wonder, Vicki, if you were ever molested in your grandmother's house."

Two Trees Creek suddenly rushed all around me. I imagined myself as a thin yellow pencil bobbing helplessly on a swell of current.

Ryan pressed on. "It makes sense when you put it all together. And it might explain why your mother acts so peculiarly around you. I've noticed that myself."

The creek rushed louder, sucking me downstream. I fought against the current and tried to pull myself upstream, toward the bridge. Toward safety.

"It could explain why you have trouble with sex." Ryan's voice rose as he warmed to his theory.

I was making progress. The sheer force of my mind cut through the water, propelling me upstream against the current. I wondered how far I had to go, how long I had to concentrate, until I would be safe.

"Vicki?"

The sudden press of Ryan's hands on mine snapped me in two. Half of me sank beneath the tumbling creek water while the other half surfaced into our bedroom at Summerwood. Confused, frightened, I snatched my hands away from Ryan and shrieked, "*Don't touch me!*"

He jumped in recoil, his eyes wide and dark with shock. I stared at him for a horrified moment. Then I buried my face in my hands and whispered, "Oh, Ryan. I'm sorry. Please, will you just go away and leave me alone?"

More frightening than tears were the dry sobs now shaking me. Like the silent screams of my nightmare, they clenched my heart and squeezed it until I thought the pain would kill me. Then, in a single burst of agony, the pain exploded, and a memory surfaced. Like an unexpected island in a clearing mist, my bedroom at Eleanor's appeared—as solid and real as if I were once again eight years old.

I knew the man who came to my room, one of the many my mother brought home and entertained in the library after I was in bed. I couldn't remember what he looked like, only the smell of his hand on my mouth and his whiskey breath on my face as he whispered urgently, "Not a sound, little lady. Now just relax. You're gonna love this."

He pulled back the covers and pushed up my nightgown, cursing softly as he struggled to get my underpants off with only one hand. I tried to get away, but he pushed me into the mattress and threatened to hurt me if I made any noise. When he finally took his hand away from my mouth, I found that I couldn't scream. I couldn't move my body at all. I lay like something dead, even when he started pushing at me and making a strange choking noise in his throat. Only my gaze moved, following the stream of moonlight from the window to the wallpaper beside my bed, where it fell on cheery sprays of cornflowers. They made room for me, and I lost myself in their quiet blue, creating a small space of escape where only I could fit.

It was the quiet blue that muted his voice whispering in my ear, "Can't help it, darlin'. You're just too beautiful. This is your fault, not mine." It was the quiet blue that covered the stabs of pain and numbed the startling new sensations that made my body writhe and jerk, while he chuckled above me in the dark. It was the quiet blue that stayed with me after he left me with a warning not to tell or something terrible would happen to me and my mother. The next morning there were bloody sheets I couldn't explain and that look of suspicion and fear that came to live in my mother's eyes whenever she looked at me.

Ryan had said I was molested, but he didn't know what he was talking about. Molestation was something that happened to rough girls who lived in poverty and had stepfathers who slept with them and made them pregnant. It didn't happen to rich girls who were well brought up and attended parochial schools. It couldn't happen to the granddaughter of Eleanor Prescott.

From the silence in the room, I assumed Ryan had honored my request and left me alone. My eyes still dry, I turned my face to the window and lowered my hands. The old oak waved eerie gray branches in the gathering dusk. I stared at it without emotion and wondered how I could have forgotten the incident for so many years. I'd never told anyone about it, yet I remembered every detail. I even remembered how I had wanted to tell my mother, how I wanted her to explain to me what the man had done. But she seemed so distant after that night, so uneasy with me that I knew I would only make her more unhappy if she knew the truth about me.

With a painful jolt, I realized that my mother already knew the truth. She had always known. And yet she never tried to help me. She hadn't protected me, and she didn't care for me afterward. She didn't care.

Bile spurted into my throat — hot and sour. I swallowed down dismay and a budding outrage at my mother's betrayal. I jerked my gaze from the window, only to jump at the sight of Ryan still sitting in his chair, watching me intently.

I stiffened but reassured myself that he couldn't know what I had remembered. Nevertheless, he stared at me with such frank speculation in his eyes that I looked away, afraid my new knowledge would somehow show and give me away.

"Ryan." I couldn't keep my voice from shaking. "I didn't know you were still here." My stomach gave a small heave, thrusting bile back into my throat. I swallowed repeatedly and pressed a hand to my forehead as Ryan rose from his chair.

"I want you to see someone when we get back to the city," he said. His voice was gentle, not condemning but deeply sad, almost wistful. "For your own sake, Vicki." He took a step toward me, but I shrank back, and he hesitated. "You want to be alone?" he asked quietly.

I dropped my gaze and nodded. He stood for a moment, his hands at his sides. Then he turned without another word and crossed the room. The door shut softly behind him.

I stared down at the quilt squares without really seeing them. My mind seemed dull, and my body so remote that I didn't feel the clammy waves rising until it was almost too late.

The quilt dropped away as I dashed for the door and threw myself into the hallway, not caring who saw me as I lunged into the bathroom and collapsed before the toilet just in time to vomit.

I clung to the cold porcelain as anger and bitterness heaved up wave after wave, erupting from a putrid pool like a geyser suddenly unearthed. Hot tears of misery mingled with the dripping acid and shook my body with sobs so deep my bones ached. The only coherent thought in my head was a prayer that doggedly repeated itself: *Please, God, take me from this world where I find no peace and no one to love me. Please, God, take me…*

I spoke the words aloud, repeatedly, cycling them like a mantra. The retching subsided, and my body temperature dropped from flaming to a sweaty chill that brought back the awful shivering. The merciless tile floor was cold and hard, bruising my knees, and made it difficult to rise. When I finally stood, a numbing calm quieted my shivers and silenced the nerves in my body one by one. The numbness crept along my limbs, into my toes and fingertips, and seeped into my brain.

With a comforting sense of unreality, I closed the bathroom door, washed my face and hands, and wiped the telltale traces of my shame from the toilet. When I finished, I gazed with dull interest into the mirror, noting the woman's pale face and enormous eyes without feeling the slightest conviction that the face belonged to me. I looked at her hands and watched her fingers flex, but I couldn't feel them. I couldn't feel her body at all because we had already separated. I had detached myself and escaped into that small, secret space where only I could fit.

Chapter Nine

The sun was up well before I was the next morning. My eyelids felt glued shut, my tongue thick in my mouth. But my body felt rested despite its sluggish response to my brain's order to wake up.

Ryan sat on the bed, holding a steaming mug in his hand.

"Time to wake up," he said. "Breakfast is over downstairs, but I salvaged a plate for you. Here, I'll get those pillows."

He helped me arrange the pillows so I could sit up against them. The smell of hot tea and bacon worked wonders in getting my eyes open and cleared some of the cobwebs from my brain. I was starving. I realized I'd had no dinner the night before.

I accepted the mug he offered and took a long sip. The tea slipped slow and hot into my body, rousing it pleasantly. I eagerly eyed the plate of food on the night table and reached for a blueberry muffin.

"Has everyone eaten already?" I asked, marveling at how sweet the muffin tasted.

"Hardly anyone is still here." Ryan laid a napkin over my stomach to catch the crumbs. "Chris and Lisa left yesterday. Lisa wanted to say good-bye, but you were already sleeping. I gave her our phone number, and she'll call you when we get back. Amanda said good-bye, too, before she left with her parents."

I remembered that this was Monday morning. Unlike

the typical weekend boarders, we were staying over one more night. Ryan planned to spend the day scouting around the construction site and finalizing his notes on local history. Unless I went with him, I would be alone today.

"How do you feel this morning?" Ryan peered into my face and nodded. "Looks like the roses are back in your cheeks." He started to lift a hand to my face but then dropped it back to his lap. "Did you sleep well?"

I nodded, munching bacon. It was heavenly—not too crisp, just the way I liked it.

"No bad dreams?" Ryan spoke carefully.

I hesitated and shook my head, avoiding his eyes. "By the way," I said, "thanks for hearing me out yesterday. I feel much better this morning. Really."

It was true. I felt rested, lighter, and stronger than I had in a long time.

Cleansed.

Ryan nodded and stood. He gave me a smile I think he meant to be cheery, but it only made him look sad. He snatched a strip of bacon from my plate and raised it in a mock salute.

"Got notes to finish up downstairs," he said. He popped the bacon into his mouth and left.

I looked down at the quilt and ran my finger over the seams, idly searching for the thread I had unwittingly begun to unravel.

* * *

The late morning sky was filling with clouds. Daylight waxed and waned as gusts of wind blew fleecy patches across the face of a remote sun.

I stood at our bedroom window and peered up through

bare oak branches at the disappearing patches of blue. A storm was brewing, certain to hit by tonight. But it would be dark in any case, for tonight would bring the first new moon of spring. Wasn't that what Elise Delacroix had said?

I turned from the window, folded my arms across my chest, and rubbed my hands up and down my shirtsleeves. Just as it hushed the feral animals in the forest, the threat of the storm jangled my nerves and prickled my flesh with goose bumps. More from habit than from conscious intent, I reached for my handbag, drew out my wallet, and probed for the old souvenir coin in the pocket behind my wedding picture.

I felt calmer as soon as I rubbed my thumb over the raised American flag and found the familiar nick in the coin's rim. On the flip side, the words "All Brothers of the Land" depicted the fair's theme in five languages: English, Spanish, Chinese, Russian, and Native American.

The door flew open and Ryan strode into the room, carrying a clipboard.

"Oh. Hi, Vicki. You're dressed." He rummaged through his briefcase and extracted a calculator and a tape measure. "Alice and I are right next door, if you want to join us." He eyed me briefly, appraisingly, before he disappeared into the passageway, leaving the door open.

Curious, I followed. The two of them were measuring off the dimensions of a large attic. Weak daylight pressed against two large windows facing east and south. Except for a few chairs stacked in a corner and a rolled-up carpet, the room was empty. Ryan's and Alice's voices echoed as they called out numbers to each other.

"Good morning, Vicki! How do you feel?" Alice stood poised at one end of the tape, her smile warm as she greeted me.

"Better, thanks, after a good night's sleep."

"Well, that's a relief. You looked like death when Ryan brought you home yesterday. I said to him you could have a touch of the flu that's been going around." She released her end of the tape as Ryan jotted down numbers on his clipboard. "I told him it's a good thing you're staying over one more night, so you can rest up."

Her expression was sympathetic, but her eyes were curious. I looked away and said nothing.

"Well, Alice, I think you could get two decent-sized rooms out of this. Or maybe a suite with a fireplace and sitting area over there. Like this." Ryan sketched on the clipboard, and Alice drew closer, looking over his shoulder and asking questions.

I wandered around the room, noticing a square of lighter floorboards near the attic's center. It looked as though a carpet had lain on that exact spot for a long time and had only recently been removed, probably the one that was rolled up in the corner right now.

I reached the south-facing window and looked out. A thick roll of clouds stretched overhead and dropped behind a distant stand of redwoods. I traced the road for about a half-mile but couldn't see where it crossed over the creek.

"Vicki?" I turned from the window as Ryan pocketed his pen. "I'm taking a run over to the site this afternoon. Would you like to come with me? Or do you think you'll be all right here by yourself?"

I glanced at Alice, but she was absorbed in Ryan's sketches as she headed for the door.

"I'll be fine, Ryan." My voice echoed, and I lowered it. "Don't worry. I'll probably do some reading and maybe lie down for a little while. You take all the time you need."

"Sure?" He raised his eyebrows. "Okay, then. Let's head into town and get some lunch. Then I'll bring you back and be off myself."

He followed Alice into the hall. I started after them, but as I approached the center of the attic, my souvenir coin tumbled unexpectedly from my hand. It bounced once, traced an arc in the square of lighter floorboards, and disappeared!

With a cry, I dropped to all fours and discovered a knothole in the flooring just large enough for the coin to drop through. I thrust my finger into the hole, but I knew there was no way I could pull the coin out. I felt my fingertip brush against it, pushing it further away.

Stunned by my loss, I leaned back and, to my astonishment, pulled up a piece of flooring about a foot long. I sat, startled, with the board dangling from my fingers. Then I realized I had exposed a tiny chamber beneath the attic floor.

Through a thick veil of dust and cobwebs, I saw the glint of copper next to some other shiny object. Gingerly, I reached in and drew out a small glass bottle. An ink bottle.

All the ink was gone, leaving a dark film crusting the inside surface of the glass. Curiosity made me bold, and I dipped my hand deeper into the cobwebs, exploring carefully with my fingers.

They brushed against something firm and smooth, definitely not wood. I found an edge and grasped the object, pulling it gently into the light. It was square and flat, wrapped in a smooth cloth, perhaps oilskin.

Too late I remembered the coin. As I pulled the package out, the coin tumbled to a lower level with a dull thud. I peered into the dark hole, but my lucky charm was gone.

Churning with a confused mix of disappointment and excitement, I turned my attention to what the coin had inadvertently purchased for me.

The package lay on the floor, filthy with dust and shouting to be opened. I eased back the folds of cloth and sucked in my breath as I saw it was a book. The red satin cover was faded and stained, but in the lower right corner the name embossed in gold was unmistakable: Katherine A. Rostnova.

"Vicki?" Ryan's voice rose from the foyer.

"Yes! I'm coming!" Quickly, I shoved the dirty oilskin and the empty inkbottle back into the hole and replaced the floorboard. Obeying an instinct I had no time to examine, I hid the book behind my back as I edged out the door and peeked over the banister. Ryan stood with one foot on the bottom step of the stairs, looking up impatiently.

"Sorry," I called. "I dropped my coin and got my finger stuck. I mean, I'll just be a minute!"

I backed into our bedroom, turned, and ran to the desk, where my satchel lay beside my handbag. I thrust the book into the satchel, which I then hid beneath the quilt folded neatly at the foot of the bed. Grabbing up my handbag and a jacket, I flew out the door and collided with Ryan, who had lost all patience and climbed the stairs to find out what was keeping me.

Chapter Ten

Katherine's journal began in the round, careful pen strokes of a child. I sat snug on the window seat in our Tree House room, the quilt tucked around my legs and the journal open on my knees. I forgot the storm-threatened afternoon as I lost myself in Katherine's narrative, thrilled at the privilege of trespassing in a world more than a century past.

25 April 1888. My name is Katherine Alexander Rostnova. Today Nicholas and I are nine years old. Nicholas is my twin brother. Auntie Ana says I am old enough to have a keepsake book like proper young ladies have. Here I am to record special events and remembrances. But does this mean I must become a proper young lady? I think not.

4 August 1888. Auntie Ana and Uncle Leon are staying with us until September. They have brought Anton, who is Auntie Ana's brother, and also Michael, her nephew. Anton is sixteen, and I hate him. He pulls my hair and laughs, and I tell Papa, but he does nothing. Anton will live with us now and help Papa with the ranch. Michael is no fun to play with. He only likes to read books and play chess with Nicholas. Dora (she is my Indian nurse) tells me I am too old to play with boys. But

I am so bored sitting in the parlor with the ladies doing embroidery. I always do my stitches wrong, and Mama makes me pull them out and do them again. I would rather ride the horses, but Papa will not allow it.

2 September 1888. All our company left except Anton because he's staying on. Monsieur Dante arrived, and Nicholas and I started lessons. Auntie Ana told Mama we should go to the new schoolhouse in town like the other children. But Papa will not hear of it. He says we are not to mix with the town children. Nicholas likes his lessons, but I want to be outside while the weather is still warm. Monsieur gets very angry with me. He says, "Be more like your brother!" Why should I want to be like Nicholas? He is so good and obedient, Mama's darling boy. He never has fun.

Christmas 1888. Papa gave Nicholas a riding crop for Christmas. Nicholas is afraid of horses, but he pretends to like them so Papa will not be angry. I am not afraid, but Papa only lets me ride on the old white mare that can barely walk. My Christmas present was a doll with moving eyes and curly yellow hair. I don't like the doll because she is beautiful, like Mama, and I am not. Papa calls me his ugly swan. I took scissors from Mama's workbasket and cut the doll's hair off. Anton saw me do it and told on me. Mama asked me why I did that, but I had no answer. She took the doll away and made me stay in my room when the Stillmans came for Christmas supper. I didn't get any supper, but later Dora brought me some berry pie in secret. I thought I was hungry but could not eat it after all.

3 January 1889. Anton stole Nicholas's new riding crop. Nicholas was scared to say anything, but I told Papa. He called Anton and Nicholas into the library and asked them. Nicholas is scared of Anton, so he said he made the riding crop a gift. I think Papa knew Nicholas was lying, but he didn't make Anton give the riding crop back. Papa likes strength better than honesty.

25 April 1889. Today is our tenth birthday. I got a new dress, and Papa bought a pony for Nicholas. Mama says maybe the pony is too frisky. She knows Nicholas is afraid of horses, but she doesn't like to tell Papa this. Nicholas is too scared to ride it. Papa tried to make him, and Nicholas started crying like a girl. I wanted to show Papa I'm not afraid. So I grabbed the reins from Nicholas and jumped up on the pony and rode it into the field. The pony was gentle and easy to ride. When I came back, I expected Papa to be proud of me. But he was furious! He pulled me off the horse and struck me down. He says I tried to humiliate him. It's not true! I only wanted Papa to see how I am not afraid and to let me be his boy instead of Nicholas.

10 February 1890. I've been calling Dora by

her full name, *tejedora,* which means "weaver." Indians go by names for what they do, like being a hunter or a painter. I call her—"Hey, *Tejedora*!"— but she doesn't care. She told me she has an Indian name that only her family knows about, but they are all dead now. She says every Indian has a secret name you never tell anyone. It's like it's really you, somehow, and if your enemies knew it, they could use it to make a wicked song about you that could kill you! I tell her I don't believe it, but she just smiles like she does when she's being a mysterious Indian. I know she won't ever tell me her secret name. I'm going to make a secret name for myself and never tell anyone. People will call me Katherine, but they'll never be able to kill me because they won't know my secret name!

19 February 1890. I thought of a good secret name for myself. It's so secret, I won't even write it down here. Ha, ha!

25 April 1890. Nicholas and I are eleven years old today. Grandfather Petrov gave us special presents. He planted a dogwood tree for Nicholas in his front yard, and he says it will grow tall and strong the way God will make Nicholas as he grows to be a man. Then he showed us a special rose bush he planted. He calls it 'Katherine' after me. He says it will have yellow petals with orange edges, and it will smell sweet to remind everyone how good I am. Grandfather always thinks I'm good. He doesn't know how bad I really am and how I think a lot of wicked thoughts. He just loves me. I wish Mama and Papa could see me the way Grandfather does.

10 June 1890. I found a baby hawk lying on the ground in the woods. I brought it home and put it in a box. It is too weak to climb out. I dug up an earthworm to feed it, but it will not eat. I want to build a big cage for it and train it to obey me. Dora says I should have left it where I found it.

11 June 1890. The baby hawk died. Dora helped me bury it in the woods where I found it. She said it would not have liked living in a cage, anyway. She said it is better to love with an open hand. I told her I don't understand that. If I didn't keep it in a cage, it would fly away, and I would never see it again. I think it's better to love something you're certain won't leave you.

30 June 1890. Nicholas likes Theresa Stillman. The Stillmans are our neighbors. When she comes over, he stammers and gets red in the face. I tease him about it, but Mama tells me to hush up. She likes Theresa, although I can't think why. Theresa is quiet and dainty and boring. I suppose that makes her a good match for Nicholas. She can sew a straight seam, but I don't think she has a brain in her head.

17 August 1890. Grandfather is dead. Right now he is lying in his coffin in the parlor downstairs, all dressed up in his Sunday clothes. I'm scared to go downstairs with him there. Papa made me go into the parlor and pray with the family, and I saw Grandfather, but it doesn't look like him at all. He had twinkling eyes and always smiled at me. His eyes are closed now, and his skin is a funny gray color. I asked Dora if his ghost can come through my door tonight. She says if it does it will be a loving ghost and nothing to be scared of. But I'm leaving a lamp burning all night just the same.

20 August 1890. We buried Grandfather behind Mama's chapel. Mr. Burbank came to the funeral and some of Grandfather's friends from his horticulture club and a lot of people I don't know. I guess he had a lot of friends. Uncle Leon came with Auntie Ana and Michael. Uncle Leon cried at the funeral, and I was embarrassed because I've never seen a grown-up man cry before. I brought some of my 'Katherine' roses and put them with Grandfather before they closed his coffin and put him in the ground.

7 September 1890. I had my first monthly bleeding. I was scared, but Dora showed me what to do. I begged her not to tell Mama, but she did, and Mama came to my room. I made her promise not to tell Papa or Nicholas. It's not fair that my brother doesn't have to go through this.

23 October 1890. Auntie Ana is here to visit

for a month. She brought Michael, but my uncle stayed in San Francisco because he is a famous artist in great demand. I think Mama told her about my bleeding because Auntie Ana keeps looking at me with a fond smile and calling me "our young lady." I'll die if she ever tells Michael. He already thinks girls are silly. He'd never stop teasing me.

25 October 1890. I asked Dora what the word "bastard" means. I heard Anton call Michael a bastard, and Michael hit him and then ran outside. He cried even though he's fourteen. I felt sorry for him. Dora says Michael's mother wasn't married to his father when he was born. Michael's mother is Auntie Ana's sister, and she died in Russia. When Auntie Ana came to California with Uncle Leon, they brought baby Michael with them and raised him. Michael always tells me his father is an English sea captain who will someday come to see us and bring jewels and silks from the Orient. He says his father will take him and Nicholas and me on his ship to see the world when we are old enough. I asked Dora about it, and she said his father will never come back. I wonder if Michael knows that?

13 January 1891. I was visited by an angel child. She came to me in a dream, on a moonbeam, fair-haired, with large clear eyes and so beautiful! I have never seen anyone as perfect as she, except perhaps Mama. I feel this morning as if the Virgin

Mother Herself has touched my lips and blessed me.

12 March 1891. Nicholas is the favorite of everyone. He is also Papa's heir. That means Nicholas will inherit the ranch when Papa dies, but Papa doesn't know how weak and puny Nicholas is. I'd run things a lot better than my brother, but Papa can't leave the ranch to me because I'm just a girl. Nicholas means everything to him and to Mama. Maybe it's because Nicholas is the good half of us and I'm the bad half. I've heard Mama tell Mrs. Stillman that Nicholas is her joy and I'm her trial.

31 March 1891. I know I disappoint Papa because I look like my Indian grandmother. He doesn't like Indians and is always harsh with the ones who work on our ranch. He calls them bad names. Mama has black hair, but it's not straight like mine. Hers is soft and curling, and she has lovely eyes like her Spanish people, not dark brown like mine and Dora's. In truth, I look more like Dora's child than Mama's or Papa's. Grandfather loved me and told me I looked like my grandmother, Morning Star. Anton calls me an ugly little squaw. He hates Indians as much as Papa. But how can Papa hate Indians so much when he is half-Indian himself? I wonder if I had blond hair like Nicholas, would I be good like him instead of being the bad half of us?

17 May 1891. Today was Emily Stillman's sixteenth birthday party. Emily wore a long, ruffled white dress and her hair piled high on top of her head with little flowers and bows in it. I can only admit this in secret, but she looked very pretty, and I was jealous. Ordinarily she's such a prig and I hate her, but today I envied her. Some young men came to the party, and she danced with them. I was not allowed to dance, of course. But when I'm sixteen, I shall have a party bigger than Emily's, and my dress will be prettier, and I'll be so beautiful that no one will recognize me. That's only four years from now.

22 May 1891. Mama is going to have another baby. Papa seems pleased. He hopes it will be a boy. I hope it will be a girl. I'd like to have a little sister to play with and dress up in pretty clothes. Maybe she will be beautiful like Mama or be blond like Papa and Nicholas. She won't look like me because Papa says I'm a throwback, and that only happens once in a generation.

4 July 1891. Today my brother Nicholas lies dead, but I swear I didn't mean to kill him! I didn't think it would work. I just wanted a chance to show them, to show Papa, that I'm as good as a boy and he should be proud of me instead of Nicholas. But now my brother is dead.

The day started with neighbors gathering at our house for the annual game shoot. The women were preparing the banquet supper when Tito came running from the woods to shout that Nicholas was badly hurt. The men brought Nicholas into the house and laid him on the sofa in the parlor. I didn't have to look at his face to know he was already dead. Doctor Goodhall said Nicholas broke his neck when he fell off his horse. He said it was quick, that Nicholas didn't suffer any pain.

Papa was beside himself with fury. He ran outside with his rifle. I followed him, begging him to come back. I watched him shoot Nicholas's horse in the head, and even after it fell to the ground dead, Papa kept shooting and shooting. I covered my ears and screamed at him to stop, but he didn't pay me any mind. When his rifle wouldn't fire anymore, Papa jumped up on Ebony Fire and rode away faster than I've ever seen him ride.

People started going home after that. Some stayed to be with Mama—she collapsed and had to be put to bed. I watched the men pick up my brother's body and carry it upstairs to his bedroom. Except for a little trickle of blood running from his mouth, Nicholas looked like he was asleep. Anton stared hard at me, his face very pale, and I wondered if he saw what happened. I was too afraid to ask him. When he left the room to follow the men upstairs, I realized I was all alone. Dora and the women were with my mother, and the men were either in Nicholas's room or on the porch discussing what happened. How can I explain to them that I never meant for my brother to die?

6 July 1891. We buried Nicholas next to Grandfather. We had to bury him quickly because it was so hot his body wouldn't keep for very long. Auntie Ana and Uncle Leon came to stay with us. Auntie Ana gave all the orders for the dinner after the funeral because Mama was out of her head with grief. The doctor is worried Mama might lose the baby. I haven't seen much of Dora because she is constantly with my mother. She moved into Mama's room and looks after her day and night. Mama did dress and attend the burial. But she went upstairs to bed afterward, so she wasn't at the dinner. Michael and I walked over to Grandfather's cottage and sat in the rose garden while we ate and talked. He asked me what happened. What could I say to him? I told him the story I was told, that Nicholas's horse bolted for some unknown reason, and Nicholas fell off and broke his neck. I didn't cry. I haven't cried at all for Nicholas. I feel dried up inside, with only pangs of guilt to remind me I'm still alive while the good half of us is dead.

30 July 1891. It has been almost a month since we buried Nicholas. Mama keeps to her rooms and will not let anyone in except Dora, not even Auntie Ana. Papa spends most of his evenings in town at The Green Bottle tavern and sometimes doesn't come home until the next day. Auntie Ana is kind to me, but she is busy running the household. She thinks I'm doing fine because I'm not crying or sick like Mama. She doesn't know I'm dead inside. She doesn't know I killed my brother.

12 August 1891. Elizabeth has come to stay with us. She is my age and sleeps in my bed with me. Elizabeth is very good and helps Auntie Ana with the household chores. Sometimes Elizabeth and I stay up late and talk. I can tell Elizabeth things I've never told anyone before, not even Dora. Elizabeth says she will never tell anyone the terrible thing I did to my brother.

16 September 1891. Auntie Ana went back to San Francisco. Mama now comes downstairs for a short time every day. She is very much changed. She is thin and pale, and her eyes are so haunted they frighten me. She has not lost the baby. Anton is managing the ranch because my father spends most of his time in town. I am relieved not to see Anton as much as I used to. Elizabeth and I always wait up for Papa and keep his supper hot for him because Mama doesn't seem to care about Papa anymore.

2 December 1891. It all started last September. Papa came home one night very late and very drunk. Elizabeth and I met him at the door and told him his supper was waiting for him. But he pushed past us to go into the library and poured himself another drink. I told him supper would make him feel better than whiskey. He suddenly whirled around and hit me hard across the mouth with the back of his hand. I didn't expect it. I fell back into the plant stand. The potted fern and I crashed to the floor, and I just lay there, stunned, in the middle of broken pottery and fern and soil. Papa snarled curses at me, and he threw his drink against the wall, breaking the glass on the wood panels. Then he charged out of the room. I heard him stagger up the stairs, and his bedroom door slammed shut. I knew then that he hates me because I'm alive and Nicholas is dead. But I didn't blame him for hitting me. Elizabeth and I decided to let the servants clean up the mess in the morning, and we went to bed.

I was sound asleep, and then wide awake because someone was in my room. I sat straight up in bed, thinking it might be Nicholas's ghost come to take his revenge on me. But someone whispered, "Hush, don't make a sound." It was Papa. Papa had never been in my room before. He sat on the bed, and I jerked my head back when he raised his hand to my face. To my surprise, his hand was gentle. He asked if my face still hurt. I lied and told him no. I knew he was still drunk because he kept stroking my cheek and not saying anything, just stroking and stroking. Then I realized it was Elizabeth he really wanted, not me.

Elizabeth put her arms around his neck, and he lay on top of her, groaning. He didn't stay long, not more than ten minutes. I pretended to be asleep, but I heard everything, the kissing and the moaning. I felt the bed shake under my body. When Papa finally left, there was a smell in the room that clung to the sheets and to Elizabeth. I knew that Papa had changed everything between Elizabeth and me. He despises me, but he loves her. And why not? Elizabeth is good and sweet, like Nicholas was. Elizabeth did not kill her brother.

Since September, Papa has made many nighttime visits to Elizabeth. She and I never speak of them, and nobody else knows. At all costs, Mama must never, ever find out.

Chapter Eleven

Following the December 2nd journal entry, I came across several pages of carefully labeled botanical sketches. I remembered Amanda telling me that Katherine had learned about native medicines and spells from her nurse. Beside each of her drawings Katherine had noted the plant's medicinal uses.

ANGELICA: tea for bleeding, cramps, and irregularity; rub root on skin rashes, bruises, and swellings, and also for protection from evil spirits.

COMFREY: poultice for insect bites, burns, skin rashes, cuts, bruises.

SOAPROOT: juice from roots on skin rashes from poison oak.

MISTLETOE: tea to prevent pregnancy or to cause miscarriage.

SAGE: gargle for sore throat.

The drawings showed superb photographic detail, with small close-ups of fruits, leaves, and roots. I could easily see that Katherine had possessed a keen artistic talent.

BLACKBERRY: juice for treatment of diarrhea.

ONION: poultice for croup, pneumonia, and chest colds.

CHERRY: tree bark makes tea for treating colds and measles.

Abruptly, the journal entries began again.

25 April 1892. I am fourteen years old today. We do not celebrate my birthday anymore since Nicholas is gone. It just makes Mama sad and Papa angry to remember. Dora gave me a blanket that she wove herself. She said the pattern in it was specially designed by her mother just for her when she was a young girl. The design is good luck for her, and she said it will bring me good luck, too. Dora was very sweet to remember my birthday.

23 September 1892. My little brother Robbie is a year old today. He is very sickly. Dr. Goodhall said he did not expect Robbie to live to see his first birthday. Papa despises Robbie, and he blames Mama for Robbie's condition. Mama and Papa hardly ever talk anymore without fighting. Papa said he could not leave the ranch to a weakling son. He has lost interest in running things and in taking care of us. Anton is twenty now, and he has taken over managing the ranch for Papa. Papa spends a lot of time in town and usually comes home drunk and mean. Nobody knows that Papa still comes to our room sometimes at night.

10 December 1892. Mama has given Dora and me permission to use Grandfather's garden workroom at the cottage. Nobody else uses the cottage now. Dora is teaching me how to distill oils and how to dry and store roots and leaves. I like being in the cottage by myself, too. I like being alone. Sometimes I go there just to sit in Grandfather's rose garden and remember how it felt to be loved. I never let Elizabeth come with me to the cottage. I like to think it belongs to me alone.

25 December 1892. We spent a quiet Christmas at home. Auntie Ana and Uncle Leon visited, and Michael brought an odious boy from school named Daryl. The two of them are impossible together. For a Christmas present, Auntie Ana gave me a color box with paints and brushes. She saw some sketches I did when she was here last summer, and she said I should try my hand at painting. Uncle Leon told me that artists run in the family. He thinks I'm gifted. I am very flattered because, of course, he is one of the most gifted artists in the world.

30 January 1893. I like painting. I know I can't paint at the house, so I set up an easel in the attic at the cottage, and I paint there during the day. I didn't ask permission, but I don't see why anyone would care. They don't care what I do. I don't have a tutor anymore since Papa says education is wasted on girls, and Robbie is, of course, too young. But I don't think Papa will spend money on a tutor for Robbie, either. Papa is a hard man and doesn't care much about any of us since The Death.

The next several pages were filled with more botanical drawings. I noticed that the next journal entry was dated a year and a half later.

26 October 1894. Yesterday I was exactly fifteen and one-half years old. I decided to celebrate by getting drunk. I sneaked a bottle of peach brandy from the dining room and drank it in the rose garden at the cottage. I expected to feel wonderful, since adults like it so much. It tasted strange, sweet and burning at the same time. I drank quite a lot. Then I felt terrible. I vomited behind the garden workroom and just lay on the ground, too sick to move. I must have fallen asleep because the next thing I knew, Dora was there, bending over me, muttering in Spanish and shaking my shoulders. I vomited again, and she took me into the cottage to wash my face and hands. Then she walked me back to the house. I felt dizzy, and my legs wouldn't move properly, but Dora kept dragging me anyway, muttering and crossing herself. We slipped in through the back door, and she got me upstairs to my room without Mama seeing me. I told her I was dying, that liquor was poisonous to young girls, just as Mrs. Stillman always said. I told her God was punishing me for my sins. But she shook her head and helped me into a clean nightgown. She fixed me a stinking tea and made me drink it. I know better than to refuse Dora's medicines. Soon I fell asleep, and this morning I woke up with a crushing headache. But I knew I would live.

7 December 1894. The rains started early this year. The roof in the tower room leaks, but Papa cares nothing about our home anymore, so no one will fix it. I could ask Anton, but I stay out of his way as much as possible. I catch him watching me every so often, like a hawk watches a field mouse. Papa no longer comes to our room at night. It seems I am now always invisible to him. I know this is probably my fault because I stay out of his way. When he is home, I often go to the cottage and paint or work on my herb collection. Sometimes I sleep there overnight. No one knows I'm gone except Dora, but she doesn't tell.

18 March 1895. Because of the damp winter, my little brother Robbie developed a lung sickness. For many days he was delirious with a high fever. The doctor came to see him and didn't want Dora to interfere with his scientific medicine. But Mama told her to go ahead and save Robbie if she could. Dora gave Robbie nettle tea and possets, and she sat by his bed for three nights, chanting and singing her Indian medicine songs. She lit candles and prayed to God and the Blessed Virgin. But she also rubbed Robbie's arms with angelica root and hung a coral shell around his neck to ward off evil spirits. Doctor Goodhall was very angry when he returned Monday morning and saw the shell. But Robbie's fever broke during the night, and the doctor couldn't deny he was much better.

Mama says Dora saved Robbie's life. Dora says God saved him, and she is just God's helper. She says God loves the earth and he loves Robbie, and she helped join them together. I don't understand her. She was raised a Catholic at the mission in San Rafael, near where Mama grew up. But she still believes Indian things that the priests say are heresy. I think she must be right and not the priests because what she does always seems to work.

3 April 1895. I spent nearly the whole day on my knees in Mama's chapel, praying to the Blessed Madonna and asking God the Father to strike me dead for my sins. But except for sore knees and eyes that are swollen from weeping, I am unharmed. I knelt without a pillow for extra penance, but it was no use. I am not clean and God the Father will not take me.

25 April 1895. Today I am sixteen years old. I am allowed to dance at parties now and wear my hair off my neck when I am in public. But these things don't matter. I have become an adult because I have taken a lover. Bruce McPherson lives on a farm northeast of town. Bruce is eighteen and leaves for Stockton soon, where his father will pay for him to go to university. Bruce is very smart in school but naïve in the ways of

women. He was very easy. I let him think it was
his idea, that I was unsure and shy. But I've had
my eye on him for weeks, planning when we
could be alone. I'm certain it was his first time, and
I admit I am surprised. Bruce is considered quite a
catch around here. He's all Theresa Stillman ever
talks about. I remember her sister Emily's
sixteenth birthday party. How I envied her! But I
was young and silly. Why should I envy her?
Emily is twenty years old and still unmarried and
still a virgin. I can have any boy I want.

19 February 1896. I am very excited because
of a new Chinese herb shop just outside of town.
Mama forbids me to go there because she believes
that Chinese folk art is of the devil. I overheard
men say that the shop is owned by a Chinese
woman and her four sons. I'm dying to find out if
she knows more about herbs and medicines than
Dora.

27 February 1896. I visited the herbalist shop.
It was dark and spooky and smelled foreign. It
was full of little drawers and bins with colored
wood chips and dried grasses and seeds. Shriveled
up figures like grotesque little humans hung on
the wall behind the counter. Rats were stretched,
stiff and dead, on wooden frames. Then the
Chinese woman herself came out through a
curtain. Although she looked old, her skin was
very smooth and shiny. She smiled and nodded at
me, and spread her hands to ask if I wanted to buy

111

anything. I stared at her, wishing for Dora and thinking Mama was right—I had no business being there. I started to back away, but then I stepped on something soft that made me cry out. It was only a rug. But it felt like I'd stepped on something living, like a human hand. I turned and ran out, swearing to the Holy Mary that I would never return!

13 May 1896. Mama is concerned that I am too much on my own. I heard her tell Mrs. Stillman that I am too old to be allowed to go about without a chaperone. She makes me stay in the parlor with her when ladies come for their tea and sewing. I hate sewing. I still get my stitches uneven. Elizabeth sews a flawless seam, but, of course, Elizabeth is perfect. I'm beginning to hate Elizabeth, with her gentle manners and goody-goody attitude. Mama thinks it is time I take some interest in charity activities, so we go together to the church in town and prepare soup and bread for the poor people around here. Most of those people don't even speak English, just Spanish or Indian. There are some Chinese, too. I wonder which are the sons of the Chinese herbalist. They keep their eyes lowered and don't look at me as I fill their bowls.

1 July 1896. Mama is too restrictive. I can't go anywhere on my own anymore. I can't even ride because no one can be spared to accompany me. Elizabeth doesn't ride, and it is one area where I feel superior to her. I could go riding with the Stillman girls, but it's no fun because they always worry about getting their hems soiled and keeping the sun from touching their delicate skin. Mama still lets me go to the cottage but only if Dora goes with me. She thinks she's protecting my virtue. She doesn't know she's too late. I've kept my secrets about Bruce McPherson and Mick Fraser and Stan Hatfield. She wants me to be pure and clean, and she prays for me daily, I know. But God already took the pure and clean part of me when He took Nicholas. Mama has never understood this.

14 July 1896. I was sitting on the Table Rock today overlooking Two Trees Creek when one of the Chinese boys appeared on the opposite bank. I didn't know his name, but I recognized him from the charity soup line. He was concentrating on the ground, hunting for roots, so he didn't notice me. I kept very still and watched him. He looked more like a ferret than a person, using his nose as well as his eyes to search the dark undergrowth along the bank. I wondered if he was like other boys — like Bruce — inside his britches. Probably, although his root might be smaller. Mama would have a fit to know I have such wicked thoughts. He vanished into the woods, and I watched the spot where he disappeared, wondering how it would be to roll with a boy who couldn't speak proper English.

20 August 1896. Kim Soo knows a lot about herbs. That's the Chinese boy I saw on the bank last month. He's a year older than I, but he hasn't any schooling. He picked up English working on the docks in San Francisco. His family came all the way from China, but his father was killed on the street in San Francisco. I think he was murdered, actually, but they don't put you in jail for killing a Chinese. That's when his mother moved their family to Springstown, to set up a shop like the one she had in China. They have seven children: four boys and three girls. Kim Soo speaks better English than any of them. He translates for his mother when people want to buy something in the shop. Mama still forbids me to go. But since I made friends with Kim Soo, I've been to the shop twice. I was silly to be afraid.

Katherine's narrative was interrupted by more descriptions and drawings of medicinal plants.

ECHINACEA: use dried root; drink decoction for treating diseases of the blood, infection, arthritis.

MEADOWSWEET: herb has almond scent to sweeten the air; drink as pain killer, brings down fever, clears the lungs.

MOONSEED: Chinese call it *fang chi*; roots of some varieties used to treat arthritis, lumbago, and reduce fever; also sedative properties. Some act as convulsive poison.

Chapter Twelve

I stared up at Isabel's beautiful face, into blue-violet eyes that gazed out silently from her place on the wall. The tour group had moved on, out of her bedroom and down the hall to visit the Rostnova nursery. I lingered behind to steal a few moments alone with Isabel's portrait.

After finishing Katherine's journal, I had felt restless. Seeing that it was not yet three o'clock, I decided to revisit Rosswood House. Ryan would not be back until dinnertime.

The walk to Rosswood House from Summerwood took about twenty minutes on a clearly marked path through the woods, not particularly difficult but eerie in the brooding stillness of the afternoon. Not a breath of wind stirred the forest underbrush; not a drop of rain relieved the heavy threat of an imminent downpour. All my senses were alert to the storm that would surely hit before nightfall.

My feet plodded silently over the soft dirt path while my mind lost itself in the reliving of Katherine's journal pages. Deciding that he could not leave the ranch to his weakling son Robbie, Alexander contracted a marriage between his daughter and Anton Kamarov, the brother of Ana. Upon his death, Alexander's estate would be held in trust for the firstborn son of his daughter's marriage. Katherine ran away, hoping to plead asylum with her Aunt Ana and Uncle Leon in San Francisco. But her father caught up with her and punished her with imprisonment in her

115

room:

>All are forbidden to speak to me. Even Dora
>has not visited me in the week since I have been
>locked in this room. I have never felt so helpless. I
>see myself becoming Anton's prisoner, enduring
>humiliations, with no hope of escape. I am utterly
>alone.

Katherine and Anton were married. Her account of her father's mysterious death on the night of her wedding was brief and factual, nothing like the drama of Elise Delacroix's story. I wondered what Katherine had really believed.

Her entries became short and erratic, often not dated. She was keeping the diary at the cottage, in the attic where no one would find it. Anton was as brutal a husband as she'd feared he would be, subjecting her to repeated "punishments" for displeasing behaviors—for running out of his preferred label of brandy, for being seen in town talking with Kim Soo, even for being too short and looking too much like "a God-cursed heathen Indian." I could feel with every page her mounting despair and helpless rage.

Then she discovered she was pregnant:

>Dora has guessed, but Anton doesn't know.
>The only power I have over him is not giving him
>a son and legal heir to my father's property. I don't
>know what I shall do. I am desperate. I want to
>run away, but there is no safe place. Wherever I
>go, Anton is sure to find me and bring me back.

>I can't keep the child a secret much longer.

Already I have loosened my waist cinch. Anton is not a fool. He will guess. I must escape or do something very soon. I have no more time.

And then:

I have a Plan. If it works, I won't have to go away. But I must be very, very careful. Even Dora must not suspect.

I turned the page, and the next entry quite literally knocked the breath out of me:

I was again visited by the woman in a dream. She stood on the rise above the bridge, looking down at me. I believe now she is the dream girl I saw all those years ago, the angel child with the fair hair. I think she wanted to tell me something, but the vision faded before she could. I had the most powerful desire to reach out and touch her, as if our joining could somehow make a new beginning for me.

* * *

My second tour through Rosswood House evoked almost continuous recall of Katherine's memories, sharp and vivid as if they were my own. In the library I wondered which of the paneled walls had shattered Alexander's whiskey glass after he struck down his daughter in a drunken rage. I imagined Katherine following Dora around the huge kitchen with her shrewd dark eyes, memorizing recipes for possets and medicinal teas. As we climbed the ornate staircase, I pictured men in riding coats and rough boots, carrying between them the lifeless body of Katherine's brother. I listened to the measured ticking of the grandfather clock and knew that, for thirty days after Alexander was found in the gully, the heavy pendulum was stopped and draped with a black sash, out of respect for the dead.

I now stood alone on the wrong side of the forbidding velvet rope, studying the portrait of Katherine's mother. Although Isabel was still a beautiful woman, up close to her image I saw the signs of care worn into her features: faint lines webbing the corners of her eyes and mouth, silver beginning to thread through the wavy black hair at her temples, hollow cheeks and dark smudges betraying long hours of grief and loneliness. I wondered why the artist couldn't have blinded himself a little to her age and preserved more of the untainted beauty of her youth. Despite the telltale marks of her unhappy life, she could not have been much older than forty when she sat for this portrait.

I stepped back a few feet, and her image softened. But I could not escape the compelling sadness in her eyes nor the wistful curve of her lips in her almost-smile.

This close to her portrait, I saw the brooch at her throat was made of white enamel, set in gold filigree and painted with a delicate spray of violets. The flowers were a deep purple, exactly the color of those in the nosegay she held in her lap. I remembered Amanda's words: "Violets were Isabel's favorite flowers."

I forced myself to leave Isabel's presence and rejoin the group now gathered in Alexander's bedroom. I followed them mechanically, my mind swirling with random, unanswerable questions. Who had finally fixed the leaky tower roof or painted the gay circus animals on the playroom wall? What had become of the blanket Dora wove for Katherine as a surprise gift on her birthday? When was the grandfather's cottage first called Summerwood? Had Michael's father really been an English sea captain, or had Michael merely created a romantic fantasy to bolster his pride?

The docent led us down the great staircase. I didn't wait for her finishing remarks but edged away from the group and slipped out the front door to the welcome rush of cold air on my overheated face. I descended the glossy cerulean steps and turned left onto a flagstone path, intent upon visiting the chapel Ryan and I had missed on the previous day.

The wind had picked up and whipped dried leaves across my shoes as I approached the formal garden. The flagstones split into two paths that ran among trim hedgerows and meticulously shaped shrubbery. Unlike the wild oak garden at Summerwood, the azaleas here were constrained into neat globes of color and texture, overhung by the lacy leaves of Japanese maples just beginning to unfurl for spring. Severely pruned rose bushes huddled together behind low borders of colorful pansies and violas of deep blue and violet.

Coming around a tall fountain made of gray stone and evidently not running water for some time, the flagstones unexpectedly rejoined into one path again. They led me the short distance to a small stone building—Isabel's chapel. My heart gave a leap of excitement as I mounted the steps and read the sign posted beside the heavy oak door: "Rosswood Chapel. Built in 1878 by Alexander Rostnova for his wife Isabel." I tried the handle, and the door swung open on surprisingly silent hinges.

Blinded by the late afternoon glare, my eyes took some moments to adjust to the gloom. I searched the vestibule in vain for a light switch; nevertheless, I shut the door against the gray daylight in the hope of discouraging other visitors. Tiptoeing down a center aisle between rows of low benches, I came up before a high wooden table that might have served as an altar but now stood bare and unused. A truly magnificent crucifix of carved wood hung on the wall above the table, the head of the suffering Christ lolling to one side under a pressing crown of thorns. I wondered if Leon Rostnova had carved it for his sister-in-law.

Drawing on years of discipline, my knee remembered to genuflect before I turned around and faced the room. Tall windows on my left were made of stained glass, but the shadowing oaks outside made the colored patterns indecipherable. I chose a bench next to the wall on the right under high square windows pushed slightly open to admit the only real sources of light and air into the room. There I sat and pulled Katherine's journal from my satchel. Squinting in the fading daylight and listening to the wind scraping oak branches across the stained glass, I reread Katherine's final entries.

Today I visited Kim Soo's mother, and all is arranged. No one saw me leave the shop. Dora suspects something, so I am avoiding her until after it's all over. Although she could help me, I dare not confide in her. That way, if something goes wrong, I will be the only one responsible. But if my plan succeeds, we will all be the better for it.

Anton stared at me over supper. I fear he suspects that I am with child. I could not eat, and I clumsily knocked over my water glass. Mama asked if I was ill, and I pleaded a headache. I excused myself from the table, went straight to my room, and locked the door. I was shaking all over, and my palms were sweating. I fear I will lose my nerve before it is time to act.

Anton's fever and chills began during the night. He pretended to be asleep when I entered his room this morning to check on his condition. As I bent down to study him, he suddenly grabbed at my waist with both his hands. I pulled away, and he was too weak to hold onto me. But he knew. He stared at me, and then he began to laugh, a terrible rasping crow of victory. I covered my ears and ran to the door, but the awful noise followed me into the hall. He thinks he has won, but he has always underestimated me. Tonight, in the darkness of the new spring moon, I shall beat him at his own game.

I turned the page and felt again the shock and disappointment of seeing only a blank page staring up at me. As before, I flipped through the remaining blank pages, hoping for a stray note that would help me understand how Katherine had resolved her dilemma.

This time my examination yielded two interesting discoveries. The first came from noticing how the book naturally opened to the page after Katherine's last entry. Raising the book for closer inspection, I noticed ragged edges peeking out from the crease where two, perhaps three pages had been torn out. When they had been removed was impossible to say. The edges were without the brown color of age, but they had also been well protected from exposure.

The second discovery was a tiny flower pressed between two pages, very close to the binding. It was a violet, its petals compressed to the point of transparency, its purple color faded but unmistakable.

Chapter Thirteen

I emerged from the chapel to a howling wind that nearly snatched my satchel off my shoulder. The promised rain had not yet broken, but the air was leaden with expectancy. Rosswood House towered beyond the garden, its tall windows reaching long bars of light into a deepening dusk.

The world suddenly brightened with a blinding electric flash. I gasped and counted ten seconds before thunder cracked and rolled from somewhere beyond the hills.

More excited than frightened, I watched trees and shrubs thrash wildly around me in the silver-gray twilight. I had an odd sense of losing my substance, as if I were a celluloid character in an old black-and-white movie. Or a phantom in a dreamscape, where nothing is real and anything is possible.

Footsteps approached on the flagstone path just beyond the fountain. For a reason I can't explain, instead of doing the sensible thing and walking toward the fountain, I shrank back into the shadow of the chapel and hid. Someone called my name just as another sheet of lightning dazzled the landscape and showed me a path, quite close at hand, leading into the woods.

Guided by instinct stronger than reason and certain as a compass, I darted onto the path and disappeared into the trees.

* * *

Of course, the path led me to the small rise overlooking the old bridge. Where else could I go but to the appointed spot where I would meet Katherine yet again, drawn to her in a space outside of time and beyond reason or explanation?

She wasn't here yet, but I would wait for her. Swept forward on the supreme confidence one feels in a dream, I covered the short distance down the rise and stepped over the warning board onto the worn planks of the bridge. As I proceeded toward the middle, a light rain began to fall. I lifted my face to the exquisite cleansing of tiny drops patting my cheeks and running in rivulets off my chin.

Another sheet of lightening lit the sky. Millions of water slivers shimmered around me, whirling for a brief moment in the wind before their electric brilliance faded. I had barely counted to one before I heard the crash of thunder, the splintering of wood, and the strangled cry of someone shouting my name.

Unexpected pain slammed into the back of my head. Stunned and blinded, I felt my body fall, floating for what seemed a long time through empty space.

The empty space seeped in through my skin and filled me, and I knew nothing. And I was nothing.

I am floating high and free near the tops of the trees when my sight returns. I look down and see men darting their flashlights over the rough ground at the creek's edge. I don't need their light to see the dangling remains of the bridge or the bits of rotten planking floating downstream and wedging themselves among the bracken. I can see quite well the body of the woman when they drag her from the water and cover her with their jackets.

Ryan rolls his jacket and presses it against the back of the woman's head. Instantly it becomes soaked with blood. I hear his words — "Hang on, Vicki! Don't leave us!" — before he opens his lips to speak.

How odd.

Now one of the men stands. He fumbles with his cell phone, pushing buttons, calling for help. But he is too late. He doesn't realize I am already floating beyond his reach.

A strong hum, like the low quiver of a cello string, begins to vibrate deep inside my chest. As the humming swells, the scene before me shrinks. Its characters fade into shadows like the end of a play. I am caught up on the darkness like a leaf on water. A strong current grabs me and hurls me into a tunnel, black and long, seemingly endless.

But now the darkness thins. The current slows. A bright mist appears in the distance with a brilliant light at its center. Gossamer curls surprisingly fragrant swirl out from the mist and enfold me like gentle arms. I nestle into them and take their fragrance inside me like a breath, filling myself with an exquisite peace as my mind shapes itself around a single thought: This is how it feels to be loved.

I am so content that I fail to notice at first when the humming returns.

It begins softly, just under my heart, and grows steadily. Too late I feel its pull, tugging me away from the tender light. The bright mist vanishes. Once again I am a leaf, bobbing and dipping on a rush of darkness as the current snatches me back into the familiar tunnel.

The humming escalates to a deafening blare, and there is suddenly another presence, another leaf swirling with me in the dark. I feel the merest brush of the other before the current wrenches us apart, throwing me with such force that all my senses collapse.

* * *

Rain drummed against a window. Flickering light played on my closed eyelids. I felt cool moisture against my skin as someone sponged my cheeks and my throat.

A woman's voice close above my ear murmured in soothing tones. To open my eyes seemed impossible, but I managed a grateful moan.

The sponging paused, and the woman's voice whispered, "Thanks be to God. She's back with us."

Part Two

SPRING

Katherine

Chapter Fourteen

Ryan Ashton frowned at the coffee grounds clinging to the inside of his paper cup. A pyramid of crumpled cups had been growing beside him in the six hours since his arrival at the Santa Rosa hospital.

Four, five... He was counting the grounds, fixed on the idea that if he counted accurately, he could keep his wife alive. *Eight, nine...* Twenty-four hours. The doctor said the first twenty-four hours were the most critical. Ryan had been allowed into the Intensive Care Unit to see her. He'd been shocked by her stillness as she lay on the bed like Snow White on her forest bier, beautiful even in sleeping death. He'd been stunned by the sudden burn of his own tears.

Eleven, twelve... Thirteen stitches. Sterile white bandages hid the wound at the back of her skull where her blood had gushed, draining life from her body with alarming speed. He couldn't get the feel of it off his hands—warm and sticky, making them slippery as he tried to cradle her head until help came. There'd been so much of it! He knew it wasn't enough to press his jacket against the wound, to shout at her above the howling wind to hang on, to stay with him.

He'd never felt so helpless.

Thirteen, fourteen... Twenty-two-years old, twenty-three next month. But sometimes Vicki seemed hardly more than a child, innocent, with her spirit oddly dormant.

He imagined her waiting for someone to come along and bring her to life with a hero's kiss. Ryan had tried to be that someone. But he had failed.

Fifteen... Or was it sixteen? Ryan crumpled the useless cup and tossed it onto the pyramid. He stretched his bloodless legs, wincing as feeling returned to them, and rubbed an open hand over his face. His eyelids felt swollen and gritty, and his back ached from slouching on the tired vinyl couch of the ICU waiting room. A cold thread of loneliness curled around his heart and tightened into a hard knot. Weak tears of frustration threatened, but Ryan refused to give in to them. Instead, he rounded his shoulders and pushed his fists into the vinyl, forcing himself to sit up straight.

A nurse appeared in the corridor and hurried toward him. She said gently, "Mr. Ashton? Will you come with me?" He rose wordlessly and raised an eyebrow. She shook her head. "There's been no change. But the doctor would like to see you."

Ryan trailed her into the ICU room and approached the bed. A large man was bending over Vicki, his powerful hands gentle as he checked her pupils and her pulse. He saw Ryan, straightened, and held out his hand.

"Ryan." The man's pleasant smile seemed out of place in the grim surroundings. "Vicki is at a level just below consciousness. I want you to sit by the bed and talk to her. Hold her hand, talk to her about anything you want, but keep talking. If she can hear you, your voice may be enough to bring her around."

The nurse placed a chair beside the bed, and the doctor stepped back as Ryan sat down and took his wife's hand. He stared at it, lying slim and warm in his. He ignored her other arm with its gauze padding and crisscross of white tape concealing the intravenous needle. He dragged his gaze from the matted tangle of her magnificent hair straggling out from under the bandage and focused on the pale perfection of her face.

"Vicki?" His voice sounded gruff from long hours of disuse and the fear squeezing his throat shut. "It's me, Vicki. It's Ryan."

He watched her eyelids for a flutter of response. But she lay like a wax doll, her shallow breathing scarcely raising the white sheet smoothed across her chest.

He sandwiched her hand in both of his and chafed it gently. "Vicki, can you hear me? Try to open your eyes now. Please, Vicki." He heard a rustle behind him as the doctor left and the nurse returned to her station. Ryan slumped a little and surrendered to a thought that had been nipping at him from the time he'd sat down: *You're the wrong person to try to reach her, Ashton. She doesn't want you. She was running away from you when she almost died.*

Painful memories he'd kept at bay for hours broke loose and swept over him. He'd returned to Summerwood to discover that Vicki had been gone for hours, and Alice made phone calls and learned that Vicki had revisited Rosswood House. Stacey's two brothers searched with him in the deepening twilight while dread thickened, ice cold, in his chest. Then there was that eerie sequence of lightning flashes that illuminated traces of her like a slide show: the chapel door standing wide open, Vicki's satchel dropped on the path that led them into the woods, and then Vicki herself teetering on the rotten planks of the bridge before falling with them into the black water.

Fresh horror and fury gripped him. He leaned close

and spoke roughly into her ear.

"Wake up, Vicki! What were you trying to do, kill yourself? Climbing up on that bridge in the middle of a thunderstorm! You can't just quit on me. I won't let you. Do you hear me? *I won't let you!* Now *open your eyes!*"

He dropped her hand and shoved back in his chair, chest heaving, and watched for a response. But her face remained smooth and still, her eyelids closed over stunning green eyes that might never look at him again. His heart lurched painfully at the thought.

Ryan gripped the seat of his chair and tried not to hear the unwelcome whispers, like the buzz of an insistent gnat in his ear: *Is it love or hurt pride that's got you so angry? What does she have to come back to? A job she hates. An indifferent family run by a tyrannical old woman. A marriage that's lukewarm at best.*

I never really listened to her, Ryan realized in a reluctant moment of clarity. *She tried to tell me, but I didn't want to hear it. This is my fault. Maybe if things were different between us, maybe if I had loved her...*

He jerked himself out of the chair, strode across the room, past the nurses' station, and before the startled nurse could speak, hurled himself into the corridor. He groped blindly along the cold wall and at last stopped to lean his head against it, dizzy from the heavy medicine smells and the torture of his guilty thoughts.

* * *

Christine Reeves glanced at the speedometer, shocked to see the needle locked on ninety. Reason won over her frantic need to push ahead, and she eased her foot off the accelerator. The Cadillac's powerful engine strained to go faster, but she dropped her speed to seventy-two, arguing with herself that she couldn't afford to get pulled over by the highway patrol. She had to get to Santa Rosa. She had to get to her daughter before—heaven forbid—it was too late.

The Cadillac's headlights reflected off the glistening pavement still wet from last night's brief but furious rainstorm. As she continued north on Highway 101, she looked for signs of dawn in the sky beyond the North Bay hills. But it was still too early. Ryan's call had awakened her from a night of fitful sleep, his words slipping into her heart like slivers of broken glass— "Vicki's had a bad fall...she's lost a lot of blood...can you come right away, in case she wakes up?"

In case she wakes up. The speedometer crept up to seventy-seven, and Christine bit her lip. *What if Victoria doesn't wake up? What if she slips away before I get the chance to tell her how sorry I am, how much I love her?*

Her face crumpled. With no one to witness her grief, she allowed herself to cry. Tears blurred the red taillights dotting the dark highway ahead, and harsh sobs hurt her chest and brought on a succession of violent hiccups.

Hold your breath, count to ten, release slowly... The hiccups subsided, and her sobs withered into quiet tears that flowed uselessly down her cheeks. God, don't let me be too late, she prayed. Keep her alive. *Keep her alive.*

Unbidden images of her daughter rose on a tender tide and filled her with a sweet ache. She saw Victoria as an infant, her tiny face crinkling with her first smile, her green eyes fixed on her mother with innocent trust. She glimpsed her at age two riding piggy-back on Jack's shoulders, laughing, and at seven when she got her first two-wheeler bike. In her mind's eye, Christine watched her daughter fly down the hill on her new red Schwinn, blond braids streaming out behind her as she crowed with excitement. Christine heard herself calling, "Not too fast, Victoria! Slow down, or you'll fall off and get hurt!"

I didn't want you to get hurt, Victoria. Fresh tears welled up. *I only wanted to protect you, to keep you safe. I never wanted to hurt you.*

I'm so sorry.

Victoria, can you ever forgive me?

The needle crept past eighty, but Christine ignored it. *Wait for me, Victoria,* she called silently. *Hold on, baby. I'm almost there.*

* * *

Eleanor Prescott stared in cold fury at the man standing before her. "This is outrageous!" She tossed her head and drew herself up, trying to minimize the twelve-inch difference in their heights. "Why wasn't I informed?"

"I'm informing you now, Eleanor." Dan Winslow spoke patiently. "Christine asked me specifically to come over early and tell you myself about Victoria. She said she'll call from the hospital with any news."

Eleanor turned on her heel and stalked to the sofa, where she sat down stiffly. Agnes appeared from nowhere with a coffee service and hot croissants.

"Thanks, dear." Dan took the tray from the housekeeper and set it on the coffee table. He glanced at Eleanor, who sat rigid, face averted, and he shook his head. "Coffee, Eleanor?"

She turned a stony face toward him and gave a curt nod but refused to meet his eyes. Dan handed her a cup and marveled at the perfection of her appearance at seven o'clock in the morning. When he had arrived at six-thirty,

133

she'd made him wait while she dressed and had her hair coiffed. She now held herself with cold dignity, like a queen granting audience to a petitioner of whom she is not particularly fond.

Dan filled a cup for himself and sat down on the sofa opposite hers, more sympathetic than offended. He knew that much of Eleanor's hauteur masked her fear of growing old and losing control of her family as well as her empire. He didn't blame Christine for leaving quietly in the middle of the night, and he didn't mind the task of informing her mother about Victoria's accident. Christine would have enough to deal with when she got to Santa Rosa without having to worry about placating Eleanor.

"Tell me everything you know." Eleanor's sudden command startled him. He steadied the cup and saucer on his knee with one hand and raised the other.

"I know very little. Christine said Ryan phoned at around three this morning and told her that Victoria had fallen and was knocked unconscious. She must have cut her head open because she lost a lot of blood and had to have stitches. They took her to a hospital in Santa Rosa." He added gently, "Ryan said it's pretty bad. She might not make it."

He sipped his coffee and settled his gaze on his cup, allowing Eleanor a moment of privacy to absorb the impact of his words. When he finally looked up, he found her green eyes glaring, her mouth pressed into a thin line.

"Well? Is that all?" Her tone was imperious, familiar to him as the voice that presided over Prescott corporate meetings.

Dan hesitated. "Yes. Christine said she'll phone when she knows more."

"But how dare she go over my head to an outsider!" Eleanor's eyes sparked. "I am the head of this family and Victoria's grandmother. I had a right to be informed first!"

Dan forced down a rising irritation. "Don't take it as an insult, Eleanor. You're not so young anymore, and the news is pretty devastating." His chin rose a little in defense of Christine. "Your daughter chose the kindest way to let you know about Victoria."

Eleanor sniffed and set down her empty cup and saucer with a clatter. "I just hope the press doesn't get wind of this," she muttered. She reached for a croissant, and her voice turned peevish. "What's wrong with the girl, anyway? Victoria's never been clumsy. Maybe she has a brain tumor. I wonder if those doctors in Santa Rosa know enough to check into the possibility."

She tore off a piece of croissant, smeared it with strawberry preserves, and pushed it into her mouth. Dan looked away, and as Eleanor unleashed another complaint, his thoughts drifted back to his phone conversation with Christine.

"Let me drive you to Santa Rosa," he'd pleaded. "You shouldn't face this alone."

"Dan, I can't ask you—" she began.

"I want to be there! Christine—"

"No." She said it with quiet finality. "I need you to tell Mother for me."

"Of course." He added, "Christine, you know I love you. Say the word, darling, and I'll drop everything to be with you—"

Agnes suddenly reappeared, interrupting his thoughts and Eleanor's tirade. "Mrs. Reeves is on the phone."

Eleanor looked up. "Did she ask for me or for Mr.

135

Winslow?" She slanted a glance at Dan.

"For you, Mrs. Prescott." Agnes offered the cordless phone to her employer and stepped back discreetly.

"Yes, Christine." Eleanor's voice was crisp, and her free hand began smoothing her slacks. "What?" Her fingers hesitated, and she nodded. "Well, thank heaven for that. Did she ask to see me?" She was silent for a few moments. "Christine, how good can those doctors be in a Santa Rosa hospital? Victoria should be at Mount Cross, here in the city. I'll arrange for it this morning." She paused again. Then, stiffly, "Well, you know best. Yes, he's here." She glanced at Dan, who was leaning forward over the coffee table. "Yes, I suppose."

She tightened her lips and passed him the phone.

"Hello, sweetheart!" Dan's relief that Victoria apparently was conscious faded the instant he heard Christine's voice. Suddenly fearful, he rose and turned his back to Eleanor. "Take your time. Tell me what's happened."

"I got here just before six," Christine told him. "Ryan, poor boy, hasn't slept or eaten since yesterday. Victoria was still unconscious, so I relieved him and sat by her bed. I held her hand and talked to her, not knowing if she could hear me. I told her about all the things we'll do together once she's recovered. I told her we'll spend a day at the wharf, just the two of us, like we did when she was young. I told her I'd buy her a shell doll. She always wanted one, you know. I don't know why I never let her have one."

Her voice broke. Dan kept silent as she struggled to regain control.

"I noticed her eyelids moving, and I called for the nurse. The doctor came, and soon after, Victoria opened her eyes." Christine choked on another sob. "Her lovely eyes. Dan, I couldn't tell Mother. Please don't tell her."

Dan's breath caught on a sudden premonition.

"She couldn't see me, Dan. She couldn't see the doctor or the nurse or Ryan when he came in and stood next to me." Christine broke into fresh sobs. "She's blind, Dan! My baby is stone blind!"

Chapter Fifteen

"I won't lie to you." Dr. Wharton spread his hands. "We've run every test I can think of. I can find no medical basis for Victoria's continued blindness and lack of speech."

Christine sat beside Ryan across the desk from the doctor. In the ten days since the accident, Victoria had been moved to Mount Cross Hospital in San Francisco and put in the care of Hal Wharton, a neurosurgeon of impeccable reputation.

"As you know," Wharton continued, "Victoria suffered a trauma to the back of the head. That's where the vision center is located. The first tests revealed some swelling, easily accounting for her inability to see." He spread his hands again. "But the edema has completely disappeared, and the cut was only superficial. She lost a lot of blood, but there appears to be no physical damage to the brain itself. In all other respects, Victoria is a perfectly healthy young woman."

"So now what?" Ryan bit off his words through clenched teeth. "Are you saying there's nothing more you can do? Doctor, we can't even communicate with her!"

Wharton held up a sympathetic hand. "Ryan, you have every reason to be frustrated, and we are by no means giving up. What I'm saying is we can find no physical cause for your wife's symptoms. I'm suggesting that we explore the possibility that her lack of sight and speech is psychosomatic."

"Psychosomatic." Christine repeated the word. "Doctor

Wharton, are you saying my daughter isn't really blind? That she's faking it?"

"No, not faking it. Her symptoms are absolutely real. But they seem to have no physical cause. That means we start looking for an emotional cause." He added, "It's not as uncommon as you might think. There's a good chance Victoria will still make a full recovery."

"You're talking about psychotherapy." Ryan spoke up beside her, his voice bright with new interest. "I think you may have hit on something. Before the accident Vicki was talking and acting very strangely. I'd even say she was close to a breakdown. I intended to make an appointment for her to see a therapist when we got back home. Then the accident happened, and I forgot all about it."

Wharton nodded. "There is a psychiatrist on staff here at the hospital I can recommend. Francine Shepherd. She specializes in neurological trauma." He pushed himself back in his chair and smiled for the first time. "Good. Then we're agreed." He rubbed his hands together. "What do you say, Christine?"

"Yes. By all means, call Dr. Shepherd." She raised her chin and rounded her shoulders. "I'm afraid it's long overdue."

* * *

Dr. Francine Shepherd reached out and touched her patient's hand, pleased when the hand didn't jerk away. It had taken three days of gentle coaxing to get the young woman to tolerate her touch. But touch was essential. With a patient deprived of both sight and speech, Francine had to rely on touch and sound to establish a bond of trust.

"I'd like to try something new today, Victoria. It's called guided imagery. First I'll play some soft music and let you get nice and comfortable. Then we'll take a little trip into your imagination. Does that sound all right?"

The young woman tensed, and Francine patted her hand. "It's easy and relaxing. I'm sure you'll enjoy it." She reached behind her and switched on the music. Strains of Mozart drifted into the room, and the young woman sat suddenly forward. A rare smile crossed her lips. *Well, there's nothing wrong with her hearing,* Francine thought. She made a note that her patient appeared to recognize Mozart.

After working the case daily for nearly a week, Francine agreed with Hal Wharton that the young woman's blind and mute state was due to emotional rather than physical trauma. Today's exercise should determine if her speech center was functioning normally. If successful, the exercise might also offer some insight into the nature of her psychological wounding.

"All right, Victoria. Lay your head back and close your eyes. That's right. Now take a big, deep breath. Hold it. Now let it out slowly…"

Francine led her patient through ten minutes of relaxation exercises, satisfied when the blond head sank deeper into the recliner and the tight mouth slackened to emit long, regular breaths.

"That's very good, Victoria. Now I want you to imagine yourself walking down a flight of stairs. Notice there is a handrail to help you feel safe." She paused. "Now you are at the bottom of the stairs. Right in front of you is a door. Can you see it?"

A slight nod of response. "Good. Now you are opening the door and walking through it, into a room on the other side. I want you to take some time and look around the room. Can you see it?"

Again, a nod of response. "Take your time." Francine counted slowly and silently to twenty. "Now, I want you to tell me what you see."

The young woman's face twitched and her eyelids moved as she scanned the imaginary room. "That's right," Francine said. "Take a good look around. Tell me what you see." Another pause met with silence. "What color are the walls in the room?"

The lips parted, and the throat worked to push out sound.

"Green," she whispered.

"The walls are green." Francine nodded with satisfaction and made a note. "Very, very good. Now, what else do you see?"

"A table by the window. Mama's sewing basket." The voice was stronger now but childlike.

"What room is this, Victoria?"

Her patient's head turned, eyes still closed and her brow furrowed. "How did you find out my secret name?" The childish voice was querulous. "I never told anyone. How does everybody seem to know?" The brow suddenly smoothed. "Are you an angel? Is that how you know? Am I in heaven?"

Francine didn't speak, and her patient began to hum along with the music. "That's Mozart, isn't it? Mama makes me practice piano every day, even when we have company. But she doesn't make Nicholas play." The slim fingers moved over imaginary keys. "This room is the parlor. Mama sews while I practice piano. Then I have permission to play on the porch until supper."

Francine watched her carefully. "If nobody knows your secret name, then what do others call you?"

The fingers stopped moving. The young woman giggled. "Why, my real name, of course. Katherine. Katherine Alexander Rostnova. But you may call me Katya."

* * *

Francine accepted a steaming mug from her colleague and watched him resettle himself in his chair. "That's about it, Max," she said. "I've put her under four times now. She always regresses herself into this child she calls Katherine. She speaks quite freely as the child, but I can't get a word out of her when she returns to the adult state."

She blew across the surface of her coffee and took a sip. "Another interesting thing: I can't get her to talk past the age of eleven or twelve. And it isn't just that she stops talking. Her whole body clams up. She literally curls into a ball and buries her head. My guess is that some kind of trauma took place around that age, and it's linked to what's frightening her now. What do you think?"

She took another sip of coffee and leaned back in her chair, comfortable in the long pause that followed. Max put the tips of his fingers together and tapped them absently against his chin, a gesture she'd seen a hundred times that meant he was deep in thought. She let her gaze wander around his office, taking comfort in its familiarity, remembering the countless times she'd come here, seeking encouragement and wise counsel. Max had been her supervisor during her internship, and over the years had become a mentor and trusted friend.

"Well, Fran." Max spoke slowly, rubbing his chin with his thumbs. "I see what you mean." He rested his chin on his steepled fingertips. "Who is Katherine?"

"I honestly don't know. I took a history from both her

mother and her husband. The name never came up."

"Do you think she's multiple?"

Francine hesitated. She had already considered and rejected this possibility, but Max might see it differently.

"I know it's too early to tell. But no, I don't think she has multiple personalities. The child Katherine shows no links to Victoria's real life. For example, as Katherine she speaks of a twin brother Nicholas and living in a home with both mother and father. Her history clearly states that she never had a brother, and her father died when she was young. And she makes no mention of her grandmother."

"So, again, who is Katherine?"

Francine shrugged. "Maybe a character Victoria got from a movie or a book. An identity to protect her from whatever is terrifying her about her real life."

"The terror that keeps her blind and mute."

"Yes. That's my guess." Francine opened the file on her lap and stared at it, as if the answers might pop out from the pages of her case notes. "I need to find out who Katherine is and why Victoria chose her identity. I think I'll ask her husband. I'm scheduled to see him tomorrow morning just before she's released from the hospital."

Max nodded, rubbing his chin again. "You mentioned that she recognized Mozart and she knows how to play the piano. Have you considered using piano as a therapy medium?"

"No, but that's a good idea." Francine frowned. "That's a *great* idea. If she were playing in her adult state, the piano might bring her out enough… Yes, I'll try it this afternoon." She grinned at her mentor. "Thanks, Max."

Max spread his hands and grinned back. "Always glad to help, Frannie."

Chapter Sixteen

Ryan caught the door with his foot and slammed it shut behind him. His hands were full of mail, which he deposited on the foyer table before dropping his briefcase and a large portfolio against the wall. He switched on the lights and noted with satisfaction the gleaming oak tables and his back issues of *Architectural Digest* neatly stacked on the bottom shelf of the étagère. Good, Emma had been in to clean. It seemed she was going to work out, unlike The Smiling Maids, who showed up haphazardly and did a skeletal job at best. He'd had to fire them because Vicki couldn't bring herself to do it; she was afraid they'd be angry with her. Ryan shook his head and frowned. That fearfulness he had taken for a charming shyness now seemed an impenetrable wall that made her as unreachable as the moon.

He pushed down useless frustration and leafed through the mail. His glance caught on an orange envelope addressed to him in a hasty scrawl. A quick look at the return address confirmed his sudden foreboding: G. Stone, New York, NY. Gina, he thought. What did she want now?

Probably more money.

He slapped the mail back on the table and strode across the room to fix a drink. He was tired and edgy, and Gina could wait. He took a sip of his bourbon-and-soda, switched on the stereo, and chose classical piano from the playlist. As the first piece began, he closed his eyes and let the music ripple up and down his spine like a keyboard, kneading the tension out of his muscles and reminding him that there was more to life than building high-rises and dealing with implacable clients like Helen Seibold. He gave himself the small gift of suspending all rational thought until the piece had finished.

When the final notes of the song died away into silence, Ryan reluctantly opened his eyes. The next song began, and he carried his drink to the foyer, picked up the mail, and made his way to the sofa. Gina's envelope lay on top of the others, screaming at him, demanding to be opened. *Gina never changes,* he thought.

He and Gina had been divorced for ten years, yet he could still hear her high-pitched whines and hysterical outbursts, which were at their worst just before the two of them decided to separate. Ryan felt weary just remembering the strain of that time — the relentless arguing, the broken china smashed in the heat of her fury, her endless string of accusations, her insults, her threats…

His gaze wandered to a photograph of Vicki. Unlike the professional glamour shots, this one had been taken by a friend at a party, and she lacked the heavy makeup and posed expressions that made her professional persona so provocative. Here her glance was shy, her smile wistful, and her hair tamed into a thick cascade that made her look like Alice in Wonderland. Vicki was so quiet, so compliant, so…different from Gina.

And so beautiful. He'd had to have her. He knew it that first night he saw her at Helen Seibold's idiotic party. His heart quickened at the memory of Helen introducing them, and Vicki turning, lifting those exquisite green eyes to his, her smile curving a luscious mouth that was made to be kissed. He was old enough to know it wasn't love, more like an intentness on physical possession that slowly burned through his body as he stood close to her in that crowded, overheated room—breathing in her light scent and listening to her soft, surprisingly shy voice telling him about her art classes and her passion for painting.

During the two months of their courtship, his desire for possession deepened into a need to protect and care for her. Admittedly, their engagement had been premature, but he was driven by the maddening paradox of her unintentional sensuality and her sexual innocence. He purposely held himself in check during the weeks before their marriage. When the hunger in his kisses seemed to frighten her, he backed off into companionable embraces and holding hands. His decision not to violate her virginity until they were married only heightened his anticipation of how carefully and thoroughly he would awaken her body to the sensual pleasure for which it was so exquisitely designed.

Even now, after nearly a year of fruitless patience and failed attempts to further their intimacy, he had difficulty admitting he had made a mistake. He hated to think he was failing at marriage a second time. Apart from their sexual incompatibility, he and Vicki seemed like a good fit. If one could believe the social tabloids and the comments of envious friends, they were the ideal couple. Not like him and Gina.

Gina. He forced himself to reach for the orange envelope and tore open the flap. Pulling out the single sheet, he skimmed its contents, tossed it aside, and got up to refill his glass. Gina was getting married again, the erratic scrawl informed him. To Clifford Baines. Ryan raised his empty glass in salute: *Poor idiot, I hope you know what you're getting yourself into.*

"Clifford's taking me to Europe." Ryan could hear the high, nasal rush of her words. "You know how I always loved to go. He's so thoughtful, so divinely romantic! But there's tons to do—shopping, getting the boutique in order so I can leave it for a month. And there's the problem of Stephanie. It would be better for her, I'm sure, if you could take her two weeks early this year. She'll miss the last week of school, but they don't do anything that last week anyway. She adores being in California with you. I really think it's in her best interest."

Ryan slammed down his glass without refilling it and paced the room, jingling the coins in his pocket and fighting down a hot surge of contempt. He didn't mind having his daughter begin her summer vacation with him two weeks early. But how like Gina to go flying off to Europe without considering anyone's needs but her own!

He glanced at his reflection in the mirror that hung over the fireplace and was startled to see a cold mask of fury swallowing his features. The blazing eyes and sour mouth annoyed him with the knowledge that Gina could still spur him into outrage, even from across the country. He was further annoyed by the mirror itself. The great ugly thing had been Eleanor's wedding gift, and Vicki felt compelled to display it even though its antique face and ostentatious frame were too much for the room. Like the old queen herself, Ryan thought. Her royal pretenses, he knew, masked an insecure old woman who lived for adulation. She was easy to charm. Unfortunately, Christine had never learned the trick, and Vicki was as defenseless as her mother against Eleanor's ruthless power tactics.

Poor Vicki never had a chance, he thought, raised in a

Judith Ingram

home with that self-made monarch and a mother who lived her life sitting on a fence. Vicki had to learn to stand her ground with those two, to make them listen to her or to send them both to blazes, like...

Like Gina? His mouth twisted at the irony. *You married Gina's opposite for a reason, Ashton.* What was that old adage? *Be careful what you wish for.*

On a muttered curse, Ryan jerked open the balcony door and stalked out into a cold wind. The night was clear, and the city lights sparkled before him as he crossed to the railing and leaned his arms on it. His gaze automatically fell on a familiar square of neighborhood park. The pleasing symmetry of its clipped hedges and softly lit paths relaxed the tangled knots in his brain and led him, quite without resistance, into memories of Gina.

They were so young when they married, so foolish, so hopelessly unsuited to one another. Both students at UC Berkeley, they ignored the warnings of friends and plunged recklessly into an elopement, swept away by idealistic dreams and intense physical attraction. Even now, Ryan could appreciate the appeal of Gina's round hips and breasts, her full-lipped mouth as sensual in a pout as it was in a smile. Her raven hair matched Italian eyes that could flash with temper one moment and flame with desire for him the next. They had played together, laughed together, and made wild love with the abandon of two young adults on the threshold of their future—supremely confident, optimistic beyond all reason.

Inevitably, Gina's temper escalated into destructive tantrums, and her pouting into secrecy and deceptions. Her consuming self-interest clashed violently with his dogged pursuit of a career in architecture. Afterwards, he realized

148

that the marriage was over long before her infidelity, before he began staying late at work every night, even before Stephanie was born.

The divorce was messy, but Ryan had agreed with Gina on one point—a mother should have custody of a young daughter. Stephanie had been a toddler at the time, and Ryan believed that, for all her self-indulgence, Gina loved her.

He'd since had reason to doubt that faith. Stephanie's life had not been easy, first caught in the backwash of their divorce, and then coping with her mother's subsequent remarriage and divorce. *I hope you're finally putting Stephanie's needs first, Gina. Baines had better be a good father to her.*

Stephanie and Vicki had not yet met. Ryan's jaw clenched as he recalled how effectively Gina had blocked his efforts to bring Stephanie out for his wedding. She had quickly planned a gala affair at the upscale boutique she owned, ostensibly to show her new line of fall fashions, and scheduled it for the same weekend as Ryan's wedding. She appealed to Stephanie to help her host the event, promising they would wear matching designer outfits and do their hair and nails exactly alike. Ryan could still hear Stephanie's voice on the phone, small and apologetic, pleading with him to understand. He understood, all right. And, as always, he gave in because he didn't want Stephanie caught in the middle. Instead, he bit his tongue, reassured his daughter, and cursed Gina in his heart.

Ryan shifted his arms on the railing. His vague plan to ask for custody of Stephanie once he and Vicki were married had soon been abandoned. At times Vicki herself seemed hardly more than a child. Caring for her was all he could manage—and he'd even failed at that. Because he couldn't give her the love she needed, she had at last removed herself to a world that effectively locked him out.

A couple walked along the street, and Ryan watched them enter the little park through a break in the hedgerow. Hand-in-hand, they started down a softly lit path but soon stopped and turned toward each other. They stepped together, and their silhouettes merged and locked for what seemed an endless moment. Ryan couldn't pull his gaze away. He held his breath and stared helplessly until his tortured lungs forced him to gulp in deep drafts of night air—so cold it burned in his chest.

The distant figure split at last into two. The couple continued their stroll, but Ryan turned away. He crossed the balcony and stepped back into his apartment, out of the wind but carrying the April cold deep inside him, lodged like a stone against his heart.

* * *

The jangle of the phone woke Ryan. He groaned and shifted his position on the sofa, hoping the noise would just stop and let him go back to sleep. But the next ring roused him further, and he twisted his head to find the clock. Almost seven. A chill trickled through the warm comfort of his sleepy brain. It might be the hospital calling. Something had happened to Vicki.

He managed to untangle his legs and get to his phone before his voicemail greeting kicked in. His heart pounded, and not just from the quick dash across the room.

"Yes?" he croaked, squinting his eyes against dazzling slices of sun reaching in through the kitchen blinds.

"Ryan? I'm sorry if I woke you." It was his mother-in-law. He stiffened, armoring himself.

"What is it, Christine?"

She burst into tears, and his heart lurched against his ribs. He gripped the phone tighter.

"Oh, Ryan! Such good news!" Joy broke through the tears in her voice, and his grip began to ease. "I spoke to the hospital a few minutes ago. I asked if I could call you myself. Victoria woke up this morning, and she's regained her eyesight! All of a sudden, just like that, she can see!"

Chapter Seventeen

Francine Shepherd stood unnoticed beside her patient's bed. The young woman seemed transfixed by the television, where a noisy game show aired, and periodically distracted by the sight of her own hands. More than once Francine observed her touching herself—her hair, her arms, her breasts—with something akin to wonder.

The nurse had informed Francine that while she was helping her patient into the bathroom that morning, the young woman had ducked through the doorway as if afraid she would hit her head. Then she'd caught sight of her reflection in the mirror and had stopped dead still, staring.

Ignoring the nurse, she had untied the neck of her hospital shift and let it drop to the floor. Her hands moved carefully over her body, over her hips and her nipples, and the soft blond mound between her legs. She had even bent down to examine her toes. When she straightened, her face glowed with delight.

The nurse didn't know what to make of it. Francine wasn't sure either.

Apparently, the session at the piano yesterday had done the trick. After initial reluctance, Victoria had warmed to the instrument and spent a good fifty minutes working through a series of pieces that left her sweating and exhausted. Unquestionably, the experience had dislodged a psychological block, for when she awoke this morning, her blindness was gone.

"Is this a program you used to watch, Victoria?" Her patient turned to her with a blank expression. She had not yet spoken, and Francine suspected that speech had not returned with her sight.

The green eyes strayed back to the screen, where a young couple frolicked in the surf. A woman's voice introduced a tampon product.

Francine tried again. "I understand you'll be staying with your mother and your grandmother for a few days." She paused. "Do you remember your grandmother's house, Victoria?"

The young woman tore her gaze away from the super-absorbency test. She plucked at her blanket.

Francine laid a reassuring hand on her arm just as Christine Reeves walked through the door.

"Victoria, darling." Christine hurried to the bed. Dark bruising around her eyes betrayed weeks of anxious nights, but this morning her smile was radiant. She bent to kiss her daughter's forehead.

The young woman shrank against the pillow and stared at her, her features tightened in alarm. Her mother checked herself and then straightened. Disappointment flicked across her face before she masked it with another smile. "You look well this morning. All ready to come home?"

The green eyes regarded her coolly. Francine gave them a moment before she spoke.

"Victoria, do you know who this is? Do you recognize your mother?"

Christine shot Francine a startled glance. She looked back at her daughter. "Victoria?" Her voice was steady,

Francine was relieved to note. "I've been coming every afternoon to see you." Her daughter closed her eyes and tilted her head as if listening. "We've—*I've* been so concerned about you. Then the news this morning; I could hardly believe it!" Her voice caught. "You are so very important to me, darling."

Her daughter opened her eyes and settled her gaze on Christine's face. Wariness softened into curiosity.

Francine cleared her throat. "Why don't you explain to Victoria what she can expect when she gets home? Tell her who will be there when you arrive, where she will sleep tonight."

Christine pulled up a chair and settled herself carefully.

"Well, let's see. Your old room is ready and waiting for you. Eleanor—your grandmother," she added, with a glance at Francine, "has ordered your favorites for lunch— beef stroganoff and strawberry blintzes for dessert. After you've rested this afternoon, we can take our tea in the sunroom. Or perhaps on the terrace if the weather is nice. It will be sunny, I think, with a cool breeze blowing off the bay."

Christine kept her tone warm and steady as she told funny stories about people they knew and promised her daughter outings when Victoria was stronger. *How different from my first impression of her,* Francine mused. At their first meeting, Christine had clutched her purse in her lap and answered Francine's questions in a tight monotone, as if every word hurt. Well, a near tragedy could bring out the best in people and repair relationships like nothing else. Christine was fortunate. In all likelihood, her daughter would eventually make a full recovery.

Confident that her patient was in good hands, Francine was preparing to leave when Victoria's husband strode into the room.

The soft stream of Christine's conversation trailed off as mother and daughter looked up at the man now standing at the foot of the bed. With his face fixed in a smile, only a tight cord of muscle in his neck hinted at his tension.

Francine turned to watch her patient's reaction to him.

She sat quite still, staring up at him with wide eyes. Christine said brightly, "Oh, look, Victoria. It's Ryan. This is your husband, darling."

Ryan shot Christine a questioning look and turned a sharp stare back on his wife. Her mouth had fallen open, and her green eyes registered mild shock. Then her gaze began to move, tracing the features of his face, lingering on his mouth before sliding down his body like a slow, intimate caress. She stared at his crotch just long enough to make him shift uncomfortably.

Her lovely mouth curved in a faint smile.

Christine rose and cleared her throat. "I'll leave you two alone, shall I? I'll be down the hall, dear, when you're dressed and ready to go." Her daughter made no response. Ryan managed a nod as Christine turned away from the bed.

"Well." Francine leaned forward to capture her patient's attention. "Victoria?" The young woman pulled her gaze from her husband with what looked like effort. "We'll see each other tomorrow. You have an appointment with me at two o'clock."

She looked dazed. Francine lifted an eyebrow.

"Ryan, you're still coming to my office before you

leave?" He, too, seemed to have difficulty focusing on anyone except his wife. He nodded wordlessly. "Good. There is one question in particular I need to ask you."

He nodded again but was already surrendering his gaze to the pull of his wife's eyes. Francine looked away discreetly and left them alone.

* * *

April sunshine splashed across the linoleum and warmed Ryan's shoes where he stood, rooted in place, staring at the impossibly beautiful woman in the hospital bed. Although neither spoke, the emotional charge running between them held him stunned—his gaze locked on hers, his breath quick and shallow. She tilted her head and slanted her green eyes at him, a smile playing at the corners of her mouth. He licked his lips and felt a pulse jump in his throat. His palms slid over the rough wool of his trousers, wiping away moisture.

Ryan cleared his throat and rocked back on his heels. Hands now in his pockets, he came alongside the bed and stood over his wife, hating the telltale heat he could feel rising up his neck.

"Your mother called this morning with the good news," he said. "I was stunned, Vicki. Tell me how it happened."

She slid her gaze from his face to his neck, where he felt a muscle jerking. Again, the corner of her mouth lifted, but she merely spread her hands and shrugged. His heart sank as he realized she still could not speak, and her gesture of helplessness roused his old protective instincts. But the hint of laughter in her eyes held him back, along with the glint of something else—something he'd never seen in her eyes before.

He spoke again, making his voice gruff to cover his uneasiness.

"You look better this morning. Rested. In fact, you're quite…lovely." He hadn't meant to say it quite like that. He pulled his hands from his pockets and gripped the bed rail. "I'm sorry. I can't have lunch with you at Eleanor's today. I have to catch a one-thirty flight to Phoenix. But I'll be back on Friday, as planned."

The laughter in her eyes died instantly, and Ryan was startled to see them clouding with disappointment. Unmistakably disappointment. He had expected relief or, at best, indifference.

His hands came loose from the bed rail and gently cupped her face. "I promise I'll be back before you even know I'm gone," he said, stroking her cheeks with his thumbs. She stared up at him with emerald eyes that seemed to widen and deepen, pulling him inside her and drawing his head down until, without meaning to, he was covering her mouth with his.

His senses abandoned him to a swirling emerald sea. Dimly, he felt her slender arms slip around his neck, pulling him deeper into the kiss. He groaned and dug his fingers into her hair, lifting her head off the pillow as his need sharpened into a tight visceral tug. Her lips parted against his, and her breath, light and sweet, slipped into his mouth. She moaned softly.

"Excuse me." Someone cleared her throat noisily. Ryan realized on some level that this was not the first time the voice had spoken. He fought his way clear of the rushing green tide and opened his eyes. The room tilted; he let his wife go and clutched the bed rail for support, swinging his head toward the voice and growling, "Well? What is it?"

A young student nurse stood at the door, visibly embarrassed. "I'm so sorry. But it's... I'm supposed to get Mrs. Ashton ready to go home."

Still shaken, Ryan nodded curtly. "Give us a moment, will you?"

The girl scurried away.

His wife lay exactly as he had released her—blond hair tumbling over the pillow, head tilted, lips parted. Her breath was light and fast, lifting her breasts under the thin cotton of her hospital gown. An image flicked across his mind of their bodies tangling on the narrow hospital bed, and Ryan took a step back, stunned by the unexpected force of his need.

"I'll...uh—" His voice shook, and her mouth curled with lazy satisfaction—like a cat licking cream from her whiskers. "I'll see you on Friday, Vicki." He ached to touch her again, but he didn't dare. Instead, he took another step back. "Till Friday."

She was still smiling when he made his escape into the corridor.

Chapter Eighteen

Eleanor paused by the library door and silently watched her granddaughter. Victoria lay stretched out on the sofa, engrossed in a television program. But then, what else would she be doing? In the five days since her release from the hospital, the girl had spent hours on end in front of that screen, watching the news, sporting events, soap operas, and talk shows. She absorbed every word as if her life depended on it. She even studied the commercials, for heaven's sake.

And that wasn't all. She'd taken to following Agnes around, her green eyes scrutinizing every move the housekeeper made. She seemed fascinated with ridiculous things like electric can openers and telephones and vacuum cleaners. And all the while her eerie muteness continued. Christine insisted there was nothing wrong with the girl that time and patience wouldn't cure, but Eleanor wasn't so sure. She wasn't giving up her brain tumor theory just yet.

Christine was another problem. Victoria's accident had triggered some alarming changes in Eleanor's daughter. For one thing, a stubborn streak was beginning to show itself far too often, especially where Victoria was concerned. Christine positively hovered over the girl, coddling her, most likely impeding her recovery. When Eleanor suggested Victoria should begin modeling again, Christine wouldn't hear of it. Moreover, she forbade Eleanor from mentioning the subject to Victoria. *Forbade* her, in Eleanor's own house! And the surprise birthday party for Victoria

159

this evening was all Christine's idea. Eleanor told her that Victoria was too old for surprise parties, but Christine had insisted. *Insisted.*

Eleanor shook her head and moved on to the study. She had work to finish before that pleasant woman from *People* magazine arrived for the interview. After all, Eleanor's own birthday gala was less than two weeks away.

At seventy-five, Eleanor was being honored by the retail industry as an entrepreneur and a feminist model of ingenuity and courage. The media couldn't seem to get enough of her story. Born Eleanor Hildegaard Rhineholdt, she was the granddaughter of German immigrants who opened a bakery on San Francisco's Powell Street in 1895. Eleanor credited her merchandising acumen to spending her childhood afternoons learning the bakery business — working the cash register and serving customers instead of playing jacks on the sidewalk or engaging in other useless endeavors. At eighteen she married her childhood sweetheart, Matthew Prescott, whose family owned a men's haberdashery a few blocks away. Although their building sustained damage in the great 1906 earthquake, the Prescott family managed to keep their business afloat, and as a young man Matthew inherited a profitable clothiers shop of fine reputation. Nevertheless, it was Eleanor's vision and aggressive strategies that turned the little shop into a multi-million dollar enterprise, first expanding into a department store, and then into a retail chain. Her success was legendary. Within a decade of establishing herself as the corporate head of Prescott's, Eleanor had bought the mansion of her dreams and taken her rightful place in the upper echelon of San Francisco society.

To her relief, the media didn't seem interested in Victoria's recent accident. And it *was* gratifying how Victoria was taking such an interest in their family history. Eleanor had seen her granddaughter poring over magazine and newspaper stories and watching every personal video Christine could supply — all the Christmases and corporate parties, and, of course, recent television interviews with Eleanor. The girl's obvious interest in her grandmother's success was really rather touching. Eleanor found herself relenting about the party.

"Oh, well," she murmured aloud. She settled herself at her expansive but impeccably organized desk. "Maybe it's not such a bad idea. I could invite that nice woman interviewer to attend." She stared at her reflection in the blank computer monitor and tapped a pencil against her chin. "I'll get her to take some photos to run with the article. After all, everyone will want to see what a close, happy family I've created."

* * *

Ryan took a long sip of the dry pinot noir and peered over the rim of his glass at the birthday guests assembled around Eleanor's dining table. Christine had been wise to keep the number relatively small. Down the table he recognized officers from Prescott's, a man and a woman from *People* magazine, some of Eleanor's cronies, and Christine's friends, including Dan Winslow. There were only a few young people, a reminder that Vicki didn't make friends easily.

He glanced at his wife sitting beside him, her head bent as she listened to a plump woman with ratted blue hair seated next to her. Ryan noted with surprise that Vicki had eaten everything on her plate, and she'd left her wineglass untouched. But then, the evening thus far had been full of such little surprises.

He couldn't get over the way she'd looked when she walked into the library, unaware that guests were waiting to spring out and shout "Happy birthday!" Her beautiful hair was twisted into a severe bun at the back of her head, not particularly unattractive, but unusual. Her face was scrubbed shiny without a hint of makeup; her clothes were elegant but plain without the accessories she always used so cleverly: no bracelets, no scarf knotted at her throat, no gold belt to accentuate her slender waist.

At the surprise chorus of good wishes, Ryan expected her to blush and withdraw into her shyness. But she'd surprised him again. After her initial shock, her face broke into a radiant smile. She moved gracefully into the knots of guests, clasping hands and smiling into each face, studying them as if memorizing their features. The impression of youth created by her scrubbed, unadorned appearance receded before her poise and confidence as she assumed with apparent ease her role as guest of honor. The paradox left Ryan feeling both amused and unsettled.

He grew even more disturbed when she spotted him across the room and began to make her way toward him. Ryan hadn't seen his wife since that disturbing scene in the hospital, which he'd convinced himself was mostly wishful thinking. But here it was again—that slanted green glint that locked her eyes with his as she drew nearer. He reached for her, intending to gather her in an affectionate hug. But before he realized what she was doing, she looped her arms around his neck, spooned her body against his, and kissed him soundly and thoroughly on the mouth.

A stunned silence settled over the room, relieved here

and there by nervous titters. A few broke into awkward applause. Ryan felt his face burn as he held her away from him, annoyed that others could see how his wife affected him. She gazed up at him with her head tilted, her mouth lifted in that feline smugness he recognized from the hospital. He raised an unsteady hand to straighten his tie and smooth his hair.

She slipped her arm around his waist and turned to face the room, smiling as she leaned her head against his shoulder. Ryan watched in amazement as glasses lifted to them in an impromptu toast. The man from *People* magazine snapped his camera in rapid succession. Christine pulled tissues from her pocket and dabbed her eyes while Dan supported her with his arm and beamed broadly. Even old Eleanor, surveying the room from her winged armchair, turned a smile on her granddaughter that could only be described as triumphant.

Victoria was unequivocally the center of attention. Moreover, she had orchestrated the moment to perfection.

And she had yet to speak a word.

* * *

Ryan came to himself and realized the dinner plates had been cleared away. Guests smiled and winked at each other as a hush fell over the table. The chandelier dimmed, and all eyes turned toward the door where a flickering reflection of light moved along the corridor wall toward the dining room.

A blaze of candles perched above a wide expanse of white icing and pink flowers floated into the room between the arms of Christine and Agnes. Ryan glanced at his wife to find that her easy poise had vanished. In its place, he could swear, were genuine shock and wonder. Tiny bright flames reflected in her eyes as her mother and Agnes placed the cake before her. Christine glanced at him for help, and together they launched the table into a chorus of "Happy birthday, dear Victoria! Happy birthday to you!"

Silence followed. The guest of honor stared into the forest of candles without moving. Even when guests began to murmur and shift impatiently, she remained frozen in her chair.

Christine bent over her daughter's shoulder. "Make a wish, Victoria darling, and blow out your candles!"

Ryan saw his wife stir and glance up at him. Tears swam in her eyes, reflecting a hundred times the twenty-three slivers of candlelight. His throat tightened as he watched her rise slowly and do something he'd never seen her do. She turned and threw her arms around Christine, locking their bodies and sobbing into her mother's neck.

Into the breathless silence of her spellbound guests, she spoke her first words in a voice barely more than a whisper: "Thank you. Thank you for my birthday...Mother."

* * *

Ryan struggled into the apartment and set down his wife's suitcases with a grunt. Glancing around the empty living room, he supposed his wife must have made it into the bedroom. He noted the bags and boxes of birthday gifts on the sofa where Victoria had unceremoniously dumped them in her eagerness to examine the apartment.

He had trailed her through the kitchen and the dining room, listening to her exclaim in that funny low voice and watching her turn the faucet on and off, open cupboards and closets to peer inside, switch on the balcony lights, and fiddle with the remote for the flat-screen television. When she stopped to finger the photos displayed in the hall, Ryan announced he was going back downstairs for the suitcases and ducked out the front door, shaking his head.

He stood in the foyer now, rubbing a hand over his tired eyes, when he suddenly heard bath water running. His watch confirmed the time as just past eleven-thirty.

What in blazes was going on with her?

Pushing the suitcases aside, Ryan dragged himself across the living room to switch on the stereo. He pushed the numbered program buttons, and soft jazz drifted into the room. He wandered around, switching off lights until there was only the dim glow from the stereo and an unexpected wash of moonlight stealing in through the balcony doors.

Ryan dropped into the corner of the sofa that wasn't crowded with gifts. He closed his eyes, leaned his head back, and invited the music into his body. In finally allowing himself to be still, he realized that he was utterly exhausted. He burrowed deeper into the cushions with a sigh and waited for sleep to claim him.

His mind, however, insisted upon jumping through a slide show of the birthday party. Perplexing snapshots of his wife rose up in succession—the way she dressed, the way she carried herself with new confidence, the way she looked straight into people's eyes when they spoke to her. None of it was like her. He relived the moment when she'd first caught sight of him, the intensity in her eyes when they'd locked onto his. He felt her arms slipping around his neck and her lips melting into his with that long, luscious kiss, and his loins tugged again in response.

Ryan groaned and pushed the images away with an

effort. Dr. Shepherd had warned him that Victoria was experiencing some kind of post-traumatic stress and could be taking refuge inside a new identity for a while. She'd asked Ryan to be patient and not to make too many demands on his wife right now, especially sexual demands.

Yeah, right, Doc. He smiled sleepily at the memory of Vicki's full breasts pressing against his chest when she'd kissed him, of her thigh brushing his more than once under the dining table. He recalled turning suddenly to find her watching him from across the room, her mouth curled in that feline smile.

The soft jazz and memories of the party began to fade as drowsiness overtook him at last. Ryan felt his spirit loosen from his body and float free, light and insubstantial as sea foam on a gentle swell of emerald tide, just before he fell asleep.

* * *

He didn't know what woke him. Soft jazz still played into the room, and he realized he was cold. He must have been sleeping for a while because the silver wash of moonlight had shifted higher, throwing a diagonal swatch across the rug right up to his shoes.

A spicy ginger scent hovered in the air. He jumped at a movement behind him and snapped his head around. A specter in white stood there, just outside the reach of the moon. He stared in breathless silence as the ghostly figure glided around the arm of the sofa to stand tall and slender before him. Moonlight from behind her cast a silver halo around her pale hair and silhouetted the curved form inside her filmy robe. Shadows obscured her face, keeping her expression secret.

In silence, she knelt before him and began to unlace his

shoes. First one foot and then the other she freed from the hot confines of leather and woolen socks. She lifted each foot in turn and laid it in the deep vale between her breasts while her hands slid up his calf, massaging inside his trouser leg up to the knee. A flush of heat broke out along Ryan's chilled skin. She bent her head over her task, and her hair hung like a silver veil, hiding what her hands were doing.

Ryan moaned and lolled his head back against the sofa cushion. The short but heavy sleep had left him dull and slow to react. Through a thick mind fog, his senses barely registered the music and the moonlight as his shirt magically unbuttoned and opened to cool air. Then warm lips trailed moisture and electric sparks down his chest, and he was helpless to know if this woman was real or a dream image his mind refused to give up. Dr. Shepherd's warning drifted against him like vapor curls and dissolved into nothing. Whoever this creature was, this enchantress who conjured wave after wave of throbbing ecstasy and melted the very bones of his body, he hadn't an ounce of will to resist her. Let her think she was this Katherine person; let her have her strange ways and her imperfect memory. *Only, please God, don't let her disappear with the moonlight. Don't let her wash through me and then recede like the tide, leaving me cold and alone on some distant shore.*

He held back her hair and searched her face, trying to read her expression. But she kept the moonlight behind her, and he couldn't tell if the gleam in her eye was one of triumph or merely a sliver of reflected light.

It didn't matter. He shut his eyes and abandoned his thoughts, surrendering himself to a rising tide that made him once again light and insubstantial as sea foam, and far from any shore.

* * *

Ryan woke to the delicious feel of sheets sliding over his naked skin. The bed bounced lightly as his wife slipped out and left him alone in it. He forced an eye open long enough to see her naked form disappear into the bathroom.

He rolled over and pulled the sheet over his head, inhaling the lingering scents of ginger spice and their lovemaking. His limbs felt drugged and his senses dull with unfinished sleep. A smile touched his lips as he slipped back into oblivion.

His body was more willing to awaken the second time. The bathroom door stood open, and the silence told him he was alone. Vicki was probably in the kitchen, fixing tea.

Vicki. Ryan stole another moment to lie with his eyes closed, reliving the smell and the feel of her. His hand absently stroked the sheet beside him where she'd curled her body into his, and exhausted and satiated almost beyond endurance, they had both finally slept.

A languorous stretch, and Ryan rose from the bed. He lingered in the shower, reveling in the hot water pummeling his muscles and washing away the last vestiges of sex and sleep. He caught himself whistling softly as he pulled a turtleneck over his head, and he grinned.

He hadn't felt this good in a long time.

The rich fragrance of coffee, bacon, and burnt toast met him as he opened the bedroom door. Vicki stood at the kitchen sink, her back to him, scraping toast. She was dressed in a yellow sweater pulled long over tight-fitting blue jeans. Instead of a neat French braid, her hair hung in a loose plait down her back.

Ryan tiptoed up behind her and slipped his arms

168

around her waist, burying a kiss in her neck. She stiffened and turned in his arms. Her green eyes regarded him, clear and uncomplicated by makeup, and her face shone with a fresh-scrubbed beauty that made his heart skip.

"Good morning," he murmured, and he planted a kiss on her shiny nose. Then he pulled her against him for a longer, deeper kiss on her mouth.

She held herself still for the kiss. But when he lifted his mouth away, she eased herself out of his arms without meeting his eyes. Puzzled, hurt, Ryan watched her return to her task of scraping the black edges from the toast. He noticed she had used the oven broiler to toast the bread instead of the electric toaster standing, covered, on the counter. Strange.

There was coffee in the pot, and Ryan poured himself a cup. He took it to the breakfast bar, where he sat down and took a sip.

"Whoa!" he sputtered. "Coffee's mighty strong, ma'am!"

His wife stopped scraping and turned to look at him. She picked up the mug sitting beside her and took a sip.

"Vicki, since when did you start drinking coffee?" Ryan couldn't remember his wife ever drinking coffee with him in the morning. In fact, he couldn't remember her ever fixing a pot before. Maybe she was trying to please him.

The thought softened his hurt, and he took another sip. "It's good, though." He watched her profile. "I like my coffee strong."

She made no response but dusted the black crumbs from her hands and reached for a plate. Ryan tried again.

"You were up early this morning. I was pretty wiped out, myself." He rippled a teasing note through his voice. But she remained silent as she arranged the toast on the

169

plate and then turned and set it before him on the bar.

He caught her hand before she could turn away. "Aren't you going to talk to me this morning?"

She looked into his eyes then, and he was puzzled to see the cool distance in hers.

"I regret I burned your toast...Ryan." She spoke in that odd, husky voice and clipped her words curiously. She stood still until he released her hand. Then she turned to retrieve the platter of bacon and scrambled eggs keeping warm in the oven. Ryan stared at her stiff back and choked down a swell of disappointment.

So, the enchantress had disappeared with the moonlight after all.

He watched the remote woman who had replaced her set the platter before him and refill her coffee mug. She came around the bar and sat primly on the high stool beside him, avoiding his eyes and helping herself to the breakfast she had prepared. He watched numbly as she bit off bacon with teeth that had nibbled his earlobes all night, and wipe her napkin across lips that had so thoroughly explored his body, they'd awakened nerves he hadn't known he possessed.

He looked away and swallowed his coffee—this time choking down a rising temper as well as disappointment. What kind of game was she playing? After so many months of putting him off, to come to him last night—oh, the memory of her, the *feel* of her—yet here she was, snow and ice again, pretending nothing at all had happened between them.

Had anything happened for her? He paused to consider, remembering the dreamlike quality of their coming together, the way the moonlight had colluded with her to keep her expression in shadow. He remembered, with sheepish honesty, his voluntary surrender to her leading, allowing himself to be taken like a virgin to a level of arousal he'd never even imagined.

And *he* was going to teach *her* the art of sexual intimacy!

The sudden, urgent tugging in his groin only annoyed him further. He quickly scooped some of the cooling eggs onto his plate and bit off a large piece of bacon. Chewing thoughtfully, he glanced sideways at his wife. She was intent on her breakfast, forking eggs into her mouth with unabashed gusto. He recalled the tightness of her jeans and wondered at her sudden interest in eating. There were times when she ate so little he feared she might have an eating disorder.

Could she be pregnant? Ryan shook his head at the thought and pushed a listless fork through his eggs. She was on the pill, and besides, their sexual intimacy had dwindled to nearly nothing over the last few months. That's why, when she'd come to him last night without a hint of reserve or embarrassment, he'd been taken so completely by surprise.

Post-traumatic stress. Assumed identity. Emotional instability. Don't make sexual demands. Dr. Shepherd's warnings forced themselves between Ryan and his breakfast, and he pushed his plate aside. Draining his coffee mug, he slid off his stool and picked up his plate.

His wife, already at the sink, was scraping leftover food into a garbage bag.

"Why aren't you using the garbage disposal?"

She met his question with a quizzical look. Ryan scraped the remains of his breakfast into the sink, turned on the cold water, and switched on the disposal. His wife jumped at the sudden grinding noise and stared suspiciously at the food and water disappearing down the drain.

"Careful of your fingers," he warned, wondering afterwards why he had said it. He switched off the disposal and let the water run a few more seconds. "There," he said.

She stood for a moment staring at the sink and chewing on her thumbnail. Ryan noticed that most of her nails had been gnawed down to the quick. *Strange.*

His wife picked up the platter and with elaborate care scraped the contents into the sink. Gingerly, she poked the food toward the drain with a fork.

It's like she's never seen this work before, Ryan thought, and he watched her switch on the disposal. It made a loud, angry noise, and he hastily turned on the faucet.

"You have to run water with it." He grabbed the tilting platter from her and set it on the counter. He switched off the disposal. "There," he said again. "That's all there is to it." He added gently, "Are you all right?"

She wiped her hands over the rough fabric of her jeans and nodded. When she looked up at him, he thought he saw a flicker of shy warmth. "Thank you, Ryan."

"You're quite welcome." He unintentionally mirrored her cool politeness. But she didn't see his frown of bafflement because she'd already turned away and was tearing at her thumbnail again with her teeth.

Chapter Nineteen

Eleanor watched in the mirror as Nora's liver-spotted hands eased the diamond tiara into the crown of her carefully arranged hair. When Nora stepped back to observe the finished work, Eleanor turned her head from side to side, catching the wink of diamonds against the dense mound of white coils. She patted the upsweep at the back of her head and allowed the maid to see her smile. Nora had done a good job. The thick Rhineholdt hair had taken Nora nearly two hours to curl, twist, and pin, but the effect was truly stunning. Best of all, the arrangement added nearly four inches to Eleanor's height.

"Excellent, Nora." Eleanor caught the maid's eye in the mirror. "You've outdone yourself."

"Thank you, Mrs. Prescott." Nora said it demurely, but her wide Swedish mouth stretched in a satisfied grin, and Eleanor knew she was pleased. Nora was the best personal maid she'd ever had. She worked a little slowly perhaps, but she was careful and loyal and efficient in her own way. Compliments like tonight were rare, Eleanor knew, but Nora didn't seem to need constant praise to keep her content at her job. Eleanor found something restful about her, and reassuring. She often astonished herself by actually looking forward to Nora's company.

"What time is it?" Eleanor asked the question for the fourth time in twenty minutes.

"Not yet five-thirty, Mrs. Prescott." Nora helped her employer out of her robe and carefully slipped the $4,500 gown from its cushioned hanger. "You've plenty of time. Mrs. Reeves and Miss Victoria are still dressing. Besides, they can't start your birthday celebration without the guest of honor."

Minutes later Eleanor stood at the center of her three-way wardrobe mirrors, casting a critical eye up and down her petite figure. The glittering gold lamé of her custom-designed gown covered her from neck to floor, billowing over her arms, fitting comfortably at the bodice, and falling from her waist in soft folds. The high neck had been deliberate, and she saw now that she had been right to insist upon it. One's eye swept naturally in an unbroken movement up the gown to the top of her hair, where the tiara sparkled like a crown. The overall effect was rich and regal. *Good*, she thought, *for tonight of all nights will be mine to reign.*

She smiled with satisfaction and returned to her dressing table.

"I'll have the emeralds now, Nora."

The maid was already bringing the familiar red velvet box. As Eleanor raised the lid and saw the green gems nestled against the blue satin lining, she felt her heart tug with a sweet ache.

"These were a gift from Matthew," she explained, as if Nora weren't already quite familiar with that fact. She traced the jewels with a red lacquered nail. "He gave them to me the night we opened our first department store." She drew out an earring and held it next to her temple, catching Nora's gaze in the mirror. "He told me even emeralds couldn't match the color of my eyes."

Her hands shook a little, and she fumbled with arthritic fingers to attach an earring to each earlobe. Nora

174

turned away discreetly and laid out items for the beaded evening bag.

Without warning, Eleanor turned on her vanity bench. "Thank you, Nora. You may go now."

Nora didn't seem offended by the abrupt dismissal. She nodded her assent and moved without a word to the door, where she paused and looked back.

"Good luck tonight, Mrs. Prescott." Her eyes crinkled at the corners with her wide smile. "And, if I may say, congratulations on your birthday. You look more royal than the Queen of England herself."

Eleanor inclined her head, and Nora left her alone. Eleanor stared at the closed door for a moment before she turned back to her mirror and studied her reflection.

Now that there was no one to watch, she allowed her shoulders to sag, and she closed her eyes in utter weariness. How she hated getting old!

Seventy-five. *Not bad for a baker's daughter, eh, Matthew?*

Eleanor opened her eyes and glanced at the middle of three photographs, framed in silver, on her dressing table. She saw herself as a young woman standing beside her husband in front of the old clothiers store on Geary Street. Matthew's lanky frame bent protectively over her diminutive one, and that boyish grin of his wrung her heart even now, as it always had. She shook her head at him, remembering how slow and cautious he always was, reluctant to accept her vision for expanding Prescott's into department stores, reluctant to move ahead into wealth and power, but acquiescing because he loved her. Matthew had always loved her.

She let her gaze wander to the other two photographs. One showed Victoria in her christening gown. She'd been a quiet baby, a quiet child, always so pensive, her head in the clouds most of the time. Eleanor felt her annoyance rise. The girl was a mystery to her. Smart and talented — that was the Rhineholdt blood rising to the surface. Eleanor had hoped to train her in the retail business, to carry on after she was gone. But in her quiet way, Victoria had resisted all of Eleanor's efforts. Instead, she took useless art classes and jumped into marriage with a man too old for her. And now, Eleanor sniffed, she sits around doing nothing with her life, not even raising children. She'll end up a disappointment to us all, just like her mother.

Christine. Eleanor grimaced and looked at the third photograph, taken when Christine and her brother were three years old. No twins had ever been more different. Luke carried the unmistakable traits of a Rhineholdt, with blond curls and wide green eyes that smiled into the camera. Luke had always been such a cheerful little boy, such a joy to his mother. Not like Christine.

Eleanor critically studied the little dark-haired girl sitting beside Luke in the picture. Still the same sour mouth and brooding eyes. Maybe if she smiled more often and relaxed that tight jaw, she'd resemble Matthew more. As it was, she looked like a dark changeling who belonged to neither of them, and Eleanor had often told her so. If God had to take one of them, why did it have to be Luke?

Eleanor's forehead creased with pain over forty years old. It was that accursed public school's fault. And, of course, Christine's. She'd picked up influenza from one of those nasty, common children and infected Luke. Then, just as he seemed to recover from the influenza, his pneumonia came on, so unexpected and intense, with a high fever that wouldn't break, and tortured breathing, and pathetic red blotches on his pale cheeks. Eleanor felt again the curl of his small fingers around hers and heard his hoarse whisper at the last: "I love you, Mommy. I don't want to go away from you."

They buried him in Sacred Heart Cemetery just six days before the twins' seventh birthday. His father had joined him thirteen months later.

Eleanor reached down absently to rub her finger under an irritating gold shoe strap. She didn't need the mirror to tell her that no tears marred the perfection of her makeup. She took grim satisfaction in knowing that she hadn't cried in years. She'd buried her tears, along with her heart, in Sacred Heart Cemetery — close to the only two people in the world she had ever loved.

* * *

Eleanor emerged from her bedroom and spied her granddaughter moving away from her down the hall, chatting with a hired hair stylist.

"Victoria!"

Her granddaughter continued a few steps. Then she stopped abruptly and turned, as if she'd just recognized her name.

That child had been acting so queerly.

"Yes?"

Eleanor raised a bejeweled hand and beckoned. "Come here, girl. Let me see you."

The stylist moved off, and Eleanor watched her granddaughter approach. She wore a shimmering gown of green and gold satin, the waist cut high and tight in an empire style, the skirt falling in straight lines to the floor. The neckline cut low across the girl's creamy bosom, which mounded in soft curves above the high lift of her bodice.

Eleanor approved the stylist's decision to pile Victoria's blond hair high, but leaving soft, loose ringlets to frame her face and trail gently down the slender curve of her long neck.

As the willowy young woman drew closer, Eleanor noted and approved the proud carriage of the Rhineholdt head. She recognized herself in the emerald eyes sparkling with excitement, and an idea flashed into her mind.

"Come with me," she snapped, covering her eagerness with a gruff tone. Her granddaughter turned without a word and followed her back into the bedroom.

"Sit down. There." Eleanor indicated the vanity bench where Nora had dressed her hair and where she herself had sat only moments before, indulging in useless self-pity.

In another moment Matthew's emeralds were settled on the creamy bosom, winking at them both in the mirror.

"Oh!" The awe in her granddaughter's voice pleased Eleanor, and she nodded as the girl's slender fingers traced the jewels with careful respect. The sparkling eyes so like her own met hers in the mirror. "They're beautiful!"

"Your grandfather Matthew gave them to me a long time ago. See?" Eleanor held one of her earlobes forward for inspection. "They match my earrings. I thought it fitting that you should wear my emeralds tonight." She allowed her gaze to stray to the young couple in the photograph, smiling eternally from inside their silver frame.

Her granddaughter rose from the bench and faced her.

Eleanor cleared her throat, embarrassed by her unexpected burst of sentimentality. "Is your mother dressed yet?" She busied her hands, shutting the red velvet box and patting the back of her hair unnecessarily. "I heard she's wearing a black gown tonight. Imagine that. She'll probably look like an old crow alongside the rest of us."

She glanced up to find her granddaughter regarding her with thoughtful eyes. The girl raised a hand to her throat and fingered the jewels again. "Thank you," she said. "Thanks for your generosity...Grandmother."

Eleanor was turning toward the door when her granddaughter's words stopped her cold. "What did you call me?" she snapped.

The girl gazed at her, unflinching.

"I never gave you permission to call me that!" Eleanor's voice rose. "You dare to disrespect me, and after this kindness I've shown you tonight?" She gestured at the girl's throat.

Her granddaughter tilted her head to one side. Eleanor thought she saw a smile play at the corners of her mouth.

"I always wanted a grandmother." The girl spoke softly, with a huskiness that was becoming familiar to Eleanor. "I'm the only person who can rightfully claim you as Grandmother, aren't I?" She didn't wait for a response but glanced at the ceiling. "I suppose I could call you Granny, if you prefer." She smiled at Eleanor's horrified expression. "Yes, I agree. You don't seem much like a *Granny* to me, either."

She walked calmly to the door and turned, her hand poised on the knob. "Mother's already downstairs. Shall we go...*Grandmother*?"

Eleanor's mouth opened and closed like a fish gulping air. Her chin rose, and her brow wrinkled in a show of wounded dignity. Tight-lipped, she brushed past her granddaughter with a rustle of satin underskirt and stepped into the hallway.

The two of them walked along the corridor without

speaking, the thick carpet muffling their footsteps. The younger woman paced herself to Eleanor's slower steps, and they reached the head of the stairs at the same time. Pausing before the descent, Eleanor gave her granddaughter a sidelong glance.

The girl's face was serene, but her eyes danced. She gave Eleanor an impertinent wink before taking the first step down.

Shocked, Eleanor froze where she stood. She stared at the shapely figure calmly descending the stairs before her, and her mouth began to twitch. Slowly, grudgingly, it widened into a grin of amused respect.

"Saints and goblins," she muttered, "if the girl hasn't got Rhineholdt spirit in her after all!"

With an effort, Eleanor tamed her grin into a practiced public smile. Head high, she followed her granddaughter down the carpeted steps, one hand raised in a royal wave at the party of upturned faces waiting in the foyer below.

* * *

The Regency Ballroom at the Bayhill Hotel sparkled with thousands of miniature white lights. They outlined the banquet tables, framed the graceful arches of the paneled walls, and twined with floral garlands draping the balustrade of the balcony, where an orchestra played to the party guests below.

From the circle of her husband's arms, Lisa Knight watched the elegant couples sharing the dance floor with them, and she marveled again at her very presence here. Ryan had been so sweet to ask that she and Chris be included in the party for Vicki's grandmother. He had kept his promise to stay in touch with them after their weekend at Summerwood Cottage. Lisa bit her lip, remembering the cost of the dress she wore. But even Chris admitted the experience was worth the cost. With him in his rented tux and her in a red Prescott gown, they looked very much like the others who had gathered in the lavish ballroom of one of the city's oldest hotels to celebrate Eleanor Prescott's seventy-fifth birthday.

Lisa couldn't get over rubbing elbows with people whose faces she recognized from the media: the mayor of San Francisco and his wife, the Alioto family, a TV news anchorwoman from Channel Four, two senators, a movie star, a professional baseball player, and the governor of Arizona. Then there were the dignitaries with unfamiliar faces who'd been pointed out to her: presidents and vice-presidents of rival stores like Macy's and Saks and Nordstrom, the archbishop of Saint Mary's Cathedral, the Wente family, renowned for their Livermore Valley winery. And on and on. After her initial awe, Lisa decided to just relax and enjoy herself. She smiled at celebrities and waiters alike because there was nothing else she could do. The evening was just that fantastic.

Champagne buzzed pleasantly in her head as she raised both hands to cradle the back of her husband's neck. She swayed her hips with his and smiled up at him. He smiled back. Then he pursed his lips in a kiss and mouthed the words "I love you."

Lisa couldn't remember feeling as good as this, ever. She snuggled her face into his neck and breathed a long, blissful sigh.

A throaty laugh close by jarred Lisa from her contented haze. She lifted her head in time to see Vicki swing by in the arms of yet another partner. Her body was tucked close against his, and she was gazing at him with a look that was…well…*seductive*.

Lisa frowned and made a clucking noise in her throat. Chris looked down and held her away so he could see her face.

"What is it, babe?"

She hesitated. "Vicki, I guess. You know we've been spending time together. I really like her. She's smart, and she's funny, and not afraid to try new things. Sometimes she's a little odd, though. And now tonight—"

Lisa bit her lip and Chris prompted her. "Yeah, tonight what?"

"Well, have you noticed how many guys she's been dancing with? And the *way* she dances…right under Ryan's nose!"

She nodded toward a corner of the room where Vicki's husband stood, hands in his pockets and head bent, listening to a large, fleshy man who gesticulated excitedly. Ryan smiled and nodded, but all the while his gaze traveled the room. Lisa saw his smile slip and his body stiffen. She shook her head and slapped Chris lightly on the arm.

"See that?"

"See what?" Chris squinted. "Holy cow, I've seen that guy Ryan's talking to! He lectured at Berkeley once. You think maybe Ryan would introduce me?"

The dance ended, and Chris turned an eager face to his wife. Lisa reached up and touched his cheek. "Men," she said softly. Then, with champagne making her bold, she surprised herself by giving him a quick, bold kiss on the mouth. At his startled smile, she took his hand and led him off the dance floor, toward the dessert buffet.

"C'mon," she said. "I know it's impossible, but I'm still

hungry."

* * *

Christine sat alone at Eleanor's table, watching the couples dip and sway on the dance floor.

No, she told herself, *what I'm really watching is Victoria making a fool of herself.*

Her frown deepened.

For the last half-hour, she'd watched her daughter dance and flirt with one attentive male after another, and none of them her husband. Christine wasn't such a prude as to think that a married woman shouldn't flirt. No, it was the *way* Victoria flirted, using her body and her eyes to signal more than the casual pleasure of a shared dance. It was the way she laughed and looked at her partner sideways, the way she trailed a finger over his black-tuxedoed shoulder and pressed her high, rounded bosom against his chest. The way her eyes lingered on him for a moment too long before she sailed off in the arms of yet another partner. Christine saw the way the men followed her daughter with their eyes, lusting after her, practically panting.

What in heaven's name could the girl be *thinking?*

She glanced at the corner where Ryan had been engaged with some person or other he knew from work. She didn't see him, and Christine felt a weak surge of hope that perhaps he'd been spared the humiliation of watching his wife's improprieties.

Then she saw him dancing with a young woman much shorter than himself. Although he smiled and talked with her, he repeatedly glanced over her head to sweep the dance floor with his gaze. When the dance ended, he stood chatting with his partner for a moment. Then he excused himself and walked away without a backward glance. *Good*, Christine thought. *At least he's not retaliating by behaving badly himself.*

Victoria, you little fool! Don't you understand you could lose Ryan — Christine tried to stop her thoughts there, but they forced their way to completion — *just like I lost Jack?*

"Here you go, sweetheart." Dan Winslow materialized in the chair beside her. "I managed to steal a pot of coffee just for us." He gave her a conspiratorial wink as he poured out two cups.

Christine smiled politely and accepted a cup. But her hand shook, and she hastily set the cup down.

Maybe Victoria really is like me.

"Christine?" Dan's voice was so close, she jumped and knocked her hand against the cup. Coffee slopped into the saucer and seeped a brown stain into the white tablecloth.

"Must be jumpy." Christine pressed a napkin to the stain, and her gaze slipped back to the dance floor. Dan's followed.

"Worried about Victoria?" His question didn't require an answer. They were both silent, watching her daughter simper into the face of her current partner and slide both arms around his waist. Dan said bluntly, "She looks like she's had too much to drink."

"She's had nothing to drink." Christine spoke without taking her eyes from her daughter. "She doesn't even drink wine anymore." She added silently, *If she were drunk, at least I could understand her behavior.*

"Well," Dan said with a sigh, "she's certainly embarrassing Ryan and her family out there."

Christine turned on him. "Don't say that! You have no idea what Victoria's been through, what she —" She stopped at his look and turned away in confusion. "Never mind, Dan." She added, in a brittle voice, "You don't want to know."

Dan's response was swift. "Try me," he urged.

The softness of his voice compelled her to look at him. His steady eyes watched her, as always seeing more than she wanted him to see. Ten months ago, she had met him for the first time, and since then she'd let him get far too close to her. For years she had prided herself on her immunity to the slick corporate suits and fortune hunters who pursued and flattered her and tried to get their teeth into the fabric of her life. She hadn't been prepared for Dan Winslow, however, a quiet widower with two grown daughters, whose imperturbable presence stood like a rock in the rushing confusion of her world. Against her better judgment, she had accepted his dinner invitations, and against her strict rules of privacy, she had allowed him an occasional glimpse of her heart. Not since Jack had she felt this needy, this vulnerable, or this emotionally out-of-control. She had never been this close to telling anyone about the dark, sordid secrets that had brought such shame into her life and pain into her daughter's.

The imminent risk of exposure terrified her.

Consequently, she answered Dan's "Try me" with a firm shake of her head, and steeled herself against his look of hurt disappointment. For Victoria's sake, as well as her own, she resolved to stick closer to her rules about keeping her privacy intact, even with Dan Winslow.

Especially with Dan Winslow.

Chapter Twenty

Ryan glared back at the red traffic light that held his Jaguar captive, idling behind the ugly rear end of an ancient yellow Volvo. He gripped the wheel with both hands and swore under his breath, feeling the powerful engine ready to leap ahead whenever the signal gave them permission to go.

Red snapped to green. The Volvo hesitated too long for his taste, and Ryan blared his horn. He felt rather than saw his wife glance at him from her side of the car.

Neither had spoken a word since they'd left the Bayhill Hotel.

Ryan saw his chance and swerved into the left lane, cutting off a BMW in his effort to pull alongside the Volvo. A voice in his head scolded him for reckless behavior, but a louder voice applauded him, affirming his right to take risks after interminable hours of minding his manners and pretending blindness to his wife's blatant humiliations.

He slammed on his brakes just in time to avoid hitting the car in front of him, which had stopped to wait for a parking space. Belatedly, its left turn signal blinked on. Unable to budge, Ryan seethed as the BMW swerved out from behind him and followed the placid Volvo through the intersection. By the time he managed to free the Jaguar and pull up to the intersection, the signal was staring red, like the twin taillights receding up the street.

Ryan muttered an oath and pounded a useless fist on the leather-wrapped steering wheel.

"You shouldn't curse," his wife admonished him primly. "Especially in the presence of a lady."

Ryan's eyes swept her with cold contempt. "What *lady?* Don't tell me it's possible to offend *your* sensibilities, *Mrs. Ashton!*"

A horn bleated behind them. Ryan jerked his gaze up to find the signal smiling green. He hit the gas, and the Jaguar lunged forward, accelerating rapidly. He scanned for the BMW, but it had vanished somewhere ahead of him.

With supreme effort he eased off the gas pedal and rolled his shoulders. He wouldn't solve anything by getting them into an accident. Besides, why was he in such a hurry to get them home? There was no way this evening was going to end on a pleasant note.

Ryan thought about the silent apartment waiting for them, and the tips of his ears burned as he remembered the intimate nights they'd been spending together, although daytime was a different story. During the day Vicki was quiet and aloof, rather like her old self but with some striking differences.

For one thing, she couldn't operate simple appliances like the iron or the dishwasher. He had come home one evening to find her on her hands and knees, scrubbing the kitchen floor with cleansing powder, and he'd had to explain about no-wax floors. His computer fascinated her, and she'd quickly learned how to access the Internet. Now, instead of asking him odd questions like who was the king of England and how much did it cost to buy a horse, she found her answers on-line. Between surfing the Web and watching TV, she seemed to spend most of her time amassing information of every kind.

Then there was Vicki herself. Ever since the accident, he'd noticed subtle differences in her. Her voice was pitched lower, rasping a little on the edges, and she spoke in the slow, concise manner of someone who had learned English as a second language. She startled him with archaic substitutes for common words — icebox instead of refrigerator, britches instead of pants or trousers. And every so often, particularly when she was excited or surprised, she'd burst out with something in Spanish. He didn't even know she spoke the language.

She walked with smaller steps and sometimes seemed afraid she'd hit her head on the door jam, as if she weren't comfortable with her five-foot-eleven-inch height. And there was the way she fixed her hair, her plain manner of dress, her sudden taste for coffee and aversion to alcohol. She even smelled different. In the absence of the new ginger spice perfume, the scent of her skin and sweat differed in a subtle way he couldn't define.

All these differences Ryan noticed and puzzled over. Keeping Dr. Shepherd's theories in mind, he tried to make sense of changes that, quite frankly, made no sense at all. Assumed identity? One that had never heard of a Big Mac or french fries and didn't know that women used maxi pads and tampons instead of cloth rags? Ryan understood how her injury could cause memory loss. But then, why would she remember how to sew on a button but not how to type on a keyboard? Know how to dig for a splinter but not how to apply a Band-Aid?

The only explanation was that Vicki truly believed she was this Katherine person from a past century, as Dr. Shepherd seemed to think. But what could possibly be the point of believing such a thing?

The psychiatrist had warned him not to pressure his wife but to support her during this period of identity confusion. She continued to see Vicki twice a week, but Ryan saw no improvement in his wife's daytime behavior. And, he had to admit, if it meant changing her nighttime behavior, then he would much rather she stayed confused.

In the weeks since Vicki had returned home, Ryan found his days repeatedly distracted by the single, embarrassingly prosaic thought of going home to have sex with his wife. Although the enchantress of the moonlight had disappeared after their first surreal night together, she had returned the following night and every night since. No matter how prim and distant she seemed during the day, come nightfall the cool personality gave way to a woman with fire in her blood and magic hands that slid over his body, knowing just where to touch him, where to tease and stroke him. Ryan felt new hope for their relationship, but because they never discussed their nighttime encounters, he could only guess at what their new intimacy meant to her.

Apparently, not much. Tonight he'd watched those same magic hands conjure lust in a queue of men she'd never seen before in her life. Even worse than her betrayal was recognizing himself in their flushed faces and laughter that was too loud, in the hungry looks that followed her around the ballroom. He felt again that lonely need that drove him into her arms night after night, seeking comfort and reassurance, and his stomach heaved in a slow, sick turn.

They were home.

Ryan blinked and tried to recall how the Jaguar had maneuvered itself into the underground garage and parked in its allotted space. His wife pulled on her door handle and gathered up her skirts, exposing a slim white ankle. He sucked in his breath and yanked his door open, bracing himself for the next phase of an evening that was far from over.

* * *

His wife preceded him into the apartment. She dropped her coat and handbag on the sofa and slipped out of her high-heeled shoes. Without switching on a light, she started for the bedroom.

"Oh, no, you don't." Ryan grabbed her arm and swung her around. "You have some explaining to do, Vicki."

"Take your hands off me!"

He debated about complying until he realized his grip was probably hurting her. He released her and took a step back.

In the dimness he saw her rub her arm, but he refused to apologize. After all she'd dished out tonight, she could stand a little pain.

They faced each other in bristling silence.

"Well?" she said at last. "You have something to say to me?"

"Baby, have you got *that* backwards! I'm waiting for *you* to explain yourself to *me*."

She stood absolutely still, a statue carved in stone. Or ice.

Little jets of rage spurted through Ryan's brain. "Okay, then. Just what were you trying to prove tonight?" He threw up his arms and saw her flinch. "I'm having trouble understanding why you felt compelled to seduce every male who came within two feet of you!"

"I don't know what you mean." In the thinning

darkness he could just make out her features, her eyes wide and staring at him.

"You think I'm blind?" he shouted. "You made a fool of yourself tonight, rubbing up against all those men like a bitch in heat. Teasing them, taunting until they couldn't keep their sweaty hands off you—" Ryan stopped himself before the trembling in his body reached his voice. He could see her mouth now, smiling in self-satisfaction. It spurred him into a final thrust of contempt. "You behaved like a slut. What's gotten into you?"

She leaned against the back of the sofa, still smiling.

"Are you upset, Ryan, because I enjoyed myself tonight? Because I received attention from attractive young men, and you were *jealous?*" She drew out the last word, and her perfect teeth gleamed in the dark. "God saw fit to give me this beautiful body." She looked down and watched her hands sweep up the sides of her hips and cup themselves under her breasts. She looked at Ryan, still cradling her breasts. "Why shouldn't I enjoy it, and let men enjoy it, too?"

Her fingertips began to trace concentric circles, narrowing to the tip of each breast. Her eyes never left Ryan's face.

"You want it right now, don't you?" she purred. "Don't you?" Her fingertips came together and traced her cleavage to the edge of her bodice. They slipped inside, just under the fabric.

She swayed toward him, a smile curling her mouth, her gaze piercing his through the darkness that still lay between them. "Why not take me, Ryan?" Her face was so close he could feel her breath on his chin. "Right here. Right now."

Her hands reached up to bring his head down, but his own shot up and caught her wrists, arresting them halfway up.

"You think you're irresistible, don't you?" Ryan hated the way his body pulsed and hardened in response to her, hated her power to arouse him—even in the face of her contempt. Hated her because he could tell, from the curve of her mouth and the gleam in her eyes, that she knew, even now, exactly what he was thinking.

He flung her away from him and stepped back, frightened by twin impulses to shake the living daylights out of her or to take her right here, on the floor behind the sofa. Either way, it was all he could do to keep his hands off her.

"You disgust me," he choked.

She leaned against the sofa and rubbed her wrists. "I know." She said it quietly, no longer smiling. "I can't say I blame you."

The nakedness of her words caught him off guard. He watched for the smirk, for that feline gleam in her eyes. But she seemed serious, even sorrowful. Baffled, Ryan spoke again, his words less venomous but still bitter.

"I won't have it, Vicki. Do you understand? You're my wife. You, and that body of yours"—he gestured toward her—"are mine. Get it? *Mine*. You belong to *me*."

"No!" She hissed the word like a snake, startling him. "This body does *not* belong to you! And *I* do not belong to you!"

She began to pace a small line in front of him, back and forth, muttering to herself: "Never again! *Never* will I submit to that kind of prison!" She faced him, and her eyes were wild. "Do you think I've come all this way just to

192

submit to the whims of another husband?" She barked a coarse laugh and went back to pacing and muttering. "Husbands are such a nuisance! So demanding, so arrogant when you give them power over you. And so difficult to get rid of!"

The hair stood up on the nape of Ryan's neck as he watched her pace like a caged animal measuring the length of her cell. He wondered if she might become dangerous, if he should call Dr. Shepherd. He did know the last thing he wanted to do was antagonize her.

"Vicki?" He spoke quietly, without moving toward her. All the same, she stopped pacing and faced him.

"Vicki? *Vicki?*" she mimicked him. Then she laughed that awful, coarse laugh again.

She jerked around suddenly and struck out across the living room. "I'm so *hot*," she whined.

Ryan took after her, suddenly afraid, wanting to stop her before she reached the patio door and the railing beyond. He switched on a lamp as he passed it, blinding them both with a painful bolt of illumination.

His wife cried out and covered her eyes.

Ryan reached her and grasped her shoulders, relieved when she didn't pull away.

"Come on, Vicki. Come sit down." She lowered her hands and allowed him to lead her to the sofa. She seated herself on the edge, and he pulled up a chair so he could sit close to her.

She looked at him with a shy expression and a trembling smile, so much like the old Vicki that his heart lurched painfully in his chest. She twisted the skirt of her gown between her hands, thoughtlessly wrinkling the fine material. With her hair coming loose from its pins and her mouth caught in that wistful smile, Ryan's old desire to protect her surged forward.

"Vicki?" His voice was gentle.

"Please don't be angry with her. She doesn't mean to be cruel. You can't imagine the terrible things she's been through. She's not trying to hurt you, Ryan. Truly. She's only — " Her words broke off at the look on Ryan's face.

They stared at each other.

"Katherine?" Ryan whispered hoarsely. "Are you Katherine?"

She looked puzzled. Then she nodded slowly.

"Yes. I can understand how you would think that. But, no, I'm not Katherine. And I'm not your precious Victoria." She looked straight into his eyes and said quietly, "I'm Elizabeth."

Victoria

Chapter Twenty-One

My eyelids felt glued shut, as if I had been asleep for years. I pried them open with some effort, and the first thing I saw was a green velvet canopy with gold tassels, decidedly ugly. Beyond it a shaft of sunshine filtered softly into the room through lace curtains. A rank sickroom smell assailed my nostrils. My muscles ached, and a sour taste in my mouth exhumed hazy memories of vomiting and shivering uncontrollably. I remembered a cool cloth sponging my face and my neck, and a woman's voice murmuring above me, soothing me in words I could not understand.

I must have dozed because the next time I opened my eyes, the shaft of sunshine had narrowed and shifted higher. I heard the gentle cadence of someone's snoring, but I couldn't make my head turn to look.

Ryan? I tried to speak his name, but my mouth wasn't working. I drifted off again, and when I next awoke, a lamp burned softly beside my head. I was lying on a bed, tucked under a warm comforter. Blinking, I tried to place the room. Summerwood?

"Ryan?" I spoke his name in a hoarse whisper. I pushed the comforter back a little and tried to sit up, and that's when I saw the hands — my hands, yet *not* my hands. These were small and brown, almost childlike, with stubby fingers and ragged nails. I sat up slowly, trailing a gaze up my sleeve of white flannel, frilled at the wrist and gathered at the shoulder. The gathering continued across the bodice, ruffled and fastened with white satin bows. A small pink seashell rested against the bows, suspended from my neck by a leather thong.

I felt weak and confused. "Ryan?" I whispered again. I hadn't imagined the snoring. It was still there, and I turned my head to the shocking sight of an enormous woman sleeping in an armchair against the wall.

Her head was bowed over her chest, her brown hands folded on her lap. Black hair liberally streaked with gray strained into a tight knot at the nape of her rolled neck. I stared in wonder at the utter size of the breasts cradling a large silver crucifix that rose and fell on the tide of her gentle snores.

The door on my left swung open. A middle-aged woman with a pleasant face stood there, peering at me over her spectacles. She broke into a delighted smile when she saw me sitting up and staring at her.

"Well! Look who's awake!" She crossed to the bed and picked up one of the hands that didn't belong to me, patting it between her own. Over the gold rims of her spectacles, her gray eyes studied my face. She nodded, and her smile widened.

"Bless you, child. It's good to have you back with us." I recognized her voice and her accent, the guttural "hk" sound in the words "have" and "back." Hers was the voice in my dream, hers undoubtedly the hand that had sponged my face.

The woman lifted the seashell from my chest and nodded toward the sleeping figure. "She hasn't left your side since you took sick." She replaced the shell and moved around the bed to shake one of the thick, folded arms.

"Dora! Dora, dear, Katya is awake. Look and see."

Katya? Who on earth was Katya? My head began to spin as my confusion hardened into solid fear.

My eyes skittered around the room, obviously someone's bedroom. I had the feeling I had been here for more than a day. But where was *here*? Who was this kind-faced woman, and who was that enormous figure slowly coming awake in the chair? The woman had called her Dora.

Dora. Katya.

Katherine.

Memory flooded back. I saw the path in the woods and the bridge where I had waited for Katherine. There was lightning and pain, and then a river sucking me through a long dark tunnel. I remembered a fragrant mist and a tender embrace I was reluctant to leave before the tunnel snatched me back. I was a leaf swirling in the darkness, and suddenly there was another leaf—we were twins twirling together, touching briefly before the current wrenched us apart, before the darkness filled me, and I awoke in...Katherine's body?

Impossible!

"Katya, dear?" I turned Katherine's head slowly. The woman's hand on Katherine's arm felt real. I smelled the lavender on her skin.

I clutched the seashell with Katherine's hand and lifted it. "It's a coral shell," I croaked. Katherine's throat was still raw from the sickness. I nodded at Dora. "She saved Katherine's life? Like she did Robbie's when he was so ill?" The woman's eyes narrowed. Katherine's bedroom began to sway and tilt.

I continued in a hoarse voice, hurting Katherine's

throat with the effort. "You don't look anything like Isabel, so I'm guessing you must be Katherine's Auntie Ana." Sleep dragged at me, making me want to close Katherine's eyes. Just before the woman's worried face shifted out of focus, I heard my funny hoarse voice whisper, "I'm pleased to meet you."

* * *

I spent much of the following day swimming in and out of dream scenarios, confused about what was real and what was imagined. From time to time I surfaced to the extraordinary sight of Katherine's bedroom and the Native American woman watching in silence from her chair. At one point the gray-eyed woman roused me to a cup of sweet tea. She smiled reassurances, but her eyes were worried as she helped me lift the cup to Katherine's lips and wiped up dribbles with a napkin.

At last I surfaced with a clear head. Weak rays of sun slanted through the window, and the armchair was empty. I was alone in the room.

I felt strong enough to venture from the bed. Throwing back the covers, I swung Katherine's legs over the side and was horrified to see them furred with fine dark hair. Like her hands, her feet were small and brown. I swung them down, and the heel of one collided with something metallic, setting up a loud clatter of spinning metal. I bent down to have a look.

A brass bowl came to rest on the floorboards beneath the bed. Good heavens, I thought, with a trickle of horror. A chamber pot!

A clammy wave pricked sweat along Katherine's skin as I stood beside the bed, wobbling a little on legs that were otherwise sturdy. Standing upright, I nevertheless felt I couldn't possibly be at my full height. I had trouble pacing my stride as I forced Katherine's short legs across a braided rug and bare floorboards. By the time I reached the cheval mirror positioned in the corner behind the door, my head was spinning and my stomach was queasy.

The image reflecting in the glass did nothing to steady me. I stared through dark brown eyes at a small, almost childlike figure in a rumpled nightgown. Her short forehead rose above a straight line of dark brows, giving her face a somber expression. Her nose was thin and sharp like her chin, her cheekbones high and broad. Her black hair was plaited down her back, but long hours of sickness had loosened it to frame her face with limp, oily strands.

I stared in dismay, and her mouth slackened to reveal small, even teeth. Gingerly I explored the rest of her mouth with her tongue and discovered a hole where a back molar was missing. I ran her small hands down the sides of her nightgown and was about to lift it when someone knocked on the door.

I spun away from the mirror and then caught my breath, for there on the threshold stood the beautiful lady of the portrait. Slender and quite tall, she wore her dark hair in a braid coiled softly on her head. Curling tendrils escaped to frame an oval face as perfect as I remembered. Her mouth was delicate, her complexion ivory and a soft rose that made the blue-violet color of her eyes even more vivid.

"Isabel." Her name escaped Katherine's lips in a long involuntary whisper. A story flashed into my mind of young Katherine taking scissors to the hair of her beautiful Christmas doll and suffering the consequences. Standing now in her unremarkable body, gazing at the perfection of her mother, I thought I understood the scissors.

* * *

"Katrina." Isabel raised shapely hands in a gesture of appeal. "Why are you out of bed?"

Her voice was light and musical with the warmth of a Spanish accent. I bathed in it as I studied her face, comparing every exquisite detail with the features I remembered from her portrait. I barely registered the dip of her finely etched eyebrows.

"Katrina, did you hear me?" She stepped toward me, and her voice sharpened. "You're shivering! Get back into bed at once!"

The room was indeed cold, and I crawled back into bed, grateful for the warmth still trapped in the sheets. Isabel found a shawl for my shoulders. Then she perched on the edge of the bed, folded her hands in her lap, and stared at me without flinching. An uneasy silence stretched until at last she spoke.

"You gave us quite a fright, Katrina." Her voice was level, but her eyes hinted at something darker. I listened to the pleasant roll of her *r*'s and tried to remember what Katherine's journal had said about Isabel's relationship with her daughter.

The musical voice continued. "You were delirious the first day, and you said some very strange things. Very strange indeed."

She rose from the bed and began to pace the room. She stopped suddenly and fixed me with a cold stare.

"Why did you do it, Katrina?"

Her sharpness surprised me. "Do what?" I said. "I don't know what you're talking about."

She jerked her head back. Anger deepened her eyes to

a cobalt blue.

"Don't play the innocent with me, young lady! I'll ask you again, and I expect an answer. *Why did you do it?*"

I gazed at her in helpless silence, all the time wondering how her frostiness could wound me so deeply.

The bedroom door opened, and we both turned our heads. The gray-eyed woman approached the bed, smiling warmly.

"Well, Katya! And how are you feeling?" She caught Isabel's look before returning her gaze to me.

"Better," I said. "But I do have to use the bathroom." The woman blinked, and I added, "Will you help me?"

Her voice was puzzled. "Bath room, dear? I shouldn't recommend a bath now, so soon after—"

"No," I interrupted. "I mean"—I groped for words—"I have to *pee*, you know?" She looked even more startled. I made clumsy flushing gestures.

Her face cleared. "Oh! There's a pot, dear, until you're steady on your feet again. Didn't you see it?"

She bent to retrieve the chamber pot from under the bed, but I grabbed her arm.

"No, not that!" She looked at me in surprise. "I mean, I'd rather..." I gestured toward the door.

The woman straightened. "You'd like me to accompany you to the necessary?"

"Yes! That's it!" I beamed with relief. The woman exchanged a look with Isabel.

"Well, if you think you're up to it." She sounded doubtful. "Sit still. I'll get your robe and slippers."

She opened the wardrobe, pulled out a blue robe, and began rummaging under the hanging garments.

Isabel retrieved slippers from under the armchair and

held them out. "Ana," she said, and the woman turned.

Ana, I thought. So I was right. This woman was Katherine's aunt.

"Here, Katya. Slip this on." The robe Ana held for me looked too small, but Katherine's arms fit into it perfectly. While Isabel watched in silence, Ana took a firm hold of me, and we crossed to the bedroom door.

Once in the corridor, I stopped short, recognizing Rosswood House. I left the support of Ana's arm to stand at the banister where I looked down on the familiar sweep of the grand staircase and the circular foyer below. Lifting my gaze, I recognized the twin hallway across the open expanse, giving off to the nursery, Alexander's bedroom, and Isabel's.

Ana touched me on the arm. "Katya, we'll have to go downstairs, I'm afraid. The one on this floor is not flushing properly." She shot me a worried look. "Are you certain you can make it?"

I gave her a confident smile. By the time we reached the bottom stair, however, I was clinging to the banister with both hands — dizzy and sweating.

"I didn't know it was this far," I muttered.

Ana shot me a glance. "Only a few steps more." She led me behind the stairs into a dimly lit corridor. "Shall I go in with you, dear?"

I shook my head emphatically and shut the door on her anxious face.

The "necessary" was a tiny room, freezing cold, with a high window hinged open to admit the gathering dusk. I sat gingerly on a discolored wooden seat above a deep porcelain bowl and stared at the floor tiles, black with mold in the corners. I pulled Katherine's slippers close together and wondered if people in her time knew about germs yet. I washed my hands with a bar of grainy soap that smelled like nothing at all. After one look at the limp towel hanging from a wooden ring on the wall, I shook off the worst of the water and wiped my hands on Katherine's robe.

Victorian decor had always charmed me, but at that moment I would have given anything for the reassuring gleam of sterile chrome, antibacterial soap, and a sturdy roll of paper towels, environmentally-friendly or not.

I opened the door to an empty corridor. I stood still, clutching the doorjamb, and tried to get my bearings. This little room hadn't been on the tour of Rosswood House. I recognized the door to the wine cellar on my left and the gunroom at the end of the hall. A lamp fixed to the wall lit the corridor with a dim yellow flame. *Gaslight?* I wondered.

Ana appeared from the direction of the kitchen. She hastened her steps when she saw me.

"You're pale as a ghost, Katya," she chided. "We must get you back to bed at once."

She led me out of the corridor. As we approached the stairs, I saw the grandfather clock, and it was like seeing the face of an old friend. Then I noticed it was silent, its brass pendulum hanging motionless and draped with a black sash. I clutched Ana's arm.

"Who's dead?" I asked.

"Oh, my dear." She covered my hand with hers. "It's Anton, Katya. He died last Monday, the night you took sick." Her gray eyes watched me cautiously. "We buried him yesterday. We couldn't wait for you to recover."

I gaped at her, trying to take it all in.

Her voice became crisp. "Your hands are like ice." She took my arm and pulled me forward. "Come along now.

Quickly."

Katherine's feet obediently climbed the stairs behind Ana, but inside her head my own thoughts were swirling. From out of nowhere came Margaret Dougan's soft Scottish brogue: *Katherine was terribly headstrong, just like her father. There was talk of her doing in her own husband...*

Why did you do it, Katrina? Isabel's accusation leaped out at me, her meaning suddenly as bold and clear as it was horrifying.

Chapter Twenty-Two

I sat in a high-backed chair surrounded by potted sword ferns, orchids, and the rich, damp smell of cultivated earth. A stone maiden poured a constant trickle of water from her bucket into a small pool crowded with water lilies. If I closed my eyes, the splash of the fountain sounded like a waterfall, completing the illusion that I was tucked away on a tropical island rather than sitting in the conservatory of Rosswood House.

Beyond the ferns a wall of windows gave a generous view of green lawn, similar to the view that the art gallery windows would give over a century later. The lawn sparkled with dew only just touched by mid-morning sun. It sloped gently to the edge of the woods where, I knew, the path to Summerwood Cottage lay.

My chair was cushioned, and I leaned back comfortably, enjoying the sensation of being clean and tidy at last. Over Dora's protests I had pleaded for and ultimately demanded a bath and shampoo after vomiting my morning toast and tea. Closing my ears to her dire warnings about bathing too soon after an illness, I instructed her to show me to the bathtub. There I lingered in the warm lilac-scented water and examined in detail the body that had suddenly become mine.

Despite her short stature, Katherine's body was extremely strong, the muscles in her legs and arms well developed. Her breasts were small and tender, and her waist thick enough to suggest a hearty appetite. As I lay back in the water, trying to submerge myself up to the chin, her belly rounded up slightly. I could just see the soft dark mound between her legs.

A sharp rap on the door caused me to rise to a sitting position with a snort of exasperation. Apparently, Dora was used to helping Katherine with her toilette, and she had not taken kindly to my insistence that she leave me alone to my bath. I had already suffered two intrusions "to see that I was not drowned" and could not prevent her from throwing open the door now and standing over me, her huge arms akimbo.

"I'm washing your back now?" It was hardly a question, for she reached immediately for the washcloth and lowered herself to her knees. She rubbed soap over the cloth and with equal ferocity, eyed Katherine's body, looking for spots I had missed.

"Sit up. Forward." She set to scrubbing Katherine's back with a vigor that made me cry out. Although she didn't speak, her grunts and sighs effectively communicated that she was vexed with me and impatient to have me out of the tub and safely dry and warm. She clucked disapprovingly at my shampooed head and crossed herself before she straightened and helped me out of the tub. Swaddling me in a white towel, she rubbed Katherine's body until the skin glowed pink. I took another towel and set to work on the dark hair, soaking up most of the water before twisting the towel into a turban. Slipping into the robe and slippers, I followed Dora down the hall to Katherine's bedroom.

A fresh nightgown lay on the bed, but I shook my head. "I feel well enough to dress and go downstairs, Dora." I added innocently, "Will you pick out something for me to wear?"

She began to fold her arms, but I deliberately turned my back and sat down at Katherine's dressing table. Pulling the towel away, I picked up a hairbrush and ran it through the damp hair. To my delight, the dark masses detangled immediately into a silky curtain that hung almost to the waist. My own blond hair was just curly and coarse enough to wrestle with the hairbrush after every shampoo, and I often wished for the courage to just cut it short. But I knew Eleanor would disapprove—she took enormous pride in my Rhineholdt hair.

Dora grumbled as she folded away the fresh nightgown and proceeded to lay out an assortment of garments on the bed. I watched curiously as she layered me with underpants, stockings, a chemise, two petticoats, and a tight-fitting black bodice with a long black skirt to match. Thankfully, she didn't bring out a corset, and the black ankle boots laced and didn't require a buttonhook. Did they use buttonhooks in Katherine's time? I wished I had paid more attention in history class.

Fully dressed, I sat down to arrange Katherine's hair. It was nearly dry, and I finger-combed it, admiring the blue-black highlights. I had started to section it for a French braid when I caught Dora's look in the mirror and hesitated. With a sigh, I dropped my hands to my lap.

Dora took up the brush and applied it to Katherine's hair with spirit. Then she twisted the dark mass into a tight knot and secured it economically with pins. I thought the effect much too severe for Katherine's already sharp features. But I smiled my thanks in the mirror and patted the taut upsweep admiringly.

Ebony earrings, a small gold crucifix, and Katherine's

gold wedding band completed the ensemble.

After my toilette, I reclined comfortably in the conservatory and was almost dozing when I heard footsteps coming down the stone steps. A young woman with a wide middle and a long black braid approached me and gave a respectful nod.

"*Señora* asks you to come to the parlor." Her voice was thick with a Spanish accent. "*Señora* Stillman and *las señoritas* have come to visit."

She didn't wait for a response but turned away, expecting me to follow. I sat still for a panicky moment while Katherine's heart quickened at the thought of my playing her role in the company of neighbors. So far I'd had good luck with Isabel, Ana, and Dora. They seemed to tolerate my peculiarities and memory lapses amazingly well. Even referring to myself in the third person didn't seem to unduly startle them.

The servant paused and threw me a questioning look. I stood up and smoothed Katherine's skirt with sweaty palms. Would her neighbors tolerate my odd behavior as well? Could I convince Mrs. Stillman and her daughters that I was the same Katherine they had known for years?

After painstaking reflection, I had already decided to keep my story to myself and pretend I was indeed Katherine Kamarov. I had seen too many horror movies of turn-of-the-century mental institutions, with their cages and lobotomies and primitive treatments, to risk sharing the truth with anyone. Katherine's illness had sapped her strength, and I intended to use that weakness to my advantage. I would feign illness or amnesia if necessary to keep myself as removed as possible from scrutiny.

I needed time to think, to get my bearings, and to

figure out what in the world I was supposed to do next.

* * *

The parlor was the prettiest and best-kept room I had seen yet at Rosswood House. Tall windows faced south, sheltered by a porch overhang and framed in heavy drapes of gold brocade. All four walls were painted green and generously hung with paintings of bright flowers and landscapes. A fireplace centered on one wall offered a cheery blaze.

The women were settled in a comfortable arrangement of sofa and armchairs around a low polished table. The servant led me to a vacant chair between Isabel and Ana. I removed the wicker workbasket from the seat of the chair, nodded politely at the circle of women, and sat down.

I stared hard at the basket on my lap and avoided the six pairs of eyes I felt fastened upon me. Heat rose to Katherine's cheeks as Victoria's old paralyzing shyness gripped me.

An older woman, clearly mother to the other three, broke the silence. "Well, Katherine. They tell me you've been at death's door." She paused until I looked up at her. "You certainly don't look it. A little pale, perhaps, but otherwise quite your usual appearance, to my mind."

I took an instant dislike to her. She was a thin, waspish sort of woman, with a high-pitched voice bordering on shrill. Hair the color of oatmeal was fisted in a knot at the back of her head. Her eyes, set close together above a long, bent nose, fixed me with a bright blue stare. She sat ramrod straight, as if her collar were hooked to the back of her chair.

I glanced at the young women seated on the sofa. Three pairs of blue eyes regarded me before the sisters resumed their sewing, leaving me to stare at the tops of three nearly identical blond heads.

Isabel's musical voice spoke up beside me. "Thanks be to God, Lillian. In His grace He gave us our daughter back, knowing we already have one in our family to mourn."

Ana's murmured "Amen" forestalled any further comment from Lillian Stillman on the subject.

A firm silence followed in which six pairs of hands busied themselves with sewing. From the wicker basket I withdrew a square of fine muslin and spread it on my lap. It was a sampler printed with the text of The Lord's Prayer surrounded by birds and flowers. The stitching was half-done and struck me as peculiar—some of the stitches were neat and precise while others were quite sloppy.

I decided to rip out the unsightly stitches and redo them. Silently blessing Sister Sonja for insisting that we learn the finer domestic arts of embroidery and needlepoint in seventh grade, I snipped off the knotted threads on the wrong side of the sampler. Then, using the blunt end of a needle, I began to pick out the stitches, one at a time, with some measure of expertise.

I had nearly freed a bluebird's wing when Lillian spoke up again.

"We were so sorry, Katherine, about your unfortunate Anton." Beside me, Isabel sucked in a breath. "How sad that you weren't able to attend your own husband's funeral. And what a mercy that you didn't lose the baby after such an ordeal."

I gasped and blurted out, "The baby! Of course! Katherine was *pregnant!*" The tender breasts, the thickened waist, vomiting tea and toast in the morning. How could I have forgotten?

I placed a hand over Katherine's stomach and looked up into a circle of frozen faces. My grin of delight faltered.

Isabel spoke in a tight voice. "Perhaps you should go upstairs and rest, Katrina. You're still not yourself—"

"Oh, let the girl be, Isabel," Lillian put in. She took up her knitting with a flourish. "It's probably just her condition. Land sakes, the time I had when I was in the family way with my Theresa there!" She nodded at the young woman seated between her sisters. "Bringing children into this world is enough to make any woman take leave of her senses!"

Lillian rambled on, but I stared at Theresa, memorizing her face to go with the name. The sister seated on Theresa's left had to be Emily, obviously the eldest. I couldn't recall the name of the youngest.

"And speaking of our Theresa"—Lillian's sharp eyes glanced around the group—"I have an announcement to make." We all looked at Theresa, who dimpled. "You remember Bruce McPherson, of course. He's been attending college in Stockton." Lillian paused, savoring her moment. "Well, he's asked for Theresa's hand, and her father has consented. They will be married come this August!"

Ana and Isabel voiced their congratulations, but I sat like a stone between them, remembering the name well. *He's all Theresa Stillman ever talks about.* Bruce McPherson, Katherine's first sexual conquest. Moreover, if I remembered correctly, a boy whose virginity she had taken.

Theresa looked at me then, and there was no mistaking the chill in her blue eyes. She knows, I thought, with a sickening drop of Katherine's stomach. My gaze slid away, and I stared at the bluebird on my lap, fighting shame and a sudden fury at Katherine.

Lillian chattered on happily. "Of course, you are all invited to the engagement party on May seventh. My nephew Raymond from Philadelphia will be here visiting." She sighed. "I haven't seen Raymond since he was in short pants, but my brother sends me pictures. A strapping young man he is, and quite eligible!"

Isabel smiled at Theresa. "Will you live hereabouts, Theresa, when you are a married woman?"

Theresa tossed her head. "We'll have a house in town," she said primly. I gathered that living in town was considered a step up in the world. "Bruce plans to start a business."

"He was always a bright, energetic boy," Isabel responded. "I'm sure he'll do very well for you both."

Lillian received the compliment with obvious pleasure. "We're all thrilled at the prospect, Isabel. Such a fine match for our Theresa!" Her smile was smug as she took up her knitting, but suddenly she flapped her arms and screeched. "Oooh! Scat, you!"

A large ginger cat had leaped from nowhere to pounce on her tempting trail of yarn.

"Henry!" Isabel scolded the cat and snapped her fingers. It patently ignored her and obviously considered Lillian's flapping part of the game. It rolled onto its back and expertly snared the yarn with all four paws, looping a segment into its mouth for a good chew.

"Filthy beast! Get away from me!" Lillian leaped from her chair and might have done murder if a small boy hadn't chosen that moment to burst into the room and rivet everyone's attention. He slid to a halt beside the sofa, dropped to his knees, and yanked up the sofa skirt to peer beneath.

"Roberto!" Isabel's sharp voice raised the boy to his feet. He stood bent like a bowstring pulled taut for imminent release. Dark hair curled damply around his flushed face, which was delicately boned like the rest of his small, graceful body. I needed no one to tell me that this was Katherine's little brother, Robbie, for he was a precise miniature of their mother.

"Where are your manners, Roberto?" Isabel nodded toward the Stillman women. "We have guests."

Robbie turned obediently and gave a stiff little bow in their direction. The youngest daughter stared at him frankly while Theresa fearfully watched her mother. It was Emily who spoke.

"Hello, Robbie. Looking for your cat?"

Lillian reseated herself stiffly. "Such a ruckus, Robert! Your pet has been very naughty. Very naughty indeed!" She held up her yarn and frowned at the dark, soggy stretch that was hopelessly frayed. "Look at this, young man! Quite ruined. That animal should be kept outside, to my mind!"

"I'm very sorry, Mrs. Stillman." Robbie's reedy voice clenched my heart in sympathy.

"It wasn't your fault, Robbie," I volunteered. "Henry was just doing what cats do. It was nobody's fault."

Robbie's startled eyes weren't the only ones that turned toward me.

"Come, Roberto," Isabel said. "You haven't seen your sister since she's recovered." She laid a hand on the arm of my chair. "Come and give her a kiss."

The boy dropped his gaze to his shoes and shuffled across the carpet toward me. When he lifted his face, I saw that his eyes were not the stunning blue-violet of his mother's. They were slate gray, tilting up slightly at the corners, like Ana's. Russian eyes.

I bent forward for his dutiful peck on Katherine's cheek and shared his embarrassment over this obviously distasteful gesture. A strained silence followed, broken at last by Henry, who emerged from beneath Lillian's chair. Tail high, the cat padded boldly across the carpet and rubbed a swath of marmalade hair across the boy's trouser leg, throat rumbling a loud purr of affection.

Robbie blossomed into life. He bent quickly, scooped the furry mass of cat into his arms, and buried a smile in its heaving side.

Isabel broke the spell of the boy and his cat. "Take Henry outside, Roberto, and play on the porch until you're called for dinner."

"Yes, Mama." Robbie fled from the room.

Isabel turned a gracious smile on her guests. "Lillian. Girls. Will you stay to take dinner with us? I should love to hear all the details for your wedding, Theresa."

Lillian hesitated, glaring at her useless yarn. "Well. Yes. Thank you, Isabel." She assumed an expression of martyred dignity, but her voice betrayed her eagerness for an audience. "The children will be married at the Community Church in town, of course. Fanny Fellhurst will do the gowns. She did such a lovely job for Emily and Theresa on their sixteenth birthdays, and she'll do the same for June when she turns sixteen next year."

June. *That* was the youngest sister's name.

Lillian droned on until the servant girl reappeared to announce dinner. We folded away our sewing projects, and Ana leaned close.

"Katya, I'm sure your mother will excuse you if you wish to go upstairs and lie down. I'll send Marta up with a tray."

The concern in her eyes touched me. "Thank you, Aunt. I do feel tired." I turned to Isabel, who nodded.

"Of course we'll excuse you, Katrina. You need your rest."

"Don't coddle yourself, Katherine." Lillian took on the tone of a practiced advice-giver. "You'll do yourself a harm if you're too weak when your time comes."

I masked my dislike with a polite nod and turned to say goodbye to her daughters.

June lifted her shoulder in a bored shrug. Theresa said nothing but stared at me with cold blue eyes. Emily busied herself with straightening a cushion and didn't turn.

I left the parlor wondering if Katherine was as popular with her other neighbors as she was with the Stillman women.

Chapter Twenty-Three

My life in Katherine's world settled into a loose routine.

The morning sickness persisted, so I took my first meal at dinner, which was their term for lunch. Overriding Dora's disapproval, I bathed daily, and to her considerable surprise did not succumb to a lung illness. I learned to dress myself, finding that Katherine's wardrobe was limited to only a few dresses and skirts, most of them black, and three pairs of shoes, two of which required mastery of the buttonhook. She owned little jewelry and wore no makeup, not even lip rouge. I discovered in her desk an inkbottle and several pens, a dozen or so sheets of fine writing paper, but no journal. Rummaging through the desk drawer, I found three papers folded into makeshift envelopes. They were not labeled, and each packet contained a different sample of dried seeds.

Isabel was remote and did not renew her accusations of the first night. She spent most of her time either in her bedroom or in the downstairs sitting room, reading or sewing while Dora worked the big weaving loom. Tuesday and Thursday afternoons she made social calls and served at charity functions. I used my pregnancy and recent illness to excuse myself from accompanying her, and to my relief she did not press me.

Ana, a brisk, efficient woman, busied herself with household affairs. The parlor, I learned, was used only to entertain guests; when not in use, its doors remained shut to keep the room clean. We had few visitors, and the silence of the grandfather clock continued to lock the house in mourning for Katherine's dead husband.

Like his mother, Robbie remained aloof. Quietly but firmly, he rebuffed my attempts to engage him in conversation. Henry, his constant companion, followed him like a dog and scorned everyone else in the household. Isabel, I noticed, paid little attention to her son. She employed a nurse to see to his needs, an older woman who kept to her room and hardly ever showed herself to me. As no children came to call and Robbie was not invited to accompany his mother on social visits, he spent his time in solitary play — drawing with beeswax crayons or erecting toy buildings in the upstairs playroom.

Rainstorms returned and remained for a week, while Katherine's body grew stronger daily. Every morning I would surface from sleep and, keeping my eyes shut, test the environment with my other senses. Each time I detected the ginger spice that scented Katherine's personal effects, and my ears picked out the patter of rain against the expansive silence of a slower-paced world. I would open Katherine's eyes to a dull gray morning and lie quietly, trying to decide how I felt about spending another day in her life.

I wondered if there was a way to return to my own world and realized that I was in no great hurry to find out. I did wonder, however, what that world was like now that I had left it.

I remembered clearly the vision of Ryan holding my limp body on the bank of Two Trees Creek. I looked dead, which would explain the dark tunnel and the fragrant mist that seemed ready to welcome me into another realm. I wondered if Katherine, like me, had died and was on her way to the white mist when our spirits touched. Had her spirit gone on to that other realm while I was returned to her earthly body? And if so, what had happened to Victoria's body?

I imagined it lying in a cold grave in Holy Cross Cemetery, beside my grandfather Matthew and my uncle Luke. With a flick of horror, I imagined suddenly returning to my own time and waking up in a coffin, buried under six feet of earth.

But the horror vanished as quickly as it came. I felt oddly certain that my presence in Katherine's life was no mistake. Even when I considered my careless wish on the old coin, I couldn't dismiss my experience as a random quirk of fate. Like the threads of Dora's emerging cloth, I was being woven into a new design that had a purpose of some kind. From that first day when I'd followed the squirrel to the old bridge, I had known that I was being drawn toward some unrevealed but very specific destination.

Well, it seemed I had arrived at that destination. The question I could not yet answer was *why*.

* * *

I chose a mild afternoon, just after the noon meal, to sneak away from the house. Isabel, looking pale and drawn, had retired to her room for a rest. Robbie was taking his usual nap, and Dora was busy at her loom in the downstairs sitting room. I heard the clunk and thump as she worked the harnesses and the beater, and I pictured her bent over her task—her face serious, her thick hands amazingly deft as she whisked the shuttle back and forth, following a rhythm in her head. The sitting room door remained shut, and the sounds of the loom masked my stealthy steps and exit through a side door.

After the gloom of the house, the gray daylight dazzled my eyes. I ran quickly across the lawn, conscious of the sitting room and conservatory windows staring at my back. Although the clouds no longer threatened rain, the ground oozed mud from a week's worth of storms as I dove into the shelter of the woods and found the path to Summerwood.

The forest seemed unchanged. All around me redwoods speared skyward, pencil-straight, arising from lush nests of saplings and sword ferns covering the forest floor. My gaze climbed their dizzying heights, and I wondered how many of these ancient trees, like the grandfather clock, would witness my passing over a century later.

A twenty-minute walk brought the cottage into view. To my shock and disappointment, it scarcely resembled the attractive bed-and-breakfast inn I remembered. For one thing, it was too small; nearly half the house seemed to be missing. Instead of a cheerful yellow, the walls were a dirty whitewash, and the windows lacked trim. I missed the neat shrubs and lawn and protective white picket fence. This porch showed boards missing, and it stepped down to a muddy path infested with weeds and rangy shrubs long gone wild. In place of the carport, a barn crouched behind the cottage, its door gaping wide.

The front door of the cottage was locked. I peered into windows, but drawn drapes kept the interior secret. I tried the kitchen door and met again with disappointment. I wondered if Katherine had kept a key hidden somewhere.

Hands on hips, I turned and surveyed the yard. A

slender, gray-limbed tree emerged from the tangled shrubbery, and I recognized the dogwood that Katherine's grandfather had planted for her brother. It chilled me to know in advance that Nicholas's tree would survive the neglect and grow to a great age while Nicholas himself had not.

I stepped down the kitchen steps and followed a path that had once been neatly edged with strips of wood. Grassy weeds nearly smothered the struggling flushes of bronze growth I recognized as rose leaves. Bending over to part the weeds, I read the rose names carved into wooden blocks still bravely erect on their posts: Morning Star, Isabel, Katherine.

Tempted to release the roses from their choking green prison, I nevertheless straightened up and turned away. I had not come here to garden, after all, but to search for Katherine's journal.

The rose garden ran alongside a section of house I did not remember. Peering in through the tall windows, I spied a high wooden worktable, neat rows of labeled drawers, and gardening tools. This had to be the garden room where Katherine worked on her herb collection. Circling to the back, I at last found a door unlocked.

The garden room was damp and cold but showed signs of recent use. Three stone steps led up into the kitchen. In the dusty quiet, I pushed through another door into a dark hallway I recognized. The parlor lay on the right, but I turned left, recalling my curiosity about the dining room that had begun as a master bedroom.

The large room at the end of the hall contained nothing save for an old brass bedstead and a battered dresser hunched against a wall. Bare windows looked out to the woods and gave light onto walls streaked with water stains and without the cheerful paper I had imagined. The little corner fireplace looked cold and cheerless.

Retreating to the hallway, I recognized Alice's pinewood sideboard standing against the wall. Further down, I came to the parlor where heavy drapes at the windows dimmed the interior of the room. Dusty white sheets draped the chairs and tables, their great muffled forms arranged as if in ghostly conversation. I crossed the bare floorboards of the foyer and nearly stepped on a small brown shape that hurled itself suddenly from under one of the sheets and ran right in front of me.

I screamed and leaped straight up into the air. The stair banister saved me, and I clung to it with both hands. Jerking my head around, I looked for my assailant. A tiny body scurried along the wall, squeaking in mousy fright. It disappeared through the kitchen door.

I leaned against the banister, limp and giggling with relief. The beautiful carvings at eye level caught my attention, and I fingered them, tracing the grooves as I climbed the stairs to the landing at the top. Instead of an archway leading into Alice's new wing of added-on rooms, a wall stood, hung with the portrait of a middle-aged man dressed in a black coat. The signature in the corner confirmed my guess that it had been painted by Leon Rostnova. This had to be a picture of his father, Petrov. I searched the weathered face for traces of the dreamer, for the man who had cared for roses and told his granddaughter she was beautiful.

When I turned away, I felt his gray Russian eyes following me, not unkindly. I walked down the hallway, past rooms later to be called Strawberry Patch and Tree

House, and arrived at the attic door. Thankfully, it opened when I turned the knob. I stood on the threshold, surprised.

I had forgotten that Katherine used the attic for an artist's studio. Like the garden room downstairs, the attic was relatively dust-free and showed signs of recent use.

Although I knew I was here for another purpose, I couldn't resist browsing among the canvases stacked against the wall. Like me, Katherine seemed to prefer oils. But unlike my timid efforts, she painted in bold strokes and strong colors.

Even without my education in art, I would have recognized her exceptional talent. Her subjects and presentation forms varied, from the photographic rendering of a horse's face to a Picasso-like figure fitted with an odd number of eyes and ears and plump breasts. She often presented several images on one canvas — a strong central figure surrounded by a half-dozen cameos rendered in charcoal. I recognized one of these central figures as Dora, her deeply textured face painstakingly reproduced in photo-accurate colors. The cameos surrounding her were like glimpses into her character — her huge bulk hunched over her weaving loom, another in her classic stance with arms akimbo, and one with her arms raised above her head — in supplication perhaps to God or to her ancestors.

I flipped through other canvases and recognized Isabel, her likeness beautiful but cold, as well as Ana and Robbie. I also found florals and some country landscapes, including a creek-side view of the Table Rock, where Katherine wrote in her journal.

Her journal.

I replaced the canvases against the wall and turned my attention to the center of the room. There an easel caught my eye and tempted me to sneak a peek at Katherine's most recent project.

I lifted the drape and clamped a hand over my mouth. My own face gazed back at me from a charcoal sketch on white paper.

Fair hair swept back gently from my temples. My eyes were sad and my mouth pensive, portraying a melancholy I had struggled very hard to conceal from others.

I lowered my hand from my mouth. Of course, Katherine had seen me, just as I had seen her. She had even mentioned me in her journal.

Her journal.

With an effort I pulled my gaze away from my own stare. Pushing a stool aside, I rolled back a thin carpet, confident of finding beneath it a loose plank with a knothole. My hand trembled a little as I thrust a finger into the hole and pulled up the plank.

Light glimmered off a glass inkbottle. With a triumphant crow, I pulled out the bottle and shook it gently, watching the dark blue liquid swirl. I reached back into the hole and pulled out a pen and a soft cloth streaked with the blue-black of many pen wipings.

I put my hand back into the hole, but it seemed empty. Dismayed, I crouched down and peered inside. I could see clearly there was no flat package wrapped in oilskin. But the light caught on something else, something that glinted with dull copper.

I reached in and pulled out the souvenir coin.

I stared at the raised American flag and ran my thumb over the old familiar nick. As if in a dream, I turned the coin over, knowing I would find the words "All Brothers of the Land" etched in five languages.

* * *

A shrill whistle jerked me out of my stupor. I turned my head, still dazed by my discovery, and heard a door downstairs slam. Moments later a man's voice yelled through the house.

"Kat! Are you here?"

Footsteps crossed the bare floor downstairs. Instinct to preserve Katherine's secret jarred me back to life. I pocketed the coin, seized the inkbottle, pen, and cloth, and jammed them back into the chamber. Dropping the plank into place, I scrambled to my feet and was just smoothing out the rug when a tall young man suddenly filled the doorway.

"Hey, brat. I thought I'd find you here."

I stared at him as he swung easily into the room on long slender legs.

"What're you doing?" He stared at the rug under my feet, and I resisted the impulse to look down and see if it was glowing neon red. But then he looked up and saw the charcoal sketch. "Hey, who's the beauty?"

He stepped up to the portrait and studied it. Then he turned a questioning look on me. He wasn't particularly handsome, I decided. His face was angular, his mouth a little too wide, although his crooked grin was appealing. Eyeglasses with thick, round lenses gave him a peering, owlish look. His hand pointing to the sketch was slender, his fingers tapered, almost girlish.

His most remarkable feature, however, was an unruly crop of orange-blond hair exactly the color of Henry's fur.

"What?" I was still dazed by my discovery. "Oh, that.

She's nobody. Just someone I...dreamed up."

"Blond and beautiful, eh? Your alter ego, maybe?"

"Alter ego?"

"You know, what Freud says. The person you're afraid to be."

"Afraid to be?"

"What are you, a parrot?"

"A parrot?"

He snorted, and his grin widened as he crossed to the window in a few long strides. He stood for a silent moment, looking out. Then he turned, hooked his thumbs over his belt, and cocked his head a little as he studied me.

"You look funny, Kat. Are you all right?"

I shook my head and groped for the stool, needing its support. "A little wobbly, I guess. It's only my first day out."

He sauntered back and draped his arm over the easel, eyeing me steadily.

"Isabel's in a snit because she didn't want you wandering off by yourself. Ana sent me to fetch you back for supper." He stared at me with an unsettling frankness and repeated his question. "What are you doing?"

I waved a vague arm at the canvases along the wall. "I was just looking. Trying to figure things out."

To my surprise, he nodded. "It's different now, isn't it?"

I gave him a sharp look. "Different?"

"Well, yes. Of course. Everything's changed." He studied me for another long moment. Then he pushed away from the easel and began to wander the room, twining and locking his fingers until his knuckles cracked. He stopped at the window again and stood with feet apart, staring out at the late afternoon. He said quietly, without turning, "Nobody blames you, Kat. Anton was a scoundrel. I'm glad he's dead."

He turned slowly and faced me. His eyes were cool and empty of feeling. I stared back, and he shrugged and put a hand to the back of his head. Smiling at the floor, he seemed about to say something else. But he merely scratched his fingers through the marmalade hair. Then he jerked himself upright and headed for the door.

"Come on. Let's get out of here. Gretchen is waiting for us."

Without a backward glance he strode through the door and headed down the passageway. I heard him lunge down the stairs, hit bottom, and pause.

"Kat! Are you coming or not?"

I rose at once, but my portrait's wistful gaze made me pause in front of the easel. Carefully I replaced the drape, veiling the face and the sad eyes, and I left the attic.

* * *

Gretchen was a sorrel mare tethered to a rail and placidly munching a lush clump of weeds. She didn't look up as we approached but continued to tear at the food with her teeth. I heard the grasses rip from the ground and watched with some trepidation as her large pink tongue shoved the greenery into her mouth.

The young man swung easily into the saddle. Then he reached down a hand to hoist me up behind him.

"Are you kidding?" I shrank from his outstretched hand and stared with alarm at the reddish-brown haunch facing me squarely at eye level. I had never ridden a horse in my life, and this one looked unbelievably huge.

The young man stared at me.

"What's the matter with you?" He reached down his

hand again. "Come on, hop up. I haven't got all day."

I looked down at Katherine's skirts and tried to imagine exactly what he expected me to do.

"What's this sudden modesty, Kat?" He chuckled. "Nobody's looking, least of all me." To prove his words, he turned his head away but kept his arm extended. "Come on, let's go."

It seemed I had no choice. Hiking up the long skirts, I gingerly placed Katherine's boot onto his resting in the stirrup. Then I clutched his arm with both hands and tried to swing my other leg up and over the saddle.

Perhaps sensing my fear, the mare whinnied and danced sideways. I slipped and fell to the ground in an undignified heap, cursing audibly.

The young man burst out laughing and climbed down from the saddle. "Sorry," he chuckled. "I keep forgetting you're in a delicate condition. Allow me."

Before I could protest, he grabbed my arms and pulled me to my feet. With a flourish he held the stirrup for my foot and then pushed me up onto the saddle. I clung with both hands to the saddle horn, terrified of slipping off the smooth leather and landing in another heap on the other side of the mare.

"You'd better sit in front." He swung himself up behind me and gathered the reins around my body. "Hey, relax." He slipped an arm around my waist and pulled me back against him. Through the thickness of her skirts, I felt Katherine's bottom resting up against his crotch and his long legs pressing against hers on either side.

He seemed unaware as he clucked at the mare through his teeth.

"All right, beauty. Let's go home."

The mare responded to the pull of the reins and headed for the forest trail. I bounced on the slippery saddle, still clutching the saddle horn for dear life, and tried not to rest against the warm body behind me. I heard a soft chuckle above my ear.

"Well, I've heard it said that carrying a babe does strange things to a woman. But I never thought I'd see you afraid of a horse. I've never seen you afraid of anything."

Even if I'd known how to reply, I didn't think I could get a word through my jaws, which jarred with every step the mare took. I kept my teeth clenched so I wouldn't inadvertently bite my tongue. Perhaps the young man thought my silence was meaningful, for he said nothing more until we were within sight of the stables behind Rosswood House. He suddenly pulled up the reins and breathed a low "Whoa" to the mare, who stopped obediently on the path.

I felt him shift behind me.

"Listen, Kat. Forget what I said back there. I had no right to speak as I did. You and Anton—well, it's none of my business."

Without waiting for a reply, he urged the mare forward, and soon we were in the stable yard. He slipped to the ground and reached up to help me down. The slender hands he fixed on Katherine's waist lifted me down with surprising ease. But they didn't linger a second longer than necessary. Without another word or glance, he turned his back, and I heard him croon to the mare as he led her toward the open stable door.

Chapter Twenty-Four

"Blast it all, Michael!" Leon Rostnova's fist pounded the snowy tablecloth and rattled Isabel's elegant dinnerware. "When are you going to start thinking for yourself? That infernal rag you call a newspaper is filling your head with nonsense that may land you in trouble one day. You mark my words, boy!"

Leon wagged a warning finger under his nephew's nose and then tugged at the starched collar confining his neck. Katherine's uncle was a compact man with a broad, powerful build that would have suited him to wrestling, and a rich baritone voice that could have shaken the rafters of the San Francisco Opera House. Thick, straight hair brushed the stiff collar that imprisoned his neck and matched exactly the silver-threaded black of his mustache and beetle brows now bristling over his sharp black eyes.

The young man who had brought me home from Summerwood leaned back in his chair and studied his uncle. "Julian Stratford's paper may be a rag, but at least it's a progressive one. He has the guts to say what's what and to print the truth instead of all that political garbage you get in *The Register*."

His uncle gave an indignant huff and shook his head disparagingly. "You know what your problem is, Michael? You never went to college."

"Well, who needs it? I don't want some stuffed shirt with his head in the clouds telling me what to read, what to do, how to think. I read what I want. I think my own thoughts."

Leon's fist pounded the table again, making me jump with the silverware. "That's *exactly* what I'm talking about! You think, all right, but you don't know how to think *correctly*."

Michael's mouth tightened. "And I suppose you do?"

"Michael." Ana's warning was soft. I glanced at Isabel, who was slicing her lamb with unruffled calm. There were five of us at the table; as usual, Robbie was eating upstairs with his nurse. I had been watching the exchange and trying to reconcile my image of the romantic Russian artist with this middle-aged man who sat red-faced and huffing at his nephew.

"You get swept up in causes, Michael," Leon growled. "You let emotional persuasions of the day dictate what's important to you. Last year you were infatuated with that new Austrian medical man, Sigmund Fraud. We heard endless arguments supporting his harebrained notions that, frankly, no decent person should even catch himself thinking. God knows what your cause will be next year."

"Freud," Michael said quietly. "His name is Freud."

Leon brushed the name aside impatiently. Then he laid his hand on the table, palm up, as if offering his nephew a glimpse of the wisdom written there.

"Simple logic will tell you, Michael, that two wrongs never make a right. Yes, the dockworkers have legitimate complaints. They don't earn a decent wage and the conditions are dangerous. It's true, the management should correct these problems. But unions are as much a corruption as unfair management. Breaking windows, setting fire to offices... I read that two office clerks, who have no say in management practices, were taken to the hospital." He held up a hand when his nephew opened his mouth to respond. "If allowed to take hold, unions will destroy democracy. A body of men cannot rule themselves if they have no sense of moral integrity in their political and economic dealings. Your unions will bring this great country of ours to its knees, son. You think about that."

Leon swept up his wine glass and dipped it at his nephew to finish off his argument. Michael stared at his plate. I saw his knuckles whiten around the handle of his fork, and I wondered what it cost him to keep his temper under control.

Without looking up, he said in a cool voice, "I believe history will prove you wrong, Uncle."

A taut silence settled over the table. Forks scraped on china, and we chewed and swallowed and coughed discreetly behind linen napkins. At long last Isabel rang a small brass bell, and Marta appeared to clear away the plates.

Isabel's smile was gracious. "Coffee, Leon? Or are you and Michael exhausted from your...exertions and wanting your beds?" She arched an innocent eyebrow.

To my surprise, Leon burst into a hearty laugh. "Sorry, Isabel, for all that spitting and hissing. But sometimes this boy gets some peculiar ideas. Picks them up from that *Clarion* he works for in the city. Julian Stratford's paper."

Dora appeared with the coffee service just as Leon reached over and ruffled his fingers through Michael's already unruly hair. His nephew didn't look up, but I saw his jaw tighten. He added sugar and cream to the cup Dora placed before him, and I watched his tapered fingers stir his coffee with a silver spoon. I wondered if he wrote for the newspaper, if he were a writer by nature. Recalling

Katherine's story of how the boy Michael had clung to the fantasy of his sea captain father returning for him, I wondered how much of the romantic child still survived in the man.

"Stratford has a lot to answer for," Leon was saying. "Filling these young pups with fantastic notions about strikes and unions and changing the world. Dangerous stuff, that."

Michael set his spoon down with a clatter. His chin came up, and my heart softened at the sudden picture of him running from the house at fourteen, crying because Anton had called him a bastard. Crying because he knew in his heart that his father was never coming back.

On an impulse I would later regret, I broke through my shyness and rose to Michael's defense.

"Uncle, everything Michael says is quite true. I can tell you with certainty that unions will not only survive in this country, but they will revolutionize the face and strength of our democracy!"

All eyes turned on me. I swallowed and looked down at my coffee, appalled by what I had just let slip.

"And just who asked you, Miss Know-It-All?" Michael's angry response brought my head up. "What makes you such an authority on wharf politics?"

Stung, I snapped back. "What makes you so touchy?"

"Politics is men's business, Katherine." He spoke carefully, as if I might have difficulty understanding his words.

"Oh. I get it." I imitated his slow, deliberate tone. "Women shouldn't venture an opinion about things they can't possibly understand."

"Well, you said it. I didn't."

"You're a chauvinist, Michael."

"A chauvinist?"

"A prime example of male egocentricity."

"Male egocentricity?"

"What are you, a parrot?"

He sucked in a breath, and his face darkened. His eyes turned dangerous.

"Now, children." Ana patted my arm. "Michael, Katya was just trying to be helpful—"

"In a pig's eye," he muttered.

"Michael!" his uncle put in. "There's no call to be uncivil."

Michael snorted. "Uncle, you—" He stopped himself. Quite suddenly he rose from his chair and gave Isabel a stiff bow. "Thank you for the meal," he said. His hands clenched and unclenched at his sides. "I'll see to Gretchen now, if you'll excuse me."

He turned abruptly and strode from the room. A moment later the front door slammed.

"Well!" Leon glanced down the table. "Can someone tell me what *that* was all about?"

Ana's response was quick. "You've been at him all day, Leon. Criticizing him, attacking his friends. He adores Julian Stratford. What did you expect?"

"I expect the boy to listen to reason. He's too sensitive by half. Always has been."

"The *boy* is twenty-six, and he can reason for himself." Ana gentled her voice. "He has to go his own way, Leon. Even if you don't agree with him."

"Humph" was all the reply she got. Leon's finger sought his shirt collar and gave it a vicious tug.

Isabel's clear voice turned our heads. "Michael is a

sensible young man, Leon." She raised her cup and gave her brother-in-law a long look over its rim. "A *good* young man. Not like"—she flicked her gaze at me—"not like...other men." Her voice took on an edge. "Count your blessings, Brother."

Leon glanced at me and flushed scarlet. He cleared his throat and poured cream into his coffee. "Yes. Well, I daresay—" He lost his words and his mustache inside his cup.

Ana clutched at her throat and said nothing.

I guessed at the thoughts behind everyone's carefully averted eyes. Nevertheless, I breathed a small sigh of relief. No one had picked up on my slip of the tongue, that stupid, careless prediction about the future of unions in America. Thank goodness for Michael's diversion.

I glanced over my shoulder at the windows and imagined Michael in the stable with Gretchen. For some reason, what I'd said in his defense had upset him. Maybe after supper I would wander over to the stable and see if I could smooth it out.

As I turned back to the table, I caught sight of Dora standing quietly near the buffet, in the shadows at the edge of the chandelier's light. She was watching me with her small dark eyes as she often did, arms folded, her expression inscrutable.

When I caught her gaze now, she narrowed her eyes until they were like twin raisins glimmering at me. Then she inclined her head and gave a decisive little nod. Still staring at me, she raised her hand and crossed herself, twice. She lifted her silver crucifix to her lips.

On silent feet she turned and left the room.

* * *

The stable smelled of warm horse, sweet hay, and the faint ripeness of manure. Michael was in the third stall, brushing Gretchen's hide with long, firm strokes, his dinner coat cast aside, his shirtsleeves rolled up to his elbows. His hair stood on end, as if he'd been raking his hands through it.

With his back to me, he talked to Gretchen in a low, confiding tone. Shamelessly I tiptoed closer to listen, the hay-strewn floor muffling my approach.

"...always knows best. For two cents, I'd move out and get my own place. But that will have to wait." The brushing took on more vigor. "First, I've got to finish writing my book. Then I've got to get Julian to take a look at it. If I could only figure out—"

I cleared my throat, and Michael jerked his head around. He gazed at me for a moment while his jaw hardened into a stubborn set. He turned back to the mare and resumed brushing.

"Go away."

I took a step closer. "Michael, what's the matter? Why are you so angry with me?"

He continued brushing, his strokes as deliberate as his silence. Gretchen stomped a foot softly.

"Michael, did you hear me?"

"Pardon me." He shouldered past me and began to work the other side of the mare's rump. Gretchen stomped again, and so did I.

"Michael, answer me! I'm trying to understand you."

"Why?" His voice was flat.

"Why? Because—" I searched for words. "Because what I said upset you, and I don't know why. I never meant to hurt you."

"You didn't." He continued to brush the mare with infuriating precision.

I bit my lip, wondering why I didn't just return to the house. But something held me in place, pushing me to take a stab in the dark.

"I know life hasn't always been easy for you, Michael."

The brushing stopped. Michael came around the mare's rump and rested his arm on it, fixing me with a cold stare.

"Why the sudden concern, Kat? What do you want?" His eyes raked me up and down. "When did you ever care about anybody but yourself?"

I stared at him. "You think I tried to get your uncle's attention at your expense, don't you?"

He shrugged. "What I think isn't your concern." His voice was cool, but his eyes flashed anger before he deliberately turned his back to me. Moving to the mare's head, he patted her neck and crooned softly.

Again I thought about leaving, but still my feet wouldn't move. Something drove me to one last thrust.

"I'm not what you think, Michael. I've…changed." My voice quavered maddeningly, and I cleared my throat. "I'm just saying I would never intentionally hurt you. You can believe it or not." I tossed my head and turned to leave.

But Michael was there ahead of me, blocking my way. I looked up into gray-green eyes fastened on me with wary speculation. I took an uncertain step back, groping against the rough wall behind me for support.

"What is going on with you?" His voice was soft, more puzzled than angry. "You haven't been yourself all evening. Next thing, you'll be telling me you've traded places with that blond beauty I saw at the cottage. Your alter ego." He saw me jump, and his eyes narrowed.

I licked Katherine's lips. "That's ridiculous, Michael." I tried to laugh, but it came out a high squeak.

He said nothing but leaned forward, studying me as if I were a bug under a microscope. I looked away, fearful of what he might read in my eyes. Neither of us spoke.

The moment seemed endless until Michael straightened and stepped aside. I darted from the stall like a frightened deer and fled into the night.

Chapter Twenty-Five

I slept late the following morning. I blamed it on the darkness of the day, for rain had returned and drummed depressingly at my bedroom window. In truth, however, my interview with Michael the night before had left me confused and shaken, disrupting my sleep.

After leaving the stable, I had paced around the garden, trying to clear my head, but it was no use. At length I slipped into the house and up to Katherine's bedroom, where I threw myself across the bed and cried tears of self-pity. For the first time, I wished I were back in my own time.

Fascinated as I was by Katherine's world, I felt overwhelmed by the daily struggle of pretending to be her, not the least of which was covering up for her indiscretions. No matter what I did, people disliked me. They thought I was cruel, selfish, disagreeable, and at times even crazy. I was navigating a minefield, never sure when an innocent step might set off another explosion.

I missed Ryan, or at least the magic circle of his protection. I missed the reassurance of strong male arms around me. My thoughts turned to Michael, to the puzzled speculation in his eyes and his anger that had unaccountably wounded me.

I rolled onto my back and tried to assess Michael's relationship with Katherine. He seemed to have a casual rapport with her, like an older brother who tolerates a pesky younger sister. But he didn't approve of Katherine.

He didn't like her. Well, he had a lot of company there.

I fell asleep wondering if Katherine had been lonely.

I awoke sometime later, grumbling because someone was shaking me roughly by the shoulder. Blinking into the light of the lamp, I saw Dora's face bending over me. A glance at the clock showed the time at nearly eleven. I allowed her to help me into a nightgown, and I watched her fold down the bedcovers. As I climbed in, I said sleepily, "Dora, where is Elizabeth?"

She didn't respond, and when I looked up at her, she was staring at me.

I repeated my question: "What happened to Elizabeth?"

Dora spread her arms in a grand gesture. "You tell me."

I was too tired to fence with her, and I said crossly, "Are you telling me that I'm supposed to know?"

She regarded me with her little raisin eyes. Then she shrugged. "Perhaps not." She bent over me and smoothed the comforter under my chin. "Elizabeth," she said, in her unhurried way. "She leaves when you come." She straightened up and peered down at me. "She's gone."

"Gone?" I repeated. "Gone where?"

Dora shrugged again. "Where you come from." She turned down the lamp and left me alone in the dark.

* * *

I ventured downstairs mid-morning to find the house quiet. I headed for the kitchen, looking for hot tea to soothe a headache and pump some life into my body. Carmen, our cook, was starting preparations for the noonday meal. She informed me that the *Señora* was ailing and keeping to her room. Leon and Michael had left early and would not return until evening. Ana was out talking to Alfred, the ranch foreman.

I took my tea into the sitting room and stared gloomily across the wet lawn, thinking about Summerwood. I had been so certain I'd find Katherine's journal in its place under the floorboard. I had no choice but to make a more thorough search of Katherine's bedroom and perhaps the old attic when the weather permitted another trip to the cottage.

A sudden memory of my own face staring at me from Katherine's merciless charcoal sketch drove me to pace the room restlessly. I wandered down the hall and into the library, which had become my favorite room in the house. I had spent happy hours curled up in one of the velvet armchairs, working my way through a slim volume of Byron's poems and making an appreciable dent in Milton's *Paradise Lost*. But today the high-backed chairs looked stiff; the rich smell of books held none of its usual appeal.

I realized that I had to talk to someone—anyone—or I'd soon be as crazy as they all seemed to think I was.

As I left the library, I caught sight of a furry marmalade body scooting up the staircase, and an idea struck me. Gathering up Katherine's skirts, I followed the cat.

Robbie was sprawled on the floor of the playroom, putting together a puzzle that looked too difficult for an eight-year-old. Henry was there ahead of me, sitting just outside the range of the boy's idly kicking feet.

I knocked lightly on the open door. "May I come in?"

The child looked up, startled, and scrambled to his feet. My heart twisted as he bent himself in a stiff little bow and said politely, "Good morning, Katya."

"Good morning. Mind if I join you?" Without waiting

for his permission, I sat on the floor and scrunched my skirts so they wouldn't interfere with his progress. "What is the puzzle supposed to be, Robbie?"

He recovered from his surprise but still eyed me suspiciously. "Angels in heaven playing musical instruments. You know, the one Uncle Leon made for me last Christmas."

"Oh, yes, of course." I picked up a piece to examine it. The picture had been painted directly onto a sheet of smooth wood, which was then cut into small interlocking pieces with a jigsaw. I wondered idly what a puzzle like this would be worth in my own time, especially if Leon had signed it.

"Can I help you put it together?" I returned the piece and glanced at Robbie. He shrugged but said nothing, resuming his belly position on the floor. Henry eyed me coldly, his ringed tail swishing.

Chalk up one more character who didn't like Katherine.

"Where is your nurse?"

Robbie shot me another surprised look. "Sleeping in her room." He tried a piece in several spots before giving up and reaching for another. "That's all she ever does."

We worked in silence for a while. Henry assumed a more settled position, and the golden eyes closed. Rain pattered on the roof, and the damp chill of the room began to seep into my muscles.

"It's very cold up here," I said. "Why don't we take the puzzle downstairs to the library, where we can have a nice fire?"

Robbie looked up from the new piece he was trying to place.

"Why do you say that?" he demanded. "You know Mama doesn't like me playing and making noise downstairs when she doesn't feel well."

I nodded, and Robbie became absorbed once more in the puzzle. We worked in silence for a few more minutes.

"This is ridiculous!" I exclaimed. I scrambled to my feet and shook out my skirts. "Come on, Robbie. Put the pieces back in the box. We're going downstairs."

Robbie sprang to his feet. "No!" He grabbed at my hand as I reached for the box. "Not unless Mama says it's all right!"

I turned my hand and took his gently. "Mama is sleeping in her room. Auntie Ana is busy with ranch business. So that puts me in charge for now." I made my smile bright. "And I say we're going downstairs."

I resisted an impulse to lay my hand along the delicate line of his cheek.

"But first," I added, squatting again and gathering pieces together, "we'll ask Carmen to make us some hot cocoa. I don't know about you, but my tummy could use some warming up!"

Robbie watched uncertainly as I scooped the pieces into the wooden box. Neither of us spoke. I retrieved a piece that had strayed close to Henry, and the cat rose with a languorous yawn. After stretching each of his hind legs in turn, he sauntered over, heedless of the puzzle pieces he stepped on, and rubbed his body against my skirts. I held myself still, allowing the cat to show me this unexpected favor, and I glanced at Robbie. His expression of surprise bloomed into wonder as we both heard the unmistakable rumble of a friendly purr.

"He's never done *that* before," Robbie breathed. His

eyes rounded as he looked at me with new respect. He hesitated a moment and then sank to his knees beside me. "Here, Katya," he said, and his smile was shy. "You missed a piece."

* * *

Leon and Michael returned in time for supper. Isabel sat in her usual place at the head of the table, gracious as always. But she looked pale, and the lines etched around her eyes and mouth had deepened.

The conversation was more amiable than on the previous night. The two men, when not embroiled over one of Michael's causes, seemed to get along quite well.

"Burned out," Leon declared. "Completely. And nobody knows what happened to them. They just up and vanished."

"What about the shop?" Ana asked. "Although I understand it didn't do much business. The sons worked local ranches for wages to keep the brood going."

"Shop's destroyed." Leon bristled his brows. "That's what makes it so obvious that the family was deliberately driven out. Somebody wanted those Chinese gone, no question about it."

I realized they were talking about the Chinese family Katherine had mentioned in her journal. I tried to recall the particulars. The family had moved to Springstown from San Francisco after their father was murdered. The mother opened a shop on the edge of town, selling herbs and oddities, and the boy Kim Soo had become friendly with Katherine. Better acquainted now with Katherine's reputation, I wondered just how friendly they had become.

Michael suddenly spoke up. "You knew the oldest son, didn't you, Katherine?"

I jumped and stared at him, wondering how much he knew about Katherine's sexual exploits. Michael's expression was guileless. We hadn't spoken since the night before.

"I knew him casually," I said. "We all saw the family at charity functions."

Ana nodded. "I always felt sorry for that family, fatherless as they were." She sighed. "It's difficult to believe someone would intentionally burn them out."

Leon pushed his salad aside and reached for his wine glass. "By the way," he said, "I heard Bruce McPherson plans to open a seed business in town. What about that?"

I swallowed hard. Did Michael know about Bruce McPherson, too? I didn't dare look at him but stared fixedly at the green beans growing cold on my plate. I took up my glass of wine, downed a large gulp, and then another. Isabel watched me, and I wondered suddenly if Katherine wasn't supposed to like wine. I brushed the thought aside, finished my glass, and waved it at her. "May I have some more?" I asked sweetly.

Ana put a cautionary hand on my arm. "I wouldn't advise it, Katya. It's not good for the baby."

"The baby and I need to relax." I shook off her hand and poured myself another glass. "Just a little. See?" I raised the glass to my lips, drained it, and grinned at her disapproving frown.

"She's getting tipsy." Michael sounded amused. "Better get that bottle out of her reach."

I glared at him, but he was right. I had enough wine in my blood already to release an imp who had been nudging me for days to do something reckless. I hiccupped and giggled, and the table fell silent as everyone stared at me.

Instead of feeling shy, however, I felt bold and enormously witty.

I gave them all the dazzling Victoria Reeves-Ashton smile. "You good people have no idea what a treasure you have sitting at your table." I set down my glass with infinite care and beamed at them. "I, Victoria, can predict the future. Go ahead. Ask me about anything. Except European history, that is." I grimaced. "I really stink at European history."

Their silence began to alarm me. "Go ahead!" I shouted. "Ask me! For example, this house will be known as Rosswood House and will become a museum. That clock out there"—I waved a hand at the door—"will still be counting off minutes a hundred years from now. Think of it, *a hundred years!* Men will walk on the moon. Scientists will propagate human life in test tubes—"

"Katrina, that's enough!" Isabel's anger cut through the pleasant buzzing in my head. Her eyes flashed and her mouth compressed into a thin line of disapproval. My gay mood abruptly dissolved. Shame and longing plunged me into a quiet pool of sadness.

"Why don't you love me, Mother?" I whispered. "All I ever wanted was for you to love me."

Isabel's eyes widened, and the pallor of her face became stark. I glanced around the table as Katherine's face crumpled with the lonely ache of my own heart. I felt exposed in the same way her charcoal sketch had exposed me.

"I think I'll go upstairs," I mumbled, and pushed back my chair. "Maybe tomorrow I'll wake up in my own bed and discover this has all been just an intensely weird dream."

There was sudden movement on the other side of the table as I struggled to my feet. Even reaching Katherine's short height seemed too much pressure for her brain; it began to swim just as Michael's hands gripped me from behind and kept me from falling to the blue and gold Aubusson carpet.

Chapter Twenty-Six

Dora woke me the following morning. She stood above my bed and clapped her hands loudly, not content to see my body writhe under the covers but waiting until my eyes actually opened and focused on her. She crossed her arms over her chest.

"*Señora* asks you to come to her sitting room," she said. "She waits there now."

I sat up quickly but regretted it as pain knifed through my brain and made me cry out. I tried to lie back down, but Dora gripped my shoulders and forced me to remain upright.

"Sit up now. Drink this." She shoved a cup of hot tea under my nose. "Drink it all."

I took the cup and watched her retrieve my robe and slippers from the wardrobe. She laid them on the bed and frowned at me.

"Drink, drink!"

"It's too *hot!*" I snapped. I set the cup clumsily on the bedside table and buried my head in my hands. "I hurt all over!"

"Too much drink last night." Dora's voice was grim. "Too much talk. *Señora* is very upset with you."

I groaned and slid my hands over the back of my head, clasping them over my neck. My memory of the previous night remained sketchy. I remembered Michael's stare and my panic over how much he knew about Katherine's sexual exploits. I remembered feeling angry at Katherine and

247

drinking a lot of wine to somehow get back at her. I couldn't remember much after that. I didn't know how I'd gotten myself upstairs to bed.

My head jerked upright at the sudden image of lying on my bed with Michael standing over me, the lamplight reflecting off his glasses. I vaguely recalled vomiting into a metal basin, but I couldn't remember who held it for me.

I groaned and shut my eyes, pressing fingertips to my temples where the throbbing had suddenly increased.

"Come, come." Dora threw back the bedcovers and pulled my legs out. I rose shakily to my feet and gripped the bedpost as a beam of white pain shot through my brain from temple to temple.

"Aspirin," I whispered. "Do you have any aspirin?"

Dora shook her head and pointed to the cooling tea. "Best for you and the baby."

I reached for the cup and sipped cautiously. The tea did nothing for my pain, but it did clear my head enough to realize that I was on my way to an interview with Katherine's mother.

Isabel and I had not shared a significant conversation since that first night when she had demanded an explanation for Katherine's crime. Sometimes I caught her watching me with a dark, unreadable look in her eyes. But she said little, as aloof with me as she was with her son.

This was the first time I had been summoned to Isabel's presence, and according to Dora, Isabel was angry about something I'd said at dinner. I recalled a vague sense of feeling witty and clever, and then…nothing.

Feeling very small, I slipped Katherine's arms into her robe and followed Dora into the hall.

* * *

Dora went ahead into Isabel's private sitting room to announce my arrival while I lingered on the threshold of her bedroom, stunned by what I saw.

Gone were the opulent furnishings of a stylish lady who enjoyed comfort and luxury. Isabel's bedroom was as stark as a prison cell, the floor bare of rugs, her bed in a state of military neatness. The beautiful curve of windows looked naked with only pull shades and no draperies. Arching above the plain white walls, the graceful dome of the ceiling seemed overly dramatic and painfully out of place, as if the room's natural beauty were being forced to deny itself for the sake of some cold vow to poverty.

The room smelled of candles. I spotted a glittering row of them offering votives beneath a picture of Mary and the infant Jesus. A prayer book and rosary lay on the bedside table. Isabel, it seemed, had already been at her morning prayers.

Dora reappeared and ushered me into the adjoining sitting room. A meager fire burned in the small fireplace, and my gaze flew instinctively to the wall above the mantel. Instead of Isabel's portrait, however, there hung a religious painting shocking in its graphic portrayal of a suffering Christ—his face twisted in agony, his eyes rolled up, his forehead running with blood from the pressing crown of thorns.

I shivered and pulled Katherine's robe close around me.

Isabel was settled on a chaise lounge, a thick blanket tucked around her legs. With her dark hair tumbling loose over her shoulders and her eyes huge against the pallor of her face, she looked young and fragile. Even in Katherine's short body, I felt as if I loomed over her, robust with health.

There was nothing fragile, however, in the way she frowned and silently indicated a chair for me or in her crisp dismissal of Dora still hovering in the doorway.

"Well, Katrina," she said coolly. "What do you have to say for yourself?"

I gulped and fingered the ties of Katherine's robe. "I know I drank too much wine," I began. "But I'm afraid most of last night is just a blur." I bit my lip and looked up. "I'm sorry if I embarrassed you. But I can't remember anything I said. If I offended you or anyone else, I didn't mean to."

Isabel stared at me for a long, silent moment before she spoke. "Losing yourself again, Katrina?" she asked softly. "From too much drink this time? Or is it your old problem?"

My old problem? Losing myself?

"I don't know what you mean…Mother."

Isabel gave a weary sigh and leaned back against the chaise lounge. She rubbed a finely boned hand across her eyes.

"All right, then." She folded her hands on the blanket and settled her gaze on me. "Tell me who Victoria is."

I jumped so violently that she flinched, and her delicate nostrils flared.

"Come now, Katrina. We already know about Elizabeth, don't we? But I've never heard you mention this other — this Victoria. She claims to have power to see into the future?"

She paused, giving me time to answer. Katherine's throat constricted so severely I could scarcely breathe, much less utter a word.

Isabel leaned forward suddenly. "It's heresy, you know. If you're making claims about having the gift of sight, you'd better have an explanation. Father Gabriel is coming to hear our confessions on Thursday. He'll certainly want to question you about these unorthodox notions."

Her beautiful eyes searched my face, and I saw fear in them. She suddenly shivered and leaned back, closing her eyes and tucking the blanket closer. She rubbed and pulled at her hands as if they were giving her pain.

I stared at her in stunned silence while the clearest thought in my head was how ill she looked.

"I'm waiting, Katrina," she said wearily, her eyes still closed. "Who is Victoria?"

I licked my lips and swallowed. "It might help if you told me what I said last night."

"Very well. You called yourself Victoria and made a prediction that our house would become a museum and the Stovolsky clock would still be running a hundred years from now." She opened her eyes and gazed at the ceiling. "Then you asked me... You said something quite unforgivable in front of our guests, family or not."

"What?" I whispered.

Isabel looked at her hands. "You asked me why I don't love you."

I stared at her in horror. Katherine's stomach churned while I cast about for words to undo the damage I had caused.

"I'm sorry I hurt you," I said gently. "As you say, I had too much to drink, and I lost myself." I paused, and added curiously, "But what did you mean by 'my old problem'? Has this happened before?"

Isabel raised her eyes to study my face. "You started losing yourself after your brother died, Katrina. And then Elizabeth came." She looked past me, into the fire. "You became like two people, one of them a saint, and the other—"

Her shoulders hunched as if to ward off pain. She stared into the fire, and I began to make sense of her words. Katherine and Elizabeth were the same person? I wondered suddenly if Elizabeth was like me, a time traveler who one day found herself waking in Katherine's body.

But no, Katherine's journal said Elizabeth lived here *with* Katherine, in the same space of time. Isabel said she came after Nicholas died, after Katherine had somehow caused her brother's death. I tried to fit the facts with what I knew about psychology. There had been a splitting of some kind, a separation into good and bad. Two personalities began to share Katherine's body, one of them a saint—

"Katherine created another personality." I spoke my thoughts aloud. "Elizabeth." I recalled the embroidery sampler, the neat stitches mixed in with sloppy, artless ones. "One personality good and loving and perfect. And the other—" I thought about Bruce McPherson, about Anton's sudden death, about the seeds I'd found in Katherine's desk drawer.

"You see?" Isabel's voice was sharp. "Even now you talk about yourself as if you were someone else. And Elizabeth, too." She leaned toward me and whispered, "So, who are you now? Are you Victoria?" Pain swam in her eyes. "Then what have you done with my daughter? *Where is Katrina?*"

The raw pleading in her voice was so unlike Isabel that it pulled me to my knees beside her chaise lounge. "Here, Mother," I whispered, wanting only to ease the pain in her eyes. "I'm here."

She gazed at me for a long moment, while her delicate mouth worked. Then she took my face gently in her hands.

"Let Father Gabriel help you, daughter. For in God's truth, I cannot. And it hurts me to see you suffer." She patted my cheek. "We have sins to pay for, you and I."

With a sigh she laid her head back and closed her eyes. "Go along now, *niña*. And fetch me Dora."

I rose with difficulty, shaken by Isabel's unexpected softening. Still feeling the warmth of her hands on my face, I turned reluctantly away and left the room to search for her old nurse.

* * *

I sat on the cold stone steps of Isabel's chapel, waiting for my turn. Katherine's mother had long ago disappeared inside with the priest and shut the door behind them. I listened but heard nothing from within, only the springtime chorus of chirping birds and the rustle of new green leaves flirting with a breeze in the treetops. A dragonfly zoomed close and hovered for an instant on rainbow wings, examining me, before darting off just as suddenly. I longed for a wristwatch and wished I'd had something to eat that morning. My stomach gave occasional howls of emptiness that could prove embarrassing during my confession.

For confession was the reason Isabel had dragged me here. All week she had been watching me, measuring my words, my expressions, and my tone of voice. I found it unnerving that she suspected me of believing myself to be someone called Victoria when she hadn't the least notion of who Victoria really was.

The chill of the stone penetrated my skirts and seeped into my bones. I rose stiffly and moved away just as the chapel door opened.

The robed figure of the priest stepped out and turned to help Isabel down the steps. She wore a dark veil, and I couldn't see her face as the priest bowed over her hand. She brushed past me without speaking and started toward the house.

"*Señora.*" The priest walked toward me, a hand extended in greeting. I interrupted his soft flow of Spanish with an apologetic smile.

"I'm sorry. I don't speak Spanish." He stopped, clearly startled. Then he gave me a smile that dazzled white against the deep tan of his face.

"My apologies, Mrs. Kamarov," he said, in perfect English. "I am Father Philippe from the mission at San Rafael. Your mother asked for her old family priest. Unfortunately, Father Gabriel is not well. He asked me to come in his stead." He stepped aside and gestured toward the chapel door. "Please. Shall we go in?"

I preceded him up the steps and recognized the small dark vestibule with its porcelain font. Recalling the severity of Isabel's bedroom, I was unprepared for, and delightfully surprised by, the beauty of the chapel room itself.

Sunlight melted through the stained glass windows on the east wall, where the forest had not yet encroached enough to cast its shadows. The plain altar I remembered in front now displayed a white linen cloth, covered in turn with a smaller cloth embroidered in rich gold and purple. Twin bowls of white lilies graced the altar, and their heady fragrance called to mind my own mother as lilies were her favorite flowers. Leon's magnificent crucifix hung on the wall above the altar, flanked on either side by colorful tapestries.

Father Philippe motioned me toward the front right corner, where two kneeling cushions faced each other for a makeshift confessional. I had not been to confession since childhood, and the sight of those kneelers started Katherine's heart pounding way up in her ears. The priest helped me kneel before he knelt himself and steepled his hands together, assuming the attitude of prayer.

"Bless me, Father, for I have sinned." I groped for the words lying buried in memory. "It has been…a long time since my last confession."

A child's voice began to prattle an old litany in my head: *Forgive me for hating my grandmother and wanting her to die. Soften my mother's heart and make her love me again. Please bring my father back to me. Please make the bear go away. Wash away my sin and make me clean like I used to be…*

I couldn't breathe. I shook my head and tried to stand. "No," I whispered. "Please. I can't do this now."

Father Philippe sprang to his feet and took my elbow. "Come and sit down, Mrs. Kamarov." He led me to one of the low wooden benches. "You are very pale." He sat beside me and rubbed my freezing hands between his own. I had a sudden, vivid memory of Ryan doing the same, of Ryan's eyes watching me with the same look of concern and mild alarm.

I gave the priest an apologetic smile. "It must be my condition," I said, and I thought the lie perfectly believable but saw speculation in his eyes. I wondered suddenly what Isabel had told him about me.

"Yes. I understand you are expecting a child." He released my hands and pushed himself back on the bench so he could rest his elbows on his knees, just as Ryan would have done. "When is your baby due?"

I wasn't sure. "Not for several months," I said evasively, squirming under the directness of his gaze. "How long have you been a priest?"

It was his turn to hesitate. "Not so very long." His eyes twinkled, and I caught myself thinking he was too attractive to be a priest. He rubbed his hands together lightly. "We don't have to treat this as a formal confession, Mrs. Kamarov. But whatever you tell me I will hold in the strictest confidence. I am your priest, and your secrets are safe with me, before God."

His deep brown eyes were solemn and full of compassion. He clasped his hands and gave me time to respond.

I still don't know what made me tell him. Perhaps it was because he reminded me so strongly of Ryan. Perhaps it was sitting together in the serene beauty of the chapel, temporarily set apart from the world outside, both mine and Katherine's. Or perhaps my secret had become too heavy to carry alone and, like the child growing inside me, compelled me to deliver it into the light of day, regardless of the risk.

For whatever reason, I told the priest everything, beginning with my first trip to Summerwood. I recounted the dreams and the painting of the two women at the bridge, and then the memory of dying and being carried into the fragrant white mist. I watched him carefully as I spoke, assessing his reaction. He listened without comment, bent forward over his knees, his hands still. Occasionally he looked up at me, but I saw neither skepticism nor fear in his eyes, only patience and rapt attention.

We must have sat for nearly an hour while sunlight

filtered through the stained glass and slid watercolor shadows across the stone floor at our feet.

"So, you see," I said, winding down from my narrative, "I keep stumbling into Katherine's misdeeds and being held accountable for things I would never do. It's very frustrating. And another thing." I bit my lip. "I have no idea how to get back to my own time. I don't even know if it's possible." I dropped my voice to a whisper. "I know I died back there at the creek. And I'm guessing that on some other plane of time Katherine must have died at the same moment. But instead of returning to her own body, I took her place. And what's more, I have a strong feeling that I've been sent here for a reason, to fulfill some kind of task." I gave him a hopeful smile. "Maybe you would know something about how that works?"

I stopped talking to let him answer. The room was suddenly very quiet, and I realized that he had not spoken a word since I'd begun my story. He rubbed his hands together lightly, thoughtfully. Still without speaking he rose and walked toward the altar where he stood, his back to me, staring up at Leon's crucifix. I watched him lower his head, and he stood motionless for several minutes while I fingered Katherine's rosary. Birdsong drifted in through the high open windows.

At last he turned and walked toward me. He frowned a little as he sat down and put his hands on his knees.

"Well. *Victoria*. I confess, I don't know exactly how to respond to you. Your tale is quite beyond my experience." He met my gaze directly. "I can tell you one thing: If God is in this, if He sent you here, then He will show you what you must do and give you the strength to do it." He patted my hand. "How terrifying this must seem to you. And how strong and brave you have been."

"I was afraid you'd think I was crazy."

He smiled faintly. "I believe in miracles, Victoria, and I believe we are all in God's hands. You said you feel part of a design. I suggest you trust your instincts. Trust that fragrant light you took inside you. It's a gift, my dear. Perhaps it holds the answers to your questions."

Chapter Twenty-Seven

I stood in Katherine's freshly bathed body before the cheval mirror in her bedroom and dolefully contemplated her reflection. The pregnancy had swallowed her waist and broadened her hips to the effect of suggesting close kinship with a ripened pear. If someone were to knock me on the head, I thought wryly, I would spring back upright like an oversized inflatable toy.

My mind's eye carved away the extra tissue, imagining Katherine's body lithe and petite before the pregnancy. Had men found her body sexually appealing? Or was there something seductive in her manner that attracted them? What did Bruce McPherson see when he looked at her?

A shudder ran through me, making me rub Katherine's arms vigorously and turn away from the mirror. *I guess I'll find out soon enough*, I thought. *I'll be facing the man himself in little more than an hour.*

This afternoon the entire neighborhood would gather at the Stillman ranch to celebrate Theresa and Bruce's engagement. Attendance was a social must. I had considered a headache, a toothache, even a fourth personality, but I knew Isabel would insist on my attendance, no matter how compelling my excuse.

I had just fitted myself with chemise and petticoats when there was a rap on the door, followed immediately by Dora's huge bulk filling the doorway. I had grown used to these intrusions and considered it a triumph that she now at least knocked before barging in on me. She assessed my progress with shrewd eyes and lumbered over to the wardrobe to pull out Katherine's best gown.

"Are you coming to the party, Dora?" The comb I ran through Katherine's damp hair sent a fine spray over the surface of her dressing table. I looked up and caught Dora watching me in the mirror.

"No, *señora*." She looked away and flicked lint from the black silk of the gown over her arm.

I watched her reflection curiously. "I guess the whole county will be there, from the way Lillian Stillman talks."

Dora didn't reply but shook out the gown and held it up. I rose from the bench and stepped into the skirt. Then I held out my arms like a child to be fitted with the sleeves. *How easily I've slipped into this role,* I thought idly, holding still so Dora could fasten the long row of buttons down my back.

With an undergirding of petticoats, the skirt gave me at least the illusion of a waist. I dropped onto the vanity bench with a sigh as Dora twisted the long hair into the usual tight knot. Katherine's dark eyes stared back morosely in the mirror from a thin face made plainer by the stark gown and severe hairstyle.

"Dora, I feel so dowdy," I whined. "Can't we do something special today? Maybe add some color or loosen the twist in my hair?"

Dora shook her head emphatically. "You are in mourning. You are a shadow until your days of grieving are over, not a flower to attract men."

"But I don't feel grief! I don't feel like mourning! And I'm sick of moping around in black like it's *me* who's dead!" I whirled around on the bench and glared at her. "You're going to fix my hair like Isabel's. Softer and prettier.

Understand?"

She shrank back, and her little eyes narrowed. "As you wish," she said stiffly.

Dora pursed her lips in disapproval but obediently pulled out hairpins, and the heavy hair fell smooth under her hands. Nimbly, she arranged a fashionable cushion of hair, secured it with pins, and then coiled a thick braid loosely above it. The effect softened the sharp angles of Katherine's features and framed her small face like a caress. Pushing aside the usual ebony earrings, I picked out a pair of ruby teardrops and hooked them into her ears, approving their pert swing. Next, I fished out a brooch set with rubies and diamonds and pinned it above the small mound of her left breast. Still not satisfied, I paraded before the footed mirror, sweeping an expert eye over her black-clad figure.

"Dora, does Isabel have any colored scarves, something with red and gold, or maybe a hunter green?"

Dora opened her mouth but then clamped it shut and left the room without a word. A few minutes later she returned with two scarves. "Ana's," she said.

I held each in turn against my bodice and chose the one with scarlet flowers nestled in green leaves. Humming a snatch of tune, I tucked the scarf into the neckline, hiding all but a frill that sprouted above the black silk like a burst of springtime and drew from Katherine's cheeks a fresh pink glow. Badgering Dora for a makeup box and ignoring her disapproving clucks, I set about applying a light touch of lip rouge and faint shadows of rose brown that deepened the dark brown of Katherine's eyes. I accentuated the blush in her cheeks and softened her brows with a light tweezing. Pleased with my results, I jumped off the bench and gave a delighted twirl.

Although she had watched the entire proceedings, Dora's eyes widened before she caught herself and lowered her gaze. I stared at her bent head and bit my lip, deciding it was time to voice a question I had been wanting to ask her for weeks.

"Dora, who do you think I am?"

She raised her head and inquired politely, "*Señora?*"

But I knew better. "You don't believe I'm Katherine, do you?" I said it softly, respectfully. She regarded me and then drew herself up with quiet dignity.

"No, *señora*. You are not she."

"Then who do you think I am?"

"You are moonseed, a holy one of the spring moon."

I don't know what I'd expected her to say. I felt behind me for the bench and sat down abruptly. "Go on," I said.

She gave me a long look. "Every spring my people pray, and the holy ones come. They teach us wisdom and lessons we cannot learn for ourselves. They come to show us their love. Sometimes the moonseed stay and become like us, as a special show of blessing and protection. But not for a long time now."

Her eyes grew wet and bright. "The night you come, Katherine, she does a very bad thing." Dora shook her head, and a single tear spilled over, bumping along the rough furrows of her cheek. "Very bad for her family. It is the night of the new spring moon, the sacred night." She stared at me, one eye still shining with its unshed tear. "Then you come to us, to walk with us and teach us." She blinked, and the tear spilled over. "You have the sacred *ojas*, eyes that have seen God. Now you must show us."

I was too stunned to speak.

Dora took one of Katherine's small hands in her own. "Grace Stillman. You must talk with Grace Stillman."

I stared into her small, inscrutable eyes, and I tried to think. Grace Stillman? Wasn't she the youngest of the Stillman daughters, the one not yet sixteen?

A rap on the door made me jump. Ana stuck her head in.

"Katya—" She broke off as I rose from the bench and walked toward her. Her startled look swept me up and down. "My goodness," she murmured, and put a hand to her throat. "Your mother sent me to fetch you, dear. The carriages are downstairs."

She pushed the door wider and stood waiting.

Dora held out my shawl and handbag. She met my gaze as I took them, and I murmured, "Grace Stillman."

She grunted her affirmative and folded her arms.

* * *

The Stillman ranch sprawled over the floor of a pleasant valley about twenty minutes by carriage from Rosswood House. Green pastures gave rise to white-fenced paddocks as we drew near the stables and outhouses. Twin rows of towering pin oaks flanked the lane, at last relinquishing their dead autumn leaves for a new spring crop. Beyond the stables, the ranch house rose into view against the green and rust backdrop of a redwood grove. More humble than its Russian neighbor, the house nevertheless gleamed like a polished apple in the May sunshine, with its fresh coat of glossy red trim and leafy hedgerows clipped neat for the occasion.

Our carriage rattled to a stop just before the front porch, and I took a moment to readjust myself after the bumpy ride. Feeling for loose hairpins, I realized that

263

Katherine's usual tight knot was probably more practical if she did much riding in carriages. But I patted the softer style lovingly and remembered, with a little flush of pleasure, Michael's startled look when he glanced up and saw me descending the stairs at Rosswood House. He merely muttered, "About time," and hurried me out the front door. Shutting me into the carriage with Isabel and Robbie, he then retreated to join his aunt and uncle in the carriage behind ours.

Leon now alighted from his carriage and came forward to help us down. Isabel, elegant as always in her black silk and enameled brooch, gave him her hand and descended gracefully. As I stepped down behind her, I was grateful to see loose hay strewn over the muddy ruts of the drive, keeping my hem and high-heeled boots clean as I turned to help Robbie.

The boy gripped my hand and would not let go, even after he reached the ground and began walking with me up the steps to the porch. Since that morning in the playroom three weeks before, Robbie had become my faithful shadow. Guided by Henry's sudden, unequivocal acceptance of me, Robbie too had gone from a suspicious reserve to a rather shy but determined effort at friendliness. On more than one occasion, he had invited me to play with his puzzles or brought me a book to read to him while he nestled against me, as content as the cat purring on his lap. He'd taken to surprising me in the library when I was reading or asking to sit by me as I relaxed on the front porch swing. To his delight, we established a daily routine of hot cocoa in the late morning and saying our prayers together before he went to bed at night.

If Isabel noticed the sudden bonding between her son

and daughter, she gave no hint. She had little to do with Robbie and spent a good deal of time in her room with the door closed. As she often appeared for meals looking pale and drawn, I began to wonder if she were merely out of sorts, as she claimed, or if she were truly ill.

Today, however, Isabel looked radiant. Even in the simple black of her gown, she shone like a jewel among the other guests, turning heads with her beauty and natural poise as she led our party into the hall to greet the guests of honor.

Lillian stood beside her husband, John, and received Isabel's hand in a formal clasp. Her smile was smug.

"Isabel. Children." Her gaze swept past Robbie and me to encompass Ana and her family. "So good of you all to come. Please allow me to present my daughter Theresa and her fiancé, Mr. Bruce McPherson."

Suddenly, I was standing squarely before the engaged couple. Theresa's blue eyes flicked over me and fell on Robbie, who was pressing into my skirt, his hand still in mine.

"Bruce," she said, "you remember Robbie Rostnova, don't you? And of course"—after the barest hesitation—"his sister, Katherine."

The young man beside her was broad-shouldered and stood well above six feet. I looked up into blue eyes made even more striking by the scarlet now flooding his face. His glance barely grazed my face and fell onto Robbie.

"Of course! The young man himself!" Bruce extended a big-knuckled hand, and Robbie looked fearfully at me before allowing his own to be swallowed in a manly handshake. "And Katherine." Bruce released Robbie's hand and stared straight at my forehead. "Always a pleasure, madam." He finished the greeting with a stiff little bow.

"Mr. McPherson," I murmured. "I'm so happy for you both."

"Thank you, Katherine," Theresa answered for them. She was clasping his hand as firmly as Robbie clasped mine. "My cousins Harry and Andrew are visiting. You remember them, don't you, Robbie?" She bent to meet Robbie's gaze at eye level. "They're at mumblety-peg out back, if you want to join them." She straightened and turned away to greet Ana and Leon.

Relieved, I let Robbie tug me toward an elegant buffet table. Between bright bowls of spring flowers, a tower of *petit fours* rose like pastel building blocks, their delicate shells laced with white piping. Twin platters offered triangles of ham and thick yellow cheese, slices of nut bread fanned like dominoes, and colorful fruit slices crusted with white sugar. I reached for a plate, hungrily eyeing a glass bowl mounded with glistening noodle salad, while Robbie secured a pink-iced sugar cookie shaped like a heart. Piling our plates shamefully high, I turned and scanned the room for a place to sit.

Isabel motioned us to empty chairs beside her. Robbie sat between us, concentrating mightily on balancing the plate on his knees with one hand as he tried to eat with the other. When two young boys burst into the room, however, his head came up to watch them, and his plate dipped to a dangerous angle. I grabbed it just as the noodle salad began to slip.

The boys were laughing and swatting at each other, rousing an indignant huff from a stout woman filling her plate as they snatched two cookies each from the buffet and devoured them.

I turned to Robbie. "Would you like to go outside and play with the boys?" He hesitated, and I saw eagerness warring with his painful shyness. Over his head I caught Isabel's eye. "Robbie can finish his plate later, can't he? I'll save it for him."

Robbie turned quickly to his mother. She looked at me in mild surprise.

"Yes, all right." She gave his trousers a token brush of her hand. "But stay clean and mind your manners, Roberto."

Robbie rose and set his plate on his chair, rescuing his cookie before he turned around. But still he hung back, clutching the cookie and glancing at the boys sideways through his lashes. They had spotted him and stood still, openly staring.

On impulse I rose and turned to Isabel. "I'm getting myself some lemonade. May I bring you a glass?"

Isabel looked up and nodded. I placed a light hand on Robbie's shoulder and urged him along with me as I made my way to the punch bowl. I focused all my attention on slowly dribbling lemonade into two glass cups and didn't look around until I heard the screen door bang. All three boys had vanished.

With a pleased grin, I carried the lemonade back to Isabel. She watched me, her expression amused.

"You handled that very well, Katrina." She took the glass I offered and held it carefully in her lap. "I hadn't noticed your taking such care of your brother before." She added, "I daresay, he is better off playing outside in the sunshine than sitting in the polite society of adults."

"I'm glad we agree." Her praise warmed me and made me bold. "I am puzzled, though, why Robbie doesn't go to school in town, where he could play with other children. It must be dull for him with only his nurse and Henry for company."

A shadow dropped over the blue-violet eyes. Isabel said nothing but raised her glass to her lips and looked away. Baffled, I moved to sit down beside her but jumped and almost spilled my lemonade when someone grasped my arm. I turned to find Lillian beaming at Isabel and fluttering a hand.

"Isabel, I'd like you to meet my nephew Raymond." She released my arm and brought forward a dark-haired man in his middle thirties. "Raymond, this is my neighbor, Isabel Rostnova."

Her nephew's ready smile was polite and his bow to Isabel gracious. But when he raised his head, he looked straight at me.

His eyes were light gray, so pale in fact as to appear almost silver. His black hair was smoothed back in the sleek fashion of the day, his mustache small and neat over a full, sensual mouth. His dark coat and silk vest, even his fingernails, were trim and immaculate.

Taking my hand, he lifted it to his lips. "And this delightful young woman?" He spoke in a honeyed baritone, his pale eyes intent on mine.

"Oh, my dear, this is Katherine Kamarov, Isabel's daughter." Lillian leaned toward him and said in a low voice, "Recently widowed, Raymond. You remember my telling you."

My cheeks stung as I withdrew my hand. But Raymond's smile remained gracious. He released me from his gaze, reluctantly it seemed, and turned his attention to Isabel. "Madam." He bowed over her hand but did not raise it to his lips as he had mine.

My face burned hotter.

"Raymond's father is my brother, Archibald Delacroix." Lillian squeezed her nephew's arm indulgently. "He's visiting us for a time, and he brings us all the news from Philadelphia society." She sighed. "I grew up there, you know. Oh, how I do miss the elegance and stimulating conversation!" Her hand fluttered by her head as if she were waving away a bee.

Isabel smiled. "What a treat for your aunt, Mr. Delacroix. You must come to dinner and entertain us with your stories." She added blandly, "Unlike Philadelphia, our countryside is so tranquil that the least little event is enough to stir up the greatest flurry of excitement and exaggerated speculation."

The corner of Raymond's mouth twitched, and I knew Isabel's barb had not been lost on him.

"I thank you for the invitation, Mrs. Rostnova," he said, with a courtly bow. "I shall look forward to the pleasure of dining with you and your family." His gaze swept me significantly.

"Oh, Raymond, look! There's Hilde and Lionel. You must come and meet them!" Nodding distractedly in our direction, Lillian grabbed her nephew's arm and tugged him toward an elderly couple whom she was flagging down with her free hand. Raymond offered us an apologetic smile displaying an even set of white teeth before he turned away. Lillian's voice shrilled, "Hilde, this is my dear nephew, Raymond Delacroix!"

Delacroix. The name stirred an elusive wisp of memory. I knew I'd heard the name recently, but I couldn't place it.

I shrugged and dismissed the thought, certain that the

memory would come back to me if it were truly important.

Chapter Twenty-Eight

As the afternoon wore on, the party guests settled into small groups. The women sat in a polite circle in the parlor, sipping lemonade from delicate glass cups and chatting pleasantly. I spied Katherine's uncle standing with a group of men, one finger perpetually tugging at his collar while he pitched his head forward attentively. Michael and another young man were squared off in a corner, engaged in a heated debate. As I watched him, Michael alternated between gesticulating wildly and raking his hands through his hair, spiking it until he resembled a ginger porcupine. The thought made me grin, and Michael suddenly caught my look. He stopped talking and stared back at me, his hands suspended in midair. His companion turned to discover the distraction, and I looked away, still grinning.

Most of the young adults had formed a separate gathering in the drawing room, adjoining the parlor where I now sat. Through the open doors, I heard them laughing and talking, but I had not been invited to join them. Instead, I sat between Isabel and Ana in the circle of married ladies and listened to their speculations about the best methods for keeping pickles crisp and the long-term consequences of a tonsillectomy. I learned everything there was to know about the new dentist in town—his wife's family history, the amount of money he had in the bank, and how many eggs his chickens were prone to lay. I stifled more than one yawn and kept blinking to clear the sleepiness from my eyes, wondering how on earth I would keep my head upright for the next hour.

I glanced around and caught Michael's eye again. He was alone, leaning his arms on the high back of a chair, grinning lazily at me. I looked away and sat up straighter, pretending interest in the current discussion of which vendor sold the best chicken feed. But it was no use. His grin was contagious, and I felt Katherine's mouth twitch. I lifted a hand to her throat and shot him a pained look, pretending to strangle.

Ana touched my arm. "Katya?" I turned in time to catch the look she gave her nephew. "Are you all right, dear?"

"Of course. A little restless, I guess."

"Well, that's to be expected, isn't it?" She patted my arm and took a sip of her lemonade. I stole a glance at Michael, but he had turned away to join his uncle. I sighed and settled in my chair, trying to refocus my attention on Mrs. Danforth, who was telling the story of how a lizard had crawled up her water pipe and appeared one morning in her bathtub, giving her the fright of her life. Although the other women tittered appreciatively, the best I could manage was a wan smile.

Piano music drew my attention to the drawing room. Through the adjoining doors I spotted the youngest Stillman daughter sitting on a piano bench, her neat blond braid straight as a plumb line down her back as she played a Mendelssohn concerto. Recalling Dora's words, I excused myself from the ladies group and approached the drawing room. The young people were separated into groups by gender, just as we were. Theresa sat among a cluster of giggling young women, and the men stood in a knot by the window, nudging each other with their elbows and erupting in raucous laughter.

I put a hand on the piano and cleared my throat.

"Grace? May I speak with you?"

The girl's hands faltered and stopped. She looked up at me in surprise.

"What did you call me?"

I started to repeat myself, but my throat closed over a sudden lump of uncertainty.

"You called me Grace. That's my grandmother's name." Her brow furrowed, and she flicked a nervous glance over her shoulder. "I'm June, Katherine."

I managed a little laugh. "Of course. June. I wanted to speak to you about where I might *find* your grandmother. There's something I've been meaning to discuss with her."

Her eyes were suspicious. "Granny's on the sun porch, I think." I hesitated, and she rose from the piano bench. "I'll take you."

I followed her into the hall. Turning a corner, we suddenly came upon Emily in the embrace of a man I did not recognize from the party. She spun around as we approached, her face reddening.

"Is Granny still on the porch?" June asked blandly.

"How should I know?" her sister snapped. She rubbed the back of her hand over her mouth and glanced at me. The man slouched against the wall with a smile I could only describe as insolent. June led me down the hall and through a screen door that opened onto a covered porch.

A white-haired woman with shriveled skin dozed in a wicker rocking chair. June approached her and touched her shoulder.

"Granny?" She straightened and turned to me. "My grandmother's sleeping, I'm afraid." She watched me nervously.

"Then I'll just sit out here for a bit. This chair looks comfortable." I moved toward a wicker armchair with a plump cushion. "Thank you, June."

The girl hesitated as I lowered myself into the chair. With a shrug, she turned away, and the screen door rasped shut behind her. Grace stirred and lapsed again into gentle snores.

The wicker creaked under the weight of Katherine's body, and then the peace of the sun porch settled around me. Slanting rays of late afternoon sun touched Katherine's hands. I felt her blood carry the warmth deeper into her body. The boys were shouting at their games around the corner of the house, and I smiled at the thought of Robbie at last abandoning his reserve and having fun. As I sank deeper into the afternoon hush, fainter sounds reached me — the drone of bees busy in the bushes below the porch, a soft wind rustling through the redwood grove behind me, the occasional crow of a rooster perhaps as confused as I was about the meaning of time.

I was beginning to drowse myself when the old woman at last stirred and opened her eyes. She stared at me vacantly, her faded brown eyes registering neither alarm nor recognition.

I leaned forward. "Grace? It's me, Katherine Kamarov." I hesitated. "I used to be Katherine Rostnova, from Ross—" I paused. "From the Russian House."

She blinked at me and slowly smiled.

"Little Katie." Her voice was feeble and cracked with age. "Such a handful! So much spirit for a girl, I told Isabel." Her face crinkled in dismay. "I'm so sorry about your brother, Katie. Nicky was a sweet boy." She sighed and

274

began to rock gently, coupling her hands in her lap and rotating her thumbs around each other. She stared out over the porch railing and didn't speak.

"So. Theresa, your granddaughter. She's getting married." I spoke loudly, trying to bring her back into conversation. She winced and turned her head.

"You needn't shout, Katie. I'm not deaf, you know." She smiled faintly. "Yes, Theresa is getting married. A fine boy, Bruce." Her face clouded. "They'd best be careful, though. Don't let them live in San Francisco. It's not far off, now. The Big One."

I leaned forward again. "The Big One, Grace? What do you mean?"

She sighed. "No one listens to me. No one understands. 'Crazy Gracie' they call me." Her thumbs accelerated around each other.

"I'm listening, Grace." A sudden hunch pitched my voice high. "Tell me about the Big One."

"It's the earthquake I've been warning everyone about for years. Not that they pay me any mind." The thumbs were now twirling and reversing, twirling forward, then backward.

"You mean," I breathed, "the 1906 earthquake?"

The twirling thumbs slowed to a stop. Grace turned to look at me.

"You believe me?"

"What else do you know, Grace?"

My eagerness seemed to frighten her, for she drew back with a suspicious look and turned away. Pressing her lips together, she began to rock again. Her thumbs resumed a cautious rotation.

Neither of us spoke. I listened to the creak of her

rocker and stared at her incessant thumbs tracing circles around each other. I took a risk.

"World War One?" My voice was soft, but the thumbs circled faster. "The stock market crash of 1929? World War Two?" The thumbs were reversing themselves, forward then backward, forward then backward. "Man's first walk on the moon?"

The thumbs stopped. Grace turned to me, her eyes wide.

"You've been that far, Katie?" She gripped my arm with surprising strength. "What else have you seen?"

Color spotted her cheeks. I hesitated, not wanting to excite her further. After a moment she released me and fell back against the rocker.

"Sometimes I dream about a white house," she said, "on a street lined with sycamores. Her husband's blue Chevy is parked in the driveway. She has two children, Janey and... I can't remember the little boy's name."

She lifted a gnarled finger and drew a shaky arc over her head. "There's a silver machine flying like a bird across the sky. And in the house a box that plays music and tells stories." She frowned. "I can't remember what they call it. There's so much I can't remember."

I sat, forgotten, while Grace murmured on about walks to the market and fixing Ovaltine for the children's breakfast. As she talked, low rays of sun slanted across her face, highlighting the moisture on her lashes and the deep etchings around her mouth. Her murmuring, like the sun's warmth, slowly dissipated, and her face took on the transparent look of old parchment. I reached forward and touched her hand.

"Grace?"

She didn't move, and her hand under my fingers was cold. Alarmed, I stood and gripped her by the shoulders.

"Grace!" I shouted, fear freezing my heart. "Grace!"

She stirred and looked up, her eyes watery and vacant.

"Grace?" I repeated softly.

But she was looking past me at images of another time, in a memory where this May afternoon and I did not exist.

* * *

I perched myself on the porch rail and watched the blazing sun dip by seconds into the distant rim of hills. I held my breath and caught the precise moment of its disappearance, when its golden fire swam and flared for the last time before sinking behind the solid silhouette of the dark land.

I was alone. Lillian had long since retrieved her mother-in-law from the rocker, scolding me for allowing the old woman to sit too long in the cooling air. Grace had remained remote, and I could get nothing more from her. My mind, however, raced with possibilities.

I was certain Grace had gone forward in time, to another woman's life, and had somehow returned. Her memory was shaky, and I couldn't tell if further questioning would satisfy my curiosity. How long she had stayed in that other time was uncertain. Nor could I determine how she had managed to return to her own time. Had it been her choice to come back?

Would I have a choice?

Once again I was that leaf bobbing on the whim of a current, powerless to steer my own course.

But if you did have the power, Victoria, would you choose to go back?

My heart twisted in a painful knot of uncertainty.

Moment by moment the sunset sky lost its brilliance. Fiery gold softened into rose and reflected off a pond not far from the house. The knot in my chest eased as I gazed at the peaceful water. "How beautiful," I murmured.

"Yes, it is," said a quiet voice behind me.

I turned sharply and would have fallen off the rail had Michael's hand not braced my arm and held me upright.

The sky reflected off his glasses, hiding his eyes. But his hand felt solid and warm on my arm as he eased me back against the post.

"I wondered where you'd gone." Michael removed his glasses and began polishing them with his handkerchief. I saw his eyelashes up close — pale with a hint of gold, almost brushing his cheek in a long sweep any woman would envy.

Perhaps feeling my gaze, he looked up at me. His gray-green eyes tilted up at the corners like Ana's, like Robbie's. Russian eyes, almost. They were rounder, hinting perhaps at his English heritage. I thought of the young boy yearning for his sea captain father to come back for him, an image not unlike the young Victoria waiting in her fantasy rose garden. My chest tightened, and I blinked back a sudden sting of tears.

Michael stopped polishing his glasses. "Kat?"

I smiled shakily and turned away just as a mallard set out across the pond. It cut through the fading rose satin of the water's surface like dressmaker shears, trailing a perfect V in its wake. Not wanting to disturb the hush, I pointed silently and watched the small figure glide into the shadows and disappear.

Michael's voice was soft behind me. "You seem so different, Kat. I don't understand it."

I didn't turn but watched the shadows around the pond deepen. I saw the first star of the evening sky.

"I thought at first I was imagining it. But it's there all the time—in your voice, your eyes, the way you carry yourself. It's in the way Robbie looks at you, and even his cat."

He touched my shoulder. I turned and slipped off the rail to face him. Wearing Katherine's high-heeled boots, I still had to look up to meet his eyes.

"Tell me I'm crazy," he said. "Tell me I'm imagining everything I see in you." Both his hands were on my shoulders. His eyes, looking soft and vulnerable without his glasses, searched mine with an intensity that set Katherine's heart fluttering in her chest.

But no, the fluttering was further down, inside her belly. I tore my gaze away from Michael's and pressed my hands over my skirt, waiting for another flutter, hoping I wasn't imagining it.

There it was again, light as butterfly wings. With a cry of delight, I grabbed Michael's hand off my shoulder and placed it over Katherine's belly.

"The baby! I feel the baby!" I clamped my hands over his to press it further against the fluttering sensation. "Wait, wait. There! Did you feel it?"

I looked up and nearly laughed at his stricken expression. There was still enough light to see he was blushing from the top of his starched collar to the roots of his unruly hair.

Without moving his hand, he managed to shake his head. "No. I didn't feel anything." He swallowed hard. "Katherine—"

"What on *earth?*" Lillian stood at the screen door, hands

on her hips, glaring at us. Michael snatched his hand away.

"Mrs. Stillman." He pulled his glasses from his pocket and slipped them on. "My cousin and I...uh...the sunset. You have a remarkable view." He glanced at me and coughed. "If you'll excuse me." With a quick little bow, he stepped off the porch and disappeared around the corner of the house.

Frowning disapproval, Lillian opened the screen door for me. She clicked her tongue, preparing to scold, just as I felt another light fluttering.

Hugging my sweet secret, I silenced Lillian with a radiant smile and slipped past her into the house.

* * *

Most of the guests had already left when we stood in the foyer, saying our good-byes. All the while I felt wrapped in a fuzzy haze of pure happiness. The flutterings had ceased, and I thought, *The baby must be sleeping now.* The notion filled me with wonder.

Isabel offered her hand to Lillian's nephew. "Then we'll see you at the house on Tuesday?"

"Yes, indeed, with pleasure, madam." His white teeth flashed in a smile. "I've heard your home is the loveliest in the county. I confess I am quite eager to see it."

Isabel retrieved her hand. "Until then, Mr. Delacroix." She turned and accepted her cloak from John Stillman.

Delacroix. Dazed as I was with my new happiness, the memory surfaced easily—Elise Delacroix, the little storyteller at Rosswood House who had thought she recognized me. *Katherine's daughter.*

I looked with new interest at Raymond as he approached and took my hand.

So, Raymond Delacroix was to be Katherine's next

husband.

"Madam." He held my fingers and looked boldly into my eyes. "Until Tuesday, Mrs. Kamarov." For the second time that day, he raised my hand to his lips.

I followed Isabel out the front door, which Michael was holding open for us. I glanced up as I passed him, but he was looking behind me, his mouth tightened in a frown. I looked down and hid my smile.

I didn't have to turn and look to know that Raymond's pale eyes were watching me as we left the house.

* * *

The dream begins as it always does. I know these trees and the moon winking at me through the treetops. It unwinds a silver path for me to follow. This, too, I have done before.

This time the path leads me to a clearing where a solitary deer grazes. She lifts her head, and as I approach her, I spy something curled at her feet – a fawn, tiny and new. The next instant I am walking along a creek, still following the silver path. To my surprise, I am carrying the fawn, so tiny it fits inside my cupped hand.

I pause on the rise above the old bridge. The fawn moves against my palm. The silver ribbon continues to uncurl before me, but I turn away and start back on the path that leads to Summerwood.

End of Book One

About the Author

Trained as a counselor, Judith Ingram writes fiction to challenge and inspire her readers with complex characters and stories laced with intrigue and romance. Her nonfiction work weaves together principles of her Christian faith with her experience of recovery from childhood abuse and damaged family relationships.

In addition to writing, Judith enjoys speaking to groups on a variety of inspirational topics. She lives with her husband in the San Francisco Bay Area and makes frequent trips to California's beautiful Sonoma County, where most of her fiction characters reside.

Please visit her at www.judithingram.com.

Please enjoy this excerpt from
Borrowed Promises
Book Two in the MOONSEED Trilogy
coming soon from Vinspire Publishing, LLC

Stephanie Ashton squinted against the painful glitter of the June sun glancing off the crinkled surface of the Pacific Ocean. As the plane arched a wide circle for its descent into Oakland Airport, her tiny window panned like a camera lens over the San Francisco Bay Area. Her heart leaped as she spotted the Golden Gate Bridge and Alcatraz Island. Mount Diablo sprawled like a sleeping giant among the East Bay hills, solid and familiar.

She didn't dare tell her mother, but Stephanie loved the Bay Area. It's where she would have grown up if her parents hadn't divorced. Where she *should* have grown up. San Francisco was beautiful, nothing like New York with its dirty streets and dark buildings, where you either had to travel in packs or stay home. She hated New York, hated the triple locks on their apartment door and the chilling way people looked right through you on the street. Hated the dazzling nightlife that teased her mother away from her most evenings.

I guess that'll change, she thought, *now that Mom's married to that creep.*

Chin in hand, Stephanie stared moodily at the gray asphalt rising rapidly to meet her plane as the engines climbed to a deafening pitch. Clifford Baines bothered her. From the first, there was something about him that Stephanie didn't trust. It made her feel weird sometimes when he looked at her, the way his eyes smiled at her like they shared some kind of secret.

She had tried to warn her mother about him, to make her understand that something wasn't right.

But who listens to a twelve-year-old?

Stephanie settled back against the leather of her first-class seat and closed her eyes, waiting for the jolt of wheels touching ground. It was time to stop thinking about Clifford Baines and the wedding and watching her mother's plane take off for Europe. In a few minutes, she'd be with her father. And Vicki.

Stephanie groaned. Why couldn't it just be the two of them, like all the other times? She loved being with her father — cooking for him, showing him new stuff on the Internet, performing her latest ice skating routine with him watching. She'd missed spending last summer with him, but her mother said it would be selfish to "intrude on the honeymooners." So she'd spent a hot, boring summer in New York. It was nothing like the summers she spent with her father. Here they rode bikes together in Golden Gate Park, ate fresh crab on the wharf, and took the boat out to Angel Island for picnics. They'd been to dog shows and circuses at the Cow Palace, and sometimes he'd shown her the new buildings and renovations he was working on. She smiled to herself, recalling the pride in his voice when he introduced her to his colleagues and the comfort of his arm around her shoulders.

Then he had to go and marry Miss Perfect USA.

Stephanie hadn't met Vicki yet, but she would have recognized her anywhere. In the strictest secrecy, she collected photos from glamour magazines and Prescott's catalogs and pored over them, memorizing the beautiful face and trying to imagine what her father must see when he looked at her. When he'd sent her photos of his wedding, Stephanie hid them, knowing the sight of them would only make her mother angry. She also hid that *People* magazine with its shot of Vicki and her father at the airport just before they took off for their honeymoon in the Bahamas. *"Retail princess marries her prince."* It was a terrible photo of her father. But Vicki looked great.

Stephanie reluctantly opened her eyes as the plane rolled neatly up to the terminal gate and stopped. The man next to her was already out of his seat, blocking the aisle as he opened the overhead compartment and struggled to remove his carry-on case. With a sigh, Stephanie dragged her backpack from under the seat in front of her and adjusted the scrunchie holding her long black ponytail.

"Uh, sir?" She cleared her throat and smiled politely at the man. He had slept for most of their flight, after three drinks at lunch, and embarrassed her with his snoring. "Can you get my skating bag down for me, please?" She scooted into the aisle beside him and pointed into the overhead. "Right there. The red one."

"Can't reach it, huh?" Chuckling at his own joke, the man swung down her bag. "There you go, short stuff."

"Thanks," she snapped, straightening to all of her four-foot-eleven-inch height. She clutched her skating bag to her chest and waited, unable to budge as other passengers jammed into the aisle, thrusting arms into coats and collecting bags and children. Eventually they began to move, funneling through a sterile corridor that spilled them into the terminal. At the sight of eager faces waiting beyond the check stations, Stephanie's feet slowed, and she shifted her backpack uneasily.

"Well, here goes nothing," she muttered.

* * *

She spotted her father right away. He was easily the best-looking man in the crowd.

"Dad!" Stephanie dropped her bag and flung her arms around him, hugging him fiercely to keep herself from crying. His jacket was soft under her cheek and smelled faintly of him.

"Hey, Stephanannie." His pet name for her made her laugh and look up into his face. His warm hazel eyes held a smile of welcome, but she noticed new lines and dark circles that hadn't been there before. *He's tired*, she thought suddenly. Then, fiercely, *He needs someone to take care of him.*

Her father kept an arm around her shoulders as he picked up her bag and led her toward the windows. "Come on, Steph. There's someone I want you to meet."

Oh, goodie. Stephanie's smile tipped into a scowl, and she looped a possessive arm around her father's waist as they approached a tall woman standing by herself, watching them.

She wasn't nearly as beautiful as her pictures, Stephanie instantly decided. Not that she wasn't pretty. Her complexion was flawless, and the green eyes were dramatic. But her trademark blond mane was pulled into an ugly knot at the back of her head, her tailored suit was expensive but plain, and her makeup was minimal—just a touch of color on her cheeks and lips, a faint mist of shadow highlighting her eyes.

Then the woman smiled. It was the same dazzling smile Stephanie had seen in photos, but so unexpectedly lovely it trapped her breath in her throat and sent a curious, sharp pain right through her chest.

"Hello, Stephanie. I'm Vicki." Her soft voice had a husky edge to it. Stephanie looked up into steady eyes that were coolly appraising her. She swallowed over twin lumps of awe and resentment.

"Hello." Stephanie pretended not to see the woman's extended hand and turned to her father. "Are we taking the BART train home, Dad? In the tube under the bay?"

He laughed and yanked gently on her ponytail. "Of course. But don't you think we should pick up your luggage first?"

"Oh, yeah." Eagerly, she turned her back on Vicki and started to pull at her father's arm. But he annoyed her by placing a light hand on Vicki's back and urging her forward with him, making them a threesome.

Stephanie glanced up to find herself still caught in that cool green gaze. She fixed her face with her nastiest New York scowl and moved ahead of them, deciding that three was definitely *not* her favorite number.

About the Author

Judith Ingram weaves together her love of romance and her training as a counselor to create stories and characters for her novels. She also writes Christian non-fiction books and enjoys speaking to groups on a variety of inspirational topics.

She lives with her husband in the San Francisco Bay Area and makes frequent trips to California's beautiful Sonoma County, where most of her fiction characters reside. Please visit her at www.judithingram.com.

Plan Your Next Escape!
What's Your Reading Pleasure?

Whether it's brawny Highlanders, intriguing mysteries, young adult romance, illustrated children's books, or uplifting love stories, Vinspire Publishing has the adventure for you!

For a complete listing of books available, visit our website at www.vinspirepublishing.com.

Find us on Facebook at
www.facebook.com/VinspirePublishing

Follow us on Twitter at
www.twitter.com/vinspire2004

and join our newsletter for details of our upcoming releases, giveaways, and more!
http://t.co/46UoTbVaWr

We are your travel guide to your next adventure!

Coming Fall 2013

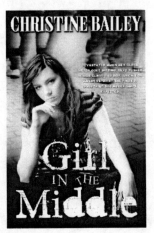

Girl in the Middle
Christine Bailey
YA Romance

Sometimes you have to be in the middle to discover what hangs in the balance.

Fifteen-year-old Skye, the middle child, finds herself wishing for a new life—one that doesn't include daily harassment from the in-crowd at Highland Creek High School. Cast into a lone existence, she wishes for a touch of extraordinary that everyone, except her, seems to have.

When her older sister goes missing without a trace, Skye gets her wish--but it's not exactly what she had in mind. And when she questions Bryan, the senior class renegade and also the last person to be seen with her sister, she finds something she never quite expected. And she ends up in the middle of a new, unwelcome role.

CPSIA information can be obtained at www.ICGtesting.com
Printed in the USA
LVOW06s1006120913

351946LV00002B/5/P